"This is ma[...]
Rachel said.

Frederick chuckled. "But it is a merry madness, do you not agree?"

Rachel looked down, as if trying to hide her face. "I would not have you disappoint your parents."

How had she uncovered the core of his dilemma? Could he surrender all his former dreams to marry Rachel? "But may a man not decide his own destiny? Must he always seek his parents' approval?"

Her brow wrinkled, as if she were considering his question. "You must count the cost, Mr. Moberly. You have more to lose than I. No doubt your father will disown you."

"Perhaps so. But what of you? I would not have you suffer on my account."

"I risk only my heart, as women have done since time began."

"If your heart suffered, I would grieve being the cause of it. As a younger son, I will inherit no part of my father's fortune. Perhaps it is time for me to earn my own."

"Why then, sir, I believe our friendship might prosper, after all."

## LOUISE M. GOUGE

has been married to her husband, David, for forty-four years. They have four children and six grandchildren. Louise always had an active imagination, thinking up stories for her friends, classmates and family, but seldom writing them down. At a friend's insistence, in 1984 she finally began to type up her latest idea. Before trying to find a publisher, Louise returned to college, earning a BA in English/creative writing and a master's degree in liberal studies. She reworked the novel based on what she had learned and sold it to a major Christian publisher. Louise then worked in television marketing for a short time before becoming a college English/humanities instructor. She has had seven novels published, five of which have earned multiple awards, including the 2006 Inspirational Reader's Choice Award. Please visit her Web site at www.louisemgouge.com.

# LOUISE M. GOUGE

## Love Thine Enemy

**Steeple Hill®**

Published by Steeple Hill Books™

STEEPLE HILL BOOKS

**Steeple Hill®**

Recycling programs for this product may not exist in your area.

ISBN-13: 978-0-373-82815-9

LOVE THINE ENEMY

www.SteepleHill.com

Printed in U.S.A.

Behold, thou desirest truth in the inward parts:
and in the hidden part thou shalt make me
to know wisdom.
—Psalms 51:6

To Kristy Dykes (1951–2008), a godly, gifted author who encouraged me to write about Florida, her home state and mine. Kristy was a beautiful Christian lady, a light in my life and in the lives of countless others. She is greatly missed by all who knew her.

Also, to my husband, David, who accompanied me on my research trips and found some excellent tidbits for this book. Thank you, my darling.

# Chapter One

St. Johns Settlement, East Florida Colony
May 1775

Through the window of her father's store, Rachel watched the Englishmen ride their handsome steeds up the sandy street of St. Johns Settlement. Their well-cut coats and haughty bearing—as if they owned the world—made their identities unmistakable.

"Make them pass by, Lord," she whispered, "for surely I'll not be able to speak a Christian word to them if they come in here." She glanced over her shoulder at Papa to see if he had heard her, but he was focusing his attention on a newly opened crate of goods.

Rachel turned back to the window. To her dismay, the two young men dismounted right in front of the store. One snapped his fingers at a small black boy and motioned for him to care for the horses.

Her dismay turned to anger. How did they know the boy could take time to do the task? Did they care that the child might be beaten by his owner if he lingered in town?

"What draws yer scrutiny, daughter?" Papa approached to look out the window. "Aha. Just as I hoped. From the cut of his clothes, that's Mr. Moberly, no mistake. Make haste, child. Go behind the counter and set out those fine tins of snuff and the brass buckles. Oh, and the wig powder and whalebone combs. Mayhap these gentlemen have wives who long for such luxuries here in the wilderness."

The delight in his voice brought back Rachel's dismay, even as she hurried to obey. Until six months ago, Papa had been a man of great dignity, a respected whaler who commanded his own ship. Why should he make obeisance to these wretches? These popinjays?

When the two men entered, the jangling bells on the front door grated against her nerves, inciting anger once more. But for Papa's sake, she would attempt to control it.

"What did I tell you, Oliver? Isn't this superb?" The taller of the two men glanced about the room. "Look at all these wares."

Rachel noticed the slight lift of his eyebrows when he saw her, but he turned his attention to Papa.

"Mr. Folger, I presume?"

"Aye, milord, I am he. How may I serve ye, sir?"

The young man chuckled. "First of all, I am not 'milord.'"

"Not yet." His companion held his nose high, as if something smelled bad. "But soon."

The taller man shrugged. "Perhaps when the plantation proves as successful as Lord Egmount's." He reached out to Papa. "I'm Frederick Moberly, sir, His Majesty's magistrate for St. Johns Settlement and manager of Bennington Plantation. This is my friend and business associate, Oliver Corwin."

For the briefest moment, Papa seemed uncertain, but then he gripped the gentleman's hand and shook it with enthusiasm. "How do ye, my good sirs? I'm pleased to meet ye both."

"And I'm pleased to see your fine store ready for business."

Moberly surveyed the shelves and counters. And again his glance stopped at Rachel.

Papa cleared his throat. "My daughter, Miss Folger."

Moberly swept off his brimmed hat and bent forward in a courtly bow, revealing black hair pulled back in a long queue. "How do you do, Miss Folger?"

She forced herself to curtsy but did not speak. The very idea, a gentleman giving a shopkeeper's daughter such honors. No doubt the man was a flatterer. The one named Corwin made no such gesture, but his intense stare brought heat to her face. Rachel could not decide which man would require her to be more vigilant.

Moberly's gaze lingered on her for another instant before he turned back to Papa. "Your store and the village's other new ones are what I've been hoping for. If St. Johns Settlement is to succeed as a colonial outpost, we must have every convenience to offer our settlers. Tell me, Folger, do you have any concerns about your shipments? With all that nonsense going on in the northern colonies, do you expect any delay in delivery of your goods?"

"Well, sir, I had no difficulty sailing down here from Boston. I expect all those troubles to be behind us soon. The rebels simply haven't the resources. I'll wager wiser heads will prevail. I'm from Nantucket, ye see, and we're loyal to the Crown."

Corwin snorted, and Moberly glanced his way with a frown.

"Ah, yes, Nantucket." The magistrate appeared interested. "From whence whalers set out to harvest the world's finest lamp oil. Will you be receiving goods from there?"

"Perhaps some, sir. My own ship will sail to and from London until things are settled."

"Good, good." Moberly nodded. "And are you a Quaker, as I've heard most Nantucketers are?"

"I was reared in the Society of Friends," Papa said. "But I don't mind wearing a brass button or a buckle."

"We don't need any dissenters here." Corwin's eyes narrowed.

"Now, Oliver, the man said he wasn't a zealot." Moberly gave Papa a genial look. "Moderation in all things, would you not agree?"

"Precisely my sentiments, sir."

Rachel inhaled deeply. She must not display her feelings. This was not Nantucket, where women spoke their minds. Nor was it Boston, where patriots—both men and women— clamored for separation from England. Until she got the lay of the land here in East Florida Colony, she must not risk harming Papa's enterprise.

"Miss Folger." Moberly approached the wide oak counter which she stood behind. "What do you think of our little settlement?"

She caught a glimpse of Papa's warning look and stifled a curt reply. "I am certain it is everything King George could wish for." She ventured a direct look and discovered his eyes to be dark gray. His tanned, clean-shaven cheeks had a youthful yet strong contour. Young, handsome, self-assured. Like the English officers who ordered the shooting of the patriots at Lexington and Concord just over a month ago.

Her reply seemed to please him, for his eyes twinkled, and Rachel's traitorous pulse beat faster. *Belay that, foolish heart. These are not your kind.*

"Indeed, I do hope His Majesty approves of my work here." A winsome expression crossed his face. "As you may know, in England, younger sons must earn their fortunes. But if we are clever and the Fates favor us, we too can gain society's interest and perhaps even its approval."

Rachel returned a tight smile. "In America, *every* man has the opportunity to earn his fortune and his place in society." With the help of God, not fate.

He grinned. "Then I've come to the right place, have I not?"

The man had not comprehended her insult in the least. How she longed to tell him exactly what she thought of his King George and all greedy Englishmen.

Papa emitted a nervous cough. "Indeed ye have, my good sir. And so have we." Again, his frown scolded her. "Now, sir, is there anything in particular we can help ye with?"

"Hmm." The magistrate effected a thoughtful pose, with arms crossed and a finger resting on his chin. "My Mrs. Winthrop requested tea, if you have some." He tapped his temple. "And something else. Oliver, can you recall the other items she mentioned?"

"Flour and coffee." Corwin's languid tone revealed boredom, perhaps even annoyance. "She wanted a list of his spices, and of course she'll want to know about those fabrics." He waved toward the crates Papa had opened.

At Papa's instruction, Rachel wrote down the items they had imported from Boston, things an English housekeeper might want. She snipped small samples of the linen, muslin and other fabrics, and wrapped them in brown paper. All the while, she felt the stares of the two men. Despite the summer heat, a shiver ran down her back while a blush warmed her cheeks.

None too soon, they made their purchases and left, but not before Mr. Moberly once again bowed to her. Why did he engage in such courtesy? Neither in England nor in Boston would he thus have honored her, nor even have acknowledged her existence.

"Well, daughter, what think ye?" Papa held up the gold guineas they had given him. "His lordship didn't even ask for credit."

"Papa, will you listen to yourself?" Rachel leaned her elbows on the counter and rested her chin on her fists. "You were raised a Quaker, yet hear how you go on about 'milord' and 'his lordship.'"

Papa harrumphed. "I suppose ye'll be after me to take up my 'thees' and 'thous' again. Ye, who abandoned the Friends yerself, going off to that other church with yer sister and her husband." He lumbered on his wounded leg toward the back room. "I should never have sent ye to Boston to live with Susanna."

He disappeared behind the burlap curtain, and soon Rachel heard crates being shoved roughly across the hard tabby floor. Sorrow cut into her. Had he not been injured on his last whaling voyage, Papa could still captain his own ship, and she would still be in Boston helping the patriots' noble cause. Instead, here she was in East Florida helping him.

He must feel as cross as she did about their differences of opinion, both about the revolution and the Englishmen. But she had not chosen to flee Massachusetts Colony to avoid the war against the Crown. How could he expect her to treat the English oppressors with civility?

"Pleasant fellow, that Folger." Frederick flipped a farthing to the Negro boy who held their horses. "Good job, lad. If you get into trouble, tell your master Mr. Moberly required your services."

"Pleasant fellow, indeed." Oliver grasped his horse's reins and swung into the saddle. "'Tis the little chit you found pleasant."

"And you did not?" Frederick mounted Essex and reined the stallion toward the plantation road. "I saw you watching her as if she were a plump partridge and you a starving man."

Oliver drew up beside him. "Of course I was watching her. Your father sent me along to this forsaken place to make sure no provincial lass sets her cap for you. And if she does, I'm to nip the budding romance."

Frederick swallowed the bitter retort. Oliver's reminder ruined the agreeable feeling that had settled in his chest the moment he set eyes on the fair-haired maiden. Here he was at twenty-three, and the old earl still treated him as if he were a boy sitting in an Eton classroom. As for the girl, she was no chit, but fully a woman, possessing a diminutive but elegant figure. Spirited, too, from the liveliness he had noticed in her fine dark eyes. But he would not say so, for Oliver would only misunderstand his generous opinion of her.

"Have no care on that account. I've no plans to pursue American women." He glanced at the rolling landscape with its sandy soil and countless varieties of vegetation. While the weather could inflict heat, lightning and hurricanes upon in-habitants, he found East Florida a pleasant paradise, as sat-isfying as any place for building his future.

"You cannot fool me," Oliver said. "Need I remind you that if you fail here, Lord Bennington will ship you off to His Majesty's Royal Navy? You'll end up wearing the indigo instead of growing it."

Frederick glared at him. "Fail? My father sent me to rescue the plantation from Bartleby's mismanagement, and that's exactly what I have accomplished. He will not be quick to snatch me home."

"You know as well as I it's moral failure he's concerned about."

Frederick gritted his teeth. How long would he have to pay for the sins of his older brothers? "Rest easy on that account. I'll not risk my business association with Mr. Folger by dallying with his daughter. However, if you will recall, we're supposed to be building a settlement here. Before we can bring English ladies to this wilderness, we must provide nec-essary services. This man Folger may have friends up north who want no part in the rebellion. We must court him, if you will, to lure other worthies to East Florida Colony, even if it means socializing with the merchant class."

Oliver regarded him with a skeptical frown. "Just be

certain you don't socialize with the little Nantucket wench while you await those English ladies."

"Enough of this." Frederick slapped his riding crop against Essex's flanks and urged him into a gallop.

The steed easily outdistanced Oliver's mare, and Frederick arrived home far ahead of his companion. At the front porch, he jumped down and tossed the reins to the waiting groom.

"Give him a cooldown and brushing, Ben. He's had a good run in this heat."

"Yessuh, Mister Moberly." The slender black man led the stallion away.

Three black-and-white spaniels bounded around the corner of the house to greet Frederick. He ruffled their necks and patted their heads. "Down, boy. Down, girls. I'm on a mission."

He took the four front steps two at a time and crossed the wide porch with long strides. The door opened, and the little Negro girl who tended it curtsied.

"Welcome home, Mr. Frederick."

"Thank you, Caddy." He pulled a confection from his coat pocket, handed it to her and patted her scarf-covered head.

Inside, he strode across the entry toward the front staircase. "Cousin Lydie, I'm home." He listened for his cousin's response. Soon the soft rush of feet sounded above him.

"Dear me." Cousin Lydie hastened downstairs, shadowed by Betty, the housemaid. "I expected you to be in the village much longer. Dinner is not yet prepared."

"Don't fret. I only announced my homecoming because I have this for you." He pulled the fabric samples from his pocket and handed them to her. "Oliver has the other items, but I wanted to give you these myself. Be quick to order the dress lengths you desire, or the vicar's wife will beat you to it." He winked at her.

"Why, sir." Cousin Lydie's gray eyes exuded gratitude as she spoke. "You're too kind."

Frederick noticed the longing in Betty's expression. The once cheerful maid had become a sad little shadow after an alligator caught her skirt and almost dragged her into the river. If Oliver hadn't shot the beast, Frederick would have had a bitter letter to write home to Father's groom to report the loss of his daughter.

"And be certain to choose something for Betty, too. Something to mark her status in the house." He felt tempted to pat the girl on the head as he had the child at the front door, but thought better of it. Such innocent contact with serving girls had been the beginning of troubles for his older brothers.

"Thank you, sir." Betty curtsied, and her pale face brightened.

"Think nothing of it."

"Mr. Moberly." Cousin Lydie insisted on addressing him formally in front of the servants. "A flatboat arrived bringing mail. Summerlin put several letters on your desk."

"Ah, very good." Frederick proceeded down the hallway to his study and sat at his large oak desk. Trepidation filled him as he lifted the top letter and broke Father's red wax seal.

As expected, he could almost hear Father's ponderous voice in the missive. The earl always seemed to find something wrong in Frederick's correspondence and scolded him about nonexistent offenses. Yet the abundant shipments of produce and the financial reports sent by Corwin confirmed everything Frederick claimed about the plantation's success.

Through the tall, open window beside him, he stared out on the distant indigo field where slaves bent over tender young plants. Last year's crop had been modestly successful, and this year should produce an abundance, perhaps even rivaling the success of Lord Egmount's nearby plantation. Why did Father doubt the veracity of Frederick's reports?

He blew out a deep sigh. Pleasing his father had always proven impossible, so he cheered himself with Mother's letter.

She chatted about a party she had given in London and said how much she missed him. As always, she thanked him for giving her widowed cousin a home where she could feel useful. Frederick would make certain he responded that Cousin Lydia Winthrop did more for him than he did for her, managing the household with skill.

Marianne's letter brought him laughter. His younger sister had rebuffed yet another foolish suitor who, despite an august title and ample wealth, possessed no wit or sense of adventure. "I shall remain forever a spinster," she wrote. Frederick pictured her dramatic pose, delicate white hand to her pretty forehead in artificial pathos. How he treasured the memories of their carefree childhood days.

The letters had done their job. Father's dire warnings had been mitigated by Mother's and Marianne's gentler words. Frederick rested his head against the back of his large mahogany chair and gazed out the window again.

In his most amiable dreams, he considered that his success in East Florida might move His Majesty to knight him, as Oliver had said. Then, in due time, he could complete the picture by returning to England to choose a woman to be his wife from one of the families who once had shunned him. But how could he win the king's favor when his own father gave only disapproval?

He recalled the words of the pretty young miss he had met two short hours ago. In America, every man had the opportunity to earn his place in society. Not be born to it, as his eldest brother had been, but to earn his fortune by his own honest sweat. More and more, that peculiar idea appealed to him, for he found great satisfaction in his work. And the sort of woman Frederick required for a wife must be willing to leave her cushioned life to establish a new home, just as Miss Folger had done for her father.

Frederick would do well to foster a friendship with the

merchant and his daughter to discover what kind of woman would make the perfect wife to bring to this savage land. Perhaps inviting the two to some sort of social gathering would be beneficial. A party such as Mother had given in London, where no expense was spared to please her guests.

Eager to enlist Cousin Lydie's help in the project, he rose from his chair, but noticed another letter bearing Father's seal lying facedown on the desk. Two reprimands? What had the old earl forgotten to scold him for?

Frederick snapped the wax and unfolded the vellum sheet, not caring if he tore it. The salutation made him blink twice.

*My dear Oliver—*

Frederick turned the missive over. Oliver's name was clearly written in Father's hand across the outside. A coil of dread tightened in Frederick's stomach. Father had never addressed *him* as "My dear Frederick."

He should not read this letter. Summerlin had left it here by mistake. Yet Frederick could not resist.

> Received your letter of December 20. You have my gratitude for your faithful reporting of the matters we discussed. I shall make my decision accordingly. Please continue your endeavors to keep my son from further overspending. As to the chit from Oswald's plantation, do all in your power to keep them apart. Gratefully, Bennington

Frederick slumped back into his chair. What matters? What overspending? What *chit?* Frederick had visited the manager of Oswald's plantation last year, but met no young woman.

And Oliver knew it. Oliver, the illegitimate son of a well-born lady, who had depended on Father's generosity since childhood. Oliver, Frederick's lifelong friend.

His hands curled into fists, crushing the heavy paper into a ball. He thrust it into the fireplace, then snatched a piece of char cloth from the box on the narrow mantelpiece. But before he could strike flint against steel to light it, other thoughts stayed his hand.

Working to subdue his anger, he pressed the page out on his desk, refolded it and then consigned it to the hidden compartment beneath his desktop. He must not let Oliver know that he had discovered his treachery.

Frederick paced back and forth across the room. All his hard work might come to nothing because Father believed Oliver's lies. He reread the earl's letter. At least Father had not called him home at once. But he must discover a way to prove himself.

The party. That was it. He would throw a grand affair and earn the friendship of the newly arrived residents of St. Johns Settlement. If they required help, he would give it. In his judgments as magistrate, he would continue to be firm but fair. He would solicit a letter of praise from his plantation physician, Dr. Wellsey, regarding the health and productivity of the slaves. He would foster friendships with the leading citizens of the growing settlement and petition for recommendations, as well.

And he would watch Oliver as a falcon watches its prey.

# Chapter Two

"Captain James Templeton. How impressive your new title sounds." Rachel sat across the table from her cousin in the parlor of the Wild Boar Inn. "Papa could have chosen no better man to succeed him as captain of the *Fair Winds*."

"Thank you, Rachel." Jamie grinned. "Of course, I've learned my trade from the best. When Uncle Lamech chose me as his cabin boy those fifteen years ago, he may have wondered how this orphaned boy would turn out."

"We will miss you, but I shall pray for a good voyage." Rachel took a sip of tea from her pewter cup. "But why must you go to London? Are there no other ports to supply Papa's store?"

"In these turbulent times, English settlers might not favor French products. And after all, London has the best merchandise." His brown eyes shone with brotherly affection. "I do wish you'd charge me with some special purchase to bring you."

"You know what I want. News of the revolution." She exhaled a sigh of annoyance. "I cannot even discuss it with Papa, for he will not listen to my opinions. With you gone, I will need to find another friend in whom I can confide…and complain to." She glanced beyond him at the British soldiers in red uniforms seated across the entry hall in the taproom.

He followed her glance, then turned back with a frown. "Don't get yourself in trouble. These soldiers are here for your good. They'll protect you and your father and every other British subject in East Florida."

"I am *not* a British subject." She leaned toward him and whispered. "When will you join us, Jamie? When will you accept that we *will* be free from British rule…or die trying?"

Now he stared into her eyes with an almost scolding look. "My dear little rebel, why do you think your father brought you so far away from the troubles? Why, you'd have been fighting alongside the militia at Concord or Lexington if you'd had your way."

She straightened as high as her short stature permitted. "When I sought to become a servant in General Gage's home, I planned to gather information to help the patriot cause."

He sat back, shaking his head. "Humph. Your feelings are always written across your face, and you never fail to speak your mind. You'd fail as a spy. You'd be discovered and hanged, but not before they wrested the name of your every accomplice from you."

She clenched her jaw and stared down at her teacup. He was wrong. She could have learned how to withhold the truth, perhaps even to lie, as Rahab in the Bible had done to save the Hebrew spies. Sometimes the desperation to do her part in the revolution ate at her soul. At other times, she felt nothing but despair that Papa had made her participation impossible.

"Dear cousin." Jamie reached over to nudge her chin. "What shall I do with you? After watching you grow into a beautiful woman, I see you slip back into the childish imp who bedeviled the crew in '68."

Rachel granted him the change of topic without protest.

"Wasn't that a grand voyage?" She smiled at the memory of dressing as a cabin boy and climbing riggings to watch for whales. Then she sobered. "But for Mama's death, Papa never would have taken me."

"Your father's never ceased his grieving." He patted her hand as if she were a child. "Please, Rachel, do not grieve him further. Forget the revolution." A frown flickered across his youthful but weathered face. "Rebellion, I should say."

She pulled back her hand. "'Rebellion' makes it sound as if the patriots are naughty children instead of sound-minded adults who have suffered enough of King George's injustices."

"Whatever you call it, just stay out of trouble."

"What trouble could I find here in this remote wilderness?"

He gave her a playful wink. "Who knows? Maybe one of these handsomely uniformed soldiers will catch your eye and you'll be married before I return."

"You may wager all the *Fair Winds*'s profits that no Englishman will ever win my hand." Again she cast a cross glance at the soldiers across the hall, who now harried Sadie, the innkeeper's daughter, demanding rum despite the early hour.

Jamie shoved away his teacup. "It'd be a winning wager, no mistake. Now, may I escort you to the store? The captain will keelhaul me if I make you late."

"He'd do no such thing to his nephew and new partner." She scooted her wooden chair backward across the plank floor. "Wait while I fetch my bonnet."

He sent her a playful smirk. "By all means, protect your face. The English value a fair complexion."

She wrinkled her nose and laughed, but not too loudly for fear of drawing the soldiers' attentions. In spite of Jamie's assurances of their protection, she had no doubt that, given the chance, they would harass her as much as they did the innkeeper's women.

As she hastened up the rickety steps to the inn's second floor, she sent up a silent prayer of thanks that soon she and Papa would move into their own more stable home above their store. Under the supervision of Mr. Patch, the carpenter from Papa's ship, the crew had labored for weeks to raise the roof and build the apartment. It was almost completed.

From her room at the end of the inn's second-story corridor, she snatched her straw bonnet from a peg on the wall. Passing the room next to hers, she heard a soft whimper through the slightly open door. She glanced toward the stairway, then peered into the room.

There, in a rough-hewn pen no more than three foot by four, sat the innkeeper's grandson, his dark, soulful eyes staring up with sudden hope when he spied her. Flies buzzed about the two-year-old's face and crawled over a dry crust of bread beside him.

"Up. Up." His winsome, tearful expression nearly undid her.

"Dear little Robby." Unable to resist his entreaty, she lifted him. "My, my, you need a change. And look at all these mosquito bites." She felt a twinge of anger that the innkeeper had not provided his grandson with mosquito netting, but perhaps he could not afford it.

Several clean diapers hung on a rope line near the window. Rachel started to call the baby's mother, but compassion filled her. No doubt Sadie was kept busy serving those awful soldiers and could not care for her child as she ought to. Laying the child on the bed, Rachel quickly changed him, cooing to him all the while.

"There, little one. I've not forgot how to do this. Gracious knows I changed my nieces and nephew often enough these past few years." And the three of them healthily plump, while this wee tyke's ribs were all too visible.

The baby whimpered as she set him back down in the pen,

a splintery structure made from an old shipping crate and far different from the sanded, polished beds her sister's children slept in. And nothing more than an old tin cup, empty at that, for a toy.

"I must go, sweet boy." Rachel thought her heart would break. "I'm certain Mama will come feed you soon."

Only by force of will could she hasten down the stairs to join Jamie in the entry hall.

"What is it, Rachel?" With a frown, he stared into her eyes. "You look distraught."

"Sadie's little one." She bent her head toward the staircase. "He spends his days alone in her room while she must fend off those dreadful soldiers."

Jamie's face softened. "You have a kind heart, cousin. Hmm, didn't Sadie say her husband is a soldier, too?"

"Aye, but that doesn't seem to protect her." She lowered her voice. "And I've learned he's serving under General Gage. Perhaps he even fought against our men at Concord."

"Rachel—"

"Yes, yes, I know." She moved past him out the inn's front door.

The East Florida heat blazed down on their covered heads as they walked the sandy road toward the sturdy wooden structure Papa had purchased for his mercantile. But Rachel could be concerned with only one matter—a poor, hungry little baby left alone in a room all day.

"I've changed my mind," she said as they reached the store. "There is something I want you to bring me when you return."

He swept off his broad-brimmed hat and gave her an exaggerated bow. "Name it, milady, and I'll sail the seven seas to obtain it."

She dipped a playful curtsy. "Why, thank you, kind sir. But there's no need for that. Just bring a toy for little Robby." She sobered. "Do you mind?"

"Anything for you, milady." He caught her hand and placed a noisy kiss on it.

"Ah, such gallantry." Caring not a whit what onlookers might think, Rachel reached up and kissed his cheek.

After a week of planning with Mrs. Winthrop, Frederick rode into town to invite more guests to his party. His first visit had been to Major Brigham, the garrison's new commander, who along with his stylish bride had responded eagerly to his invitation. Several others also promised to attend. With a similar response from the merchants, the party would be complete.

Frederick rode past the inn and saw the innkeeper's wife and daughter hanging laundry on a line. Mrs. Winthrop had been aghast when he had suggested inviting them, and now her wisdom was confirmed as he observed their unkempt appearance and heard their uncouth language.

A half mile from the inn, he spied Miss Folger with a brawny fellow who was bent over her hand like an adoring swain. The young lady then reached up to kiss the man's cheek, and an odd pang coursed through Frederick's chest. Did she dole out kisses to every man, or was this one a particular friend? He shook his head. Why should it matter to him?

The fellow straightened and offered his arm, and the two entered Folger's Mercantile. Frederick tethered his horse to a post under a nearby oak tree and followed them inside.

The door had no sooner shut behind him than the three inside turned to him in surprise. Was that a glare emanating from the young lady's face, or were her eyes merely adjusting to the inside light, as were his?

"Good morning, sir." Mr. Folger limped forward to welcome him. "How can I help ye?"

"Good morning, my good man. Miss Folger." Frederick

removed his hat, nodded to the father and daughter, and cast an inquisitive glance toward the big man behind Folger.

"Ah, ye've not met my partner." Folger urged the man forward. "Mr. Moberly, this is my nephew, Captain Templeton, who now commands my old ship."

The younger captain's steady gaze was a clear and bold appraisal of Frederick.

In an instant, the air seemed sparked with invisible lightning. Instinctively, Frederick took on the unassuming pose he had perfected as the youngest of four sons to keep from being whipped into his proper place. Hating himself for it, he nonetheless feigned amiability and reached out to shake the other man's hand rather than meet his challenge and put him in *his* place. Who was this man that he would boldly stare at a superior?

"Captain Templeton," Frederick said.

"Moberly." Templeton's guarded frown softened as they shook hands. "You've done a right fine job in building St. Johns Settlement. Perhaps we can do business in the future."

"Indeed?" Frederick glanced at Folger.

"Aye." The older man's broad smile suggested his eagerness to foster a friendship among the three of them. "A wise man's always on the lookout for good business associates."

"Well said." Frederick wondered if he had been mistaken about the younger captain's earlier demeanor.

The conversation turned to weather, the war up north, anticipated shipping problems, the feasibility of planting more citrus groves and prices of goods. All possible storms were dispelled as the three men enthusiastically expressed their concerns and opinions as if they had been in trade together for years. The amity in the air felt good after Oliver's betrayal.

He noticed Miss Folger had busied herself with the bolts of lace and ribbons behind the counter. With her back to him, he could see the delicate lines of her ivory neck, with a few blond curls escaping from her mobcap to trail over the white collar of her brown dress.

Templeton must have caught the direction of his gaze, for he cleared his throat. "Did you wish to speak with my cousin?" His tone sounded like the growl of a protective bear.

Irritation swept through Frederick, but again, he was all amiability. "Indeed, I did."

She turned around, puzzlement lifting her eyebrows into a charming arch. "To me?"

Frederick hesitated. "Perhaps I should say to you and your father." He nodded to Templeton. "And now to you, as well."

Folger appeared more than a little pleased. "Say on, sir."

"I am planning a dinner party for those whom I consider the leading citizens of this community and surrounding areas. I should like to invite you and Miss Folger—" He included Templeton with a quick glance. "All three of you to join us one week from Saturday at my plantation."

Their stunned expressions nearly sent Frederick into a schoolboy's guffaw. Did these people know nothing of parties? Had they never received such an invitation?

"Why, that's quite an honor, sir." Folger straightened as if he had been knighted by the king himself. "Of course I accept."

"And you, Miss Folger? Will you attend with your father?"

Her wide-eyed gaze darted from him to her father to Templeton and back to him again. "Why, I—I haven't anything to wear to such a grand occasion."

"Why, Rachel, what a thing to say in front of these gentlemen." The color deepened in Folger's ruddy cheeks. "As if yer papa couldn't provide a proper gown for ye."

The young lady's corresponding blush bespoke her modesty, a pleasing sight.

Frederick looked at Templeton. "And you, captain?"

Templeton shook his head. "I thank you, sir, but I'm afraid

I'll be on my way to London by then. I'm setting sail from Mayport in a few days."

"Ah, I'm sorry to hear it." Frederick found himself meaning those words. After those first sparks had been extinguished, the fellow had inspired a certain confidence.

As for doing business with him, Frederick had much to consider. After Oliver's betrayal, how could he ever trust another man? Especially an American.

## Chapter Three

"Can ye beat that?" Papa stared after Mr. Moberly as he rode away. "Inviting us to a dinner party. Calling us 'leading citizens.'"

Jamie raised one eyebrow and traded a glance with Papa. "A good opportunity."

"What do you mean?" Rachel looked from one to the other. Was this another of those secrets they kept from her, things they called "men's matters"?

"Why, business, daughter." Papa took up his shipping log and quill and made notes. "'Tis a great honor for Mr. Moberly to stamp his approval on us. It'll bring more customers."

"Indeed it shall." Jamie leaned back against the counter and crossed his arms. "Now what do you suppose I could bring from London to further foster his good opinion?"

Papa tapped his quill against his chin. "Hmm. He hires ships to deliver the plantation's products to England and bring back what's needed here." He stared out of the window for a moment. "I've got the notion they'd like to increase the population with decent folk, more tradesmen and such, not the lowlife camp followers that plague the regiment, nor the Spanish who stayed on after England seized these lands."

"Humph," Rachel said. "Please do not tell me you want Jamie to import more Englishmen, tradesmen or no. It is beyond enough that English sympathizers from the Carolinas are arriving here every week."

"And welcome to them." Papa bent toward her in his paternal fashion. "The more that come from South Carolina and Georgia, the better it will be for everyone, for they'll understand the land more than an Englishman. And consider this. King George gave the good citizens of New England plenty of opportunities to populate both East and West Florida. Ye can see how few have accepted his invitation."

"And, if not American colonials," Jamie said, "why not more English?" He sent Rachel a brotherly smile. "The ordinary Englishman's no threat to your patriot cause, especially way down here in East Florida. They're like Uncle Lamech here, people who want a chance to build a life in a new place."

"Yes, so you both have said. Never mind that they will all be willing to join a militia in support of the Crown." Rachel would not add that she had never wanted a life in a new place. Papa had announced she would accompany him to East Florida, and that was that. With a sigh, she ambled across the room toward the material display and ran a finger over a bolt of fabric. "Papa, will you let me take a length of this mosquito netting to protect Sadie's baby? He's a mass of bites this morning, poor boy."

"And how's Sadie to pay for it, might I ask?" Papa had returned to his accounting and now peered at her over his reading spectacles, eyes narrowed.

Rachel lifted her chin and stared back, mirroring his look. She had backed down in the discussion about the English, but she would not back down in this matter. For countless seconds, she faced his "captain" glare that had always made his whalers tremble.

Jamie coughed and hummed a flat tune, then drummed his fingers on the counter. The hammers of the men working on the living quarters echoed above them. A bird of some sort sent out a plaintive cry in the marshes behind the store.

Papa did not flinch, nor did Rachel.

"If you do it for the least of these—" she began.

Papa slammed his logbook shut. "What shall I do with ye, my girl? Given yer head, ye'd give away the entire store."

Pulling the bolt from the display, Rachel hurried to his side and placed a kiss on his gray-stubbled cheek. "Perhaps Mr. Moberly will make more purchases with his gold guineas. That should balance everything out."

She glanced at Jamie, whose face had reddened in an obvious attempt to stifle his amusement. She never would have put up such a fight in front of any other of Papa's crew. Measuring out an appropriate length of the sheer material, she cut, folded and wrapped it. "May I take it over right away?"

"There's a limit to my surrender, daughter. Look." Scowling, he pointed out the window. "Customers are headed this way. Ye can take it when ye go for yer noon meal." His expression softened. "Have ye noticed the mosquitoes come out in the evening? The tyke will be fine until then."

"Thank you, Papa."

Jamie left, and customers entered to shop. Several soldiers came to purchase tobacco, and one bought a new pipe. An Indian family, speaking in their Timucuan language, studied the various wares and selected a large cast-iron pot. The tanner's wife bought a box of tea. One of the slatterns who followed the soldiers eyed the finer fabrics with a longing eye. Repulsed by her sweaty smell but also filled with pity, Rachel watched the woman move lazily among the displays. Papa greeted one and all as if they were old friends, even taking time to learn a few native words from the Indians.

The morning passed quickly, and soon Papa gave Rachel

a nod. She placed her bonnet over her mobcap, fetched the wrapped mosquito netting, and then hastened out the door.

The sun stood at its zenith like an angry potentate pouring fiery wrath upon all who dared to venture beneath him. Perspiration slid down Rachel's face and body, stinging her eyes and dampening everything she wore. Perhaps she should ask Jamie to bring her a new parasol from London, for her old one was bent and tattered.

As she passed the large yard beside the inn, she heard a commotion—Sadie's shrill voice screeched for help above the chaotic squawking of chickens and geese. Rachel hurried around the corner of the clapboard building, where she saw the young woman tussling with a soldier amidst the innkeeper's fowls, a plump goose the object of their struggle.

"Let 'er go, ya blunderhead." Sadie tried to kick the red-uniformed man, without success. "Ya've no right to take 'er."

The man cursed and continued to grasp the goose's neck. "Gi' way, girl. I've a right as the king's soldier to take what I need."

"Ya've got yer own provisions in the regiment," cried Sadie.

Her sob cut into Rachel's heart, stirring memories of the time a brutish soldier invaded her sister's house and took food from the children's plates. Then he had threatened Rachel and Susanna with something far worse. Enraged by the recollection, she dashed toward the altercation.

"Brazen wench, let go." The soldier cuffed Sadie on the face, but though she cried out, she held on to the goose.

"Stop it, you horrid monster." Rachel dropped her package and, with hardly a thought of what she was doing, grabbed a length of wood from the nearby woodpile and slammed it into the man's ear. Her hands stung from the blow, and she dropped the weapon as his tall, black leather cap flew to the ground.

"Ow!" He grabbed his ear and released the now-dead beast. Turning to Rachel, he glared at her with blazing eyes and took a menacing step toward her.

*Lord, what have I done?* Terror gripped her, and she searched for an escape.

But he glanced beyond her and stopped.

"What's all this?" A familiar English voice resounded with authority behind her.

Rachel turned to see Mr. Moberly astride his horse, staring down his aristocratic nose at the scene. His gray eyes flashed like a shining rapier in the shadow of his broad-brimmed hat. Despite the day's heat, a strange shiver swept through her body.

"Good thing ya come along, gov'ner." The soldier tugged at a lock of his hair in an obeisant gesture. "This wench refuses me a soldier's right to provision, and this 'un…" He waved at Rachel. "She done assaulted a king's soldier, is what she done." He stepped toward her as if about to return the blow. "'Tis a hangin' offense."

"Take another step—" Moberly bent forward and pointed his riding crop at the soldier "—and you'll be the one to hang."

The man stopped, his eyes wide. Rachel could see his fear in his slack-jaw expression. Did Moberly really have that kind of power?

"Chiveys, gov'ner," Sadie cried, "he just killed one o' Ma's brood geese."

"I've a right to take provision as needed." The soldier retrieved his tall cap and shook off the sand clinging to it. He winced as he placed it above his bloody ear.

"I shall speak to Major Brigham about the matter." Moberly dismounted. "I shall also see he requires you to repay the innkeeper for the loss of his goose."

"Repay—?"

"Are you contradicting me?" Moberly's stately posture forestalled any appeal.

"No, sir, yer lordship." The man stood straight and lifted his hand into a salute.

"What is your name, private?"

"Buckner, sir."

"Well, now, Buckner, get back to your duty." Moberly pointed the riding crop toward the street.

"Yes, sir." The soldier hastened around the corner of the inn and disappeared from sight.

Moberly stepped near Sadie, and his stern expression softened. "Hurry to pluck and dress it, girl, so it won't be a complete loss."

Her face still flushed, Sadie cast a confused look at Rachel and then at Moberly. "Aye, sir. I'll do that." She curtsied to each of them. "Thank you, miss." And away she dashed.

Moberly now gave Rachel a gentle smile, and she thought the heat might flatten her on the spot. Gratitude for his rescue warred within her heart against her scorn for all things English.

"I must say, Miss Folger, I have never seen a lady quite so, um, bold in defense of a less fortunate soul." His gray eyes twinkled. "But I must also say I quite admire you for it."

"Indeed? I did no more nor less than the citizens of Lexington and Concord this past month when your British soldiers attacked them." Rachel could not believe her own words. The man had just saved her from assault.

Puzzlement swept across his face, as if he had no idea of the matter. "I beg your pardon?" Then his eyebrows raised in clear comprehension. "Ah. I see. May I surmise you favor the cause of the thirteen dissenting colonies?" His thoughtful expression held no condemnation or disdain.

Before she could respond, the injury to her left hand began to sting, and she looked down to see several splinters embedded in her bloody palm.

"Why, Miss Folger, you've been wounded in battle." He stepped forward and seized her hand to inspect it. A frown creased his forehead. "I shall send my personal physician immediately to make certain no infection sets in. If left untended, this sort of wound can become quite serious, especially here in the tropics." He drew a white silk handkerchief from his waistcoat and wrapped it around the injury. "This should protect it until he arrives."

Shame dug into her. Had she misjudged this man? She pulled her hand away.

"Thank you, sir, but please don't trouble yourself." She tried to brush past him, but his large horse stood in the way. Confusion filled her. She spied the forgotten package of material.

Anticipating her direction, he hastened to retrieve it and held it out.

"Yours?"

"Yes." She took it in her uninjured hand. "Thank you."

"May I escort you to your destination?"

Rachel's pulse raced. A hundred arguments warred within her, yet she felt a strange, strong impulse to accept. Was this nudging from the Lord? "Yes. Thank you. To the inn."

He offered his arm, and she set her bandaged hand on it, wincing slightly at the pain.

"You must accept my apology for that soldier's conduct." Mr. Moberly's tone rang sincere, reinforced by his troubled frown. "I shall speak to his commander. You may trust me when I promise we shall have no conflict between citizenry and soldiers here in St. Johns Settlement."

Once again, the day's heat almost proved her undoing. *Lord, I've judged this man without knowing anything about him. That's nothing less than a sin. Please forgive me.*

They walked to the front of the inn, and Mr. Moberly tethered his horse to a post. "Are you always this quiet?" His tone betrayed amusement.

She again took his offered arm. "Papa would say I am all too loquacious."

"Ah, I see. Then I shall have to spend more time in your company to ascertain who the true Miss Folger is."

As they passed through the open door, his posture transformed from relaxed to imperious. He surveyed the taproom, where a half-dozen soldiers sat drinking. Then, in a voice raised so they could hear, he said, "Miss Folger, you and your father may count me as your friend. If you need anything at all, send one of these fellows to my plantation." He waved his riding crop toward the soldiers. "And you shall have it post-haste." He took her injured hand and placed a gentlemanly kiss on it. "Good day, dear lady."

Filled with wonder, Rachel watched him depart. A good Englishman. An aristocrat who treated her with dignity. Who, through one simple sentence or two, had made clear to these brigands that she and Papa must be respected. Surely the word would pass through the entire regiment, and her fears of mistreatment could be set aside.

"Chiveys, Miss Folger, what do you think o' that?" Sadie stood at her elbow. "The gov'ner's a right decent fellow, ain't 'e?"

Rachel shook off her stupor. "Why, yes, Sadie. I do believe you are right."

Frederick barely noticed the landscape as he rode slowly back to his plantation. How could one brief encounter with a dark-eyed beauty answer all his questions about the sort of woman he must marry?

He had caught a glimpse of the brawl behind the inn, not realizing who was involved, and had ridden around the building in time to see Miss Folger strike the soldier. In that instant, he knew two things. First, her courage could not be matched in any titled young lady he had known in his life. Second, his position as magistrate demanded that he protect this young woman from the irate soldier. Because of the troubles up north, Major Brigham might be offended by Frederick's actions, but he would stand by them.

And then there was a third thing he knew…and felt as deeply as any truth he had ever encountered. He did not need to ask Miss Folger for advice on the type of young lady to marry, for she herself embodied everything he could ever desire: beauty, spirit, wit, pluck and more. The list seemed endless.

Was he mad? Possibly. Impetuous? No doubt. Yet, at this moment, Frederick's heart felt so light, he longed to turn Essex back to the settlement, where he might spend more time in Miss Folger's delightful company.

But that whimsical impulse was cut short by the specter of Oliver and his lies to Father. He had invented an imaginary female at the Oswald Plantation. Well, now Frederick's attention had been captured by a real, living young lady, and he must do all within his power to keep Oliver from destroying his chances with her…and from telling Father about her.

# Chapter Four

"**O**h, Señorita Rachel, this lace, it is very beautiful." Inez carefully stitched the delicate white trim to the neckline of the blue gauze gown. "Your papa, he is generous to make such expense for you." Her dark eyes shone with appreciation for the fabric. "He wants you to look nice for the party, *sí?*"

Rachel sat beside her newly hired servant in the corner of the store and hemmed the gown's striped panniers. Inez had already moved into the kitchen house behind the store and awaited the day when Rachel and Papa would take up residence in their apartment over the store. When he announced he had hired someone to cook and launder for them, Rachel had been delighted and more than a little surprised at his willingness to bear such an expense.

Now Papa had once again set aside his frugal ways for the party and insisted she use an expensive fabric. Rachel didn't know what to make of his interest in her clothing. Perhaps her claim to have no appropriate gown for the party wounded his pride, especially spoken in front of Mr. Moberly.

"So you think *el patrón's* fiza…" Inez wrinkled her forehead, then shrugged. "Fiza-something."

"His physician?" Rachel asked.

"*Sí,* the fiz-iz-cion." Inez laughed, and the age lines around her eyes deepened. "The one who fix your hand. He will be at the party, no? This one, he is not married, is nice to look at, is not so old for—" She gave Rachel a sly look. "Hmm. Maybe Inez say too much?"

"Not at all. You may speak freely when you and I are alone." Rachel studied her stitches to make certain they gathered the delicate fabric without puckering it. "But perhaps you don't understand the English. Dr. Wellsey is a member of the gentry and no doubt regards himself as being above a shopkeeper's daughter. For my part, I would not consider receiving the attentions of an Englishman."

"No?" Inez stared at her. "You do not like the English?" She busied herself with the lace again, muttering to herself in Spanish.

"What is it, Inez?"

"Have we not agreed, señorita, *Dios* has love for every man? *Jesu Christo,* He die for every man?"

"Yes, of course."

"Then if we do not like the English, is the love of *Dios* in us?" Maternal warmth glowed in Inez's eyes. "Does He not say to love others as He love us?"

Rachel concentrated on her work without answering. Inez had not abused her freedom to speak her thoughts, and her words conveyed great wisdom.

In truth, Rachel had hated the English for as long as she could remember. They stole from the colonists, both in taxes and in seizing men and property for their own use. Yet she had not considered that God might love them, as He did every soul. Her Quaker mother would be disappointed in her, for she had taught Rachel the Bible verse Inez quoted.

The jangle of the bell over the front door startled her from her thoughts.

"Hello, is anyone here?" Mr. Moberly stood inside the

door, hat in hand, blinking his eyes as everyone did to adjust to the dimmer store light after being out in the sun.

"Yes, sir." Rachel set aside her sewing and hurried to greet him. "How may I help you?"

"Miss Folger." His smile seemed almost boyish. "Good afternoon."

"Yes, sir. How may I help you?" *You just asked him that.* She gazed up into his dark gray eyes, transfixed by the intense look he returned. At the memory of his rescuing her from the soldier, she felt her cheeks grow warm. Now, as then, she thought perhaps some Englishmen might not be purely evil. His black hair was swept back in a queue, but one stray lock curled over his forehead like an unruly, and utterly charming, black sheep.

"I, well, um," he said, "I wondered how your father's business is faring. I have been telling everyone they should patronize your store. Even written the news of your establishment to other plantations along the St. Johns River. Settlers have done without many necessities and nearly all luxuries here in the wilderness and waited a long while for a proper mercantile close by…" He pursed his lips. "Now who's being too loquacious?"

Rachel laughed. Her face grew hotter. To think he had recalled her silly comment. "Papa will be pleased to hear that you are, um, pleased."

"Yes." He glanced around the store and then back at her. "Ah, I should have asked straightaway. How is your hand?" His right hand moved toward her slightly, then retracted, as if he would take her injured one but thought better of it. "Did Dr. Wellsey serve you…well?" He grinned.

"Oh, indeed, he did." Forbidding herself to laugh again, Rachel flexed her fingers to show the hand was on its way to complete recovery. "Although I must say he seemed to regard my little injury as a scientific experiment." The pleasant young doctor had never once looked at her face and seemed disappointed at the ease with which the splinters came out. "But, gracious, the smell of that salve." She waved her hand beneath her nose at the memory.

"Dreadful stuff, I agree." Mr. Moberly gave her a comical frown. "Yes, the good doctor is a serious scientist. But a competent physician must be, do you not think?"

"Why, I've never considered—"

"What's this?" Papa's voice boomed from behind Rachel as he entered from the back room. "Ah, Mr. Moberly. What can I do for ye today?"

Jamie followed close behind Papa and raised an eyebrow to question Rachel. She shrugged one shoulder and hoped Mr. Moberly did not see their silent communication. For some strange reason, she felt an urge to remind the Englishman that Jamie was her cousin, not a suitor. But why should he care about such things?

"Good afternoon, Mr. Folger." Mr. Moberly extended his hand. "Mrs. Winthrop has sent me for thread and, oh, several other items. I can't recall them all." He pulled a crumpled paper from his pocket and handed it to Rachel. "Do say you have everything she wrote down, Miss Folger, so I may continue to recommend this establishment for its many and varied wares."

"Yes, sir." Rachel walked to the counter and pressed the paper flat with her hand so she could read it. Mr. Moberly reminded her of a little boy who had not yet learned to be entirely neat, but she found it charming. Darning needles, twenty ells each of red and blue bunting, cinnamon, black pepper, several shades of thread, plus other needs. She gathered the items on the front counter but kept her ears open to the men's lively conversation.

"I did not know if I would see you again, Captain Templeton." Mr. Moberly's tone was jovial, as if chatting with an old friend. "Were you not to sail to England this week?"

"I'll sail day after tomorrow, weather permitting." Jamie's expression brightened to match Mr. Moberly's. "But since you've been here for some time, I hoped to ask your advice about the merchandise I should bring from London."

"Of course." Mr. Moberly clapped Jamie on the shoulder. "This is truly fortuitous. We have had many newcomers whose needs we failed to anticipate. I shall make a list for you."

"Very good." Jamie grinned. "List as you will, and I'll obtain it. And if you give me a letter of introduction, I shall be pleased to call upon any of your associates for you."

"I shall prepare that letter this very day. Do you have time to ride to my plantation this afternoon?"

"Sir, that is most agreeable." The last reservation fled from Jamie's expression, replaced by a broad smile.

"Excellent." Mr. Moberly perused several items on display: knives, flintlock pistols, a barrel of cast-iron nails. "While I am here, I should like to enlist your assistance."

Rachel's ears tingled, and she leaned closer to the men.

"Ask as ye will, sir," Papa said.

"A dissident agitator has entered our settlement and tried to stir up sympathy for the rebellion in Massachusetts and the other colonies." Mr. Moberly toyed with a length of rope coiled for sale. "The chap slips into the Wild Boar Inn or Brown's Tavern and makes a few remarks while men are in their cups, then slips away before anyone can apprehend him."

Rachel's heart raced. Another patriot, right here in St. Johns! She must learn his identity and try to contact him.

"Of course, no man here is of that mind." Mr. Moberly settled a placid smile on Papa and Jamie.

"Not that I've discerned," Papa said.

"Certainly not." Jamie sent Rachel a warning scowl. She wrinkled her nose in return.

"In any event, a reward awaits the man who can supply any information leading to his apprehension."

The men continued their business discussion, and by the time Rachel had assembled and packaged all of Mr. Moberly's purchases, they seemed to be lifelong friends. The gentleman paid Papa, bowed to her and afterward left the store.

"Don't that beat all?" Papa crossed his arms and watched Mr. Moberly leave. "Looks like the path is smooth before us."

"To be sure." Jamie sent a glance Rachel's way. "With Moberly's letters, we'll have access to the best products London can offer."

"Indeed we will." Papa moved behind the counter and pulled out a logbook. "Now let's take a look at those figures."

The two men hovered over the book and continued their discussion of Jamie's imminent voyage. To Rachel's annoyance, they never once mentioned the dissident agitator.

She wished they would include her in their consultations, but most often, they shooed her away. Her heart torn between wanting Mr. Moberly to come back and longing to go find the patriot right away, she returned to her corner. Inez was stitching the last inches of lace to the gown's neckline, and Rachel resumed her own work. With their shoulders almost touching, Rachel felt Inez shake and looked over to see the older woman working to hide her mirth.

"Shh. What is it?" Rachel glanced toward Papa. As kind-hearted as he was, he had no patience with chatty or giggling servants.

Inez leaned toward her and whispered, "Señorita, I think we both make mistake."

"Oh?"

"*Sí.* My mistake is thinking the physician is for you. No, no. It is *el patrón* who admires my mistress, and more than a little."

"What nonsense. Mr. Moberly is an English aristocrat. He would never consider…*admiring* me." Rachel sniffed at the thought of it. "Furthermore, as I said before, I would never receive the attentions of an Englishman."

"Mmm—mmm." Inez hummed softly. "From the happiness I see in your eyes, mistress, you have receive them whether you wish it or not."

Rachel forced herself to frown. "What nonsense."

But if the notion were truly nonsense, why had her face felt hot the entire time the gentleman spoke to her? Why had she felt keen disappointment when Papa and Jamie entered the store? And why did her heart now pound as if trying to leap from her chest?

Nonsense. Utter nonsense.

While Mrs. Winthrop prepared a list of household needs, Frederick carefully penned the letter to Father recommending Captain James Templeton as a worthy business associate. While he had nothing to lose after Father's last correspondence, he did not wish to further anger him. Despite a bit of rusticity, Templeton had an air about him that Father should admire, as one might esteem a capable horse handler or even a household steward. The captain possessed clear eyes that seemed to hold no hidden motives, unlike Oliver, who had always been a bit sly.

How ironic that Frederick had never noticed Oliver's wiliness. Yet since he had read Father's revealing letter, Frederick began to recall many instances where his innocent antics had brought unwarranted censure. But only when Oliver was involved.

Perhaps he was mad to entrust to Templeton the rebuilding of his own reputation with Father. But at this point, the captain's good reference was all he had.

Templeton arrived midafternoon. Frederick met him in the drawing room and welcomed him like a brother.

"You've a fine house, sir." The captain surveyed the room with interest, but no envy clouded his tone or expression. "I've often thought to build a house, but the sea's been my home since boyhood. I don't know if I could abide solid ground beneath me for too long."

"You may have the sea, sir. I gladly welcomed the feel of that solid ground after my stormy voyage across the Atlantic to East Florida."

They both chuckled, but before Templeton could offer a rejoinder, Oliver sauntered into the room. Frederick reluctantly made introductions.

"Well, captain," Oliver said, "what brings you to our humble home?"

Templeton's eyes narrowed for an instant, but he seemed to purposefully brighten his expression. "Just a bit of private business with Mr. Moberly."

Frederick withheld a laugh. His new friend was no fool. How quickly he had seen through Oliver's facade.

"Then let us adjourn to my study." Frederick enjoyed the dark look on Oliver's face. "You will excuse us, Oliver."

"Of course." Oliver's terse tone came through clenched teeth.

Once in the study with the door closed, Templeton stared at Frederick, an earnest look in his eyes. "Moberly, you don't know me well, but let me advise you not to trust Corwin." He gave his head a quick shake. "Something about him—"

"Yes, I agree." To think this man had seen it in less than five minutes. Perhaps as first mate to Captain Folger and now a captain himself, he had honed his skills in human understanding, whereas Frederick had taken a place of leadership only a few short years ago. He still had much to learn.

He sat at his desk, retrieved his letters and lists, and checked them once more to be sure all was in order before applying his seal. "Thank you for taking these to my family. I hope the introduction will serve us both well."

"I'm honored that you trust me." Seated opposite him, Templeton took them in hand, all the while appearing to search for words. "I sense you are a trustworthy man, too, Moberly, and therefore I must address a subject of some concern."

Frederick swallowed hard. He wanted to be open with this man, but he was so used to posing to achieve advantage that he hardly knew how to be genuine. Perhaps in that manner he had been playing the same game as Oliver. But at least he had never betrayed anyone.

"Say on, friend." He felt as if he had just unlocked his soul.

Templeton's brown eyes bored into his. "My cousin Rachel, Miss Folger, is like a sister to me. Captain Folger raised us together, and I couldn't love a sister by birth any more than I love her." He studied the letters in his hand, yet seemed not to see them. Again, he stared at Frederick. "If harm of any sort should come to her, whether to her person or to her heart, I'd have to require it of the man responsible for her grief."

Frederick's lower jaw fell slack, and he closed it as casually as possible while overcoming his shock. "I find Miss Folger to be a remarkable young lady, one whom I admire far too much to grieve in any way." He offered a half smile. "You may count on me in your absence to require it of anyone who might think to harm her."

Templeton's gaze softened. "I believe you."

An unfamiliar sense of comradeship filled Frederick's chest. Before he could speak his gratitude, Templeton added, "I hope Lord Bennington knows what an extraordinary job you've done in developing St. Johns Settlement. If he doesn't know it now, he will after I've finished talking with him."

Again warmth filled Frederick almost to bursting. "I am grateful, captain, more than you can know."

They stood, shook hands, and then proceeded to the front of the house. After another handshake, Templeton set his hand on Frederick's shoulder.

"Please know that the Almighty will be receiving my frequent petitions on your behalf."

Frederick coughed away the emotion that threatened to overwhelm him. "And I shall pray for you, as well." An onlooker might think them lifelong friends. "God speed you on your way."

He stood on the porch and watched Templeton ride away on a lop-eared mule. The chap did not ride any better than Frederick kept his footing on a ship. But their new friendship soothed away some of the ache left by Oliver's betrayal.

As if conjured by his thoughts, Oliver appeared beside him on the porch.

"Hmm. I wonder if his departure will put a stop to the seditious gossip in the taverns."

Frederick would have struck him if the suggestion had not sent a sting of suspicion through his chest.

## Chapter Five

"Papa, the heel of my shoe has loosened." Rachel would not mention that she had helped it to that condition. "May I go to the cobbler?"

Seated behind the store counter, he took off his spectacles and peered over his logbook. "Aye, 'tis best not to delay such repairs, else it'll cost more. We've no customers, so hurry along." He glanced down the length of her skirt, which covered her shoes, and wrinkled his forehead.

For a moment, Rachel thought he might have comprehended her ruse. She shifted from one hidden foot to the other and gave him a bright smile. "Thank you. I shall return as quickly as possible." She turned to go before he could change his mind.

"Avast." He stood and crossed his arms.

"Yes, sir?" Her pulse quickened.

"Whilst ye're there, see if the cobbler can make ye some slippers to match yer new gown." From his tone, he could have been ordering her to swab the deck. He sat down, put on his spectacles and studied the logbook again.

Yet his words brought a blush of confusion and shame to Rachel's cheeks. "Slippers?"

"Aye." He did not look up. "I'll not have ye tramp through a fancy plantation house in yer old shoes."

Surprised again by his generosity, she nonetheless hurried from the store and up the street, glancing at the various structures as she passed. While much needed to be done to transform the settlement into a true town, the streets had been laid out and cleared, and tabby foundations now supported numerous wooden buildings in various stages of completion.

In the distance, Rachel noticed a group of people loitering in the village's common. One tall figure in a wide-brimmed hat stood above the crowd. Mr. Moberly! Her feet—and her heart—tried to carry her toward the gathering, but she forced herself to turn aside at the cobbler's building two blocks from Papa's store.

As she stepped inside, the heavy smell of oiled leather almost pushed her back into the street. She inhaled shallow breaths and glanced around the small front room, where lasts, buckles, buttons, needles and countless other shoemaking supplies covered three tables.

The middle-aged cobbler looked up from his work and acknowledged her with a nod. "Miss Folger, what can we do for you today?" He rose to greet her.

"Good morning, Mr. Shoemaker. Would you be so kind as to fix my heel?" She slipped it off and held it out.

He turned it in his hands. "Tsk. Looks like someone tried to pry the heel off with a nail." Carrying it back to his workbench, he began his repairs.

Rachel moved across the bench from him. "Is Mrs. Shoemaker well?"

"Yes, thank you. She and the children are working in the kitchen house. Shall I call her?"

"No. No doubt she is too busy to chat." Rachel glanced around and saw no fabric for slippers, but another matter held priority. "Tell me, sir, what prompted your removal from

Savannah to this wilderness? Surely the city had sufficient work for a cobbler."

"Humph. Let those rebels look to their own feet." He hammered her shoe with considerable force. "After they tarred and feathered Judge Morgan for speaking against their wicked rebellion, any sensible man would take his family elsewhere." He held up the repaired shoe and rubbed it with an oil-stained cloth. "Just let those rebels dare come to East Florida. We're raising a militia here, and there'll be no mercy for any who rise up against the Crown."

Rachel gulped back a tart reply. Clearly this man was not the unknown patriot seeking to stir up sympathy for the cause. She would have taken her shoe and left, but Papa would only send her back. Ordering the slippers helped her collect her emotions. Mr. Shoemaker agreed to send his oldest daughter to Papa's store for the needed fabric, and the two men would negotiate the payments.

Glad to leave the stuffy shop, she breathed in the warm, fresh breeze drifting down the street. To her right, loud voices drew her attention to the common. She glanced at Papa's store and back toward the crowd. Once again her feet seemed determined to carry her there. This time she did not deny the impulse.

To her relief, several women from the settlement and nearby plantations stood among the men on the newly planted grass poking through the dark, sandy soil. She stayed at the edge of the crowd, surprised to see Mr. Moberly seated at a rough table beneath a spreading oak tree. He was writing in a leather-bound ledger. So this was how he dispensed his duties as magistrate. Rachel's feet once again seemed to move of their own will, drawing her closer to him.

In front of Mr. Moberly's table stood a barefoot young man in rags with his hands tied behind his back and fear in his eyes. Nearby stood a man whom Rachel recognized as the owner of a small plantation close to the village. He held in his arms a plump pink piglet that wiggled and squealed until he covered it with a burlap bag.

Laughter and rude comments from the crowd nearly sent Rachel on her way, but she could not bring herself to leave. Surely the Lord had directed her steps to this place so she might learn more about Mr. Moberly through his judgments.

She noticed two red-coated soldiers beside a hangman's noose that dangled from a branch of the vast tree, and an icy shiver ran through her from head to toe. Several yards away, out in the sun, newly made wooden stocks suggested a less severe sentence. But in this East Florida heat, who could endure even that?

A storm of emotions swirled through Rachel. The young man must have stolen the piglet. Such a crime must not go unpunished. Praying for justice and mercy, she found herself barely able to breathe.

Frederick felt the urge to squirm like the hapless young man who stood bound and trembling before him. He hated holding court, hated making judgments, hated having the eyes of everyone in the settlement look to him for wisdom. Why Father had arranged for him to be the magistrate, he could not guess. And with Oliver leaning against the trunk of the oak tree, arms crossed and chin lifted, Frederick felt certain whatever he did would be reported to the earl…and would be wrong.

Heretofore, the disputes had been easy to solve: uncertain boundary lines, drunken brawling, that sort of nonsense. But the theft of a pig must be dealt with severely. In England this thief most likely would be hanged. Surely in this remote part of East Florida, where men sometimes were forced to do desperate things in order to survive, English law need not be enforced to its fullest extent. And after reading of former

Governor Grant's harsh decision in a similar case where he sentenced the hapless servant to death by hanging, Frederick shrank from inflicting such an unforgiving sentence. Should a Christian not offer mercy and redemption to the miscreant?

Frederick surveyed the crowd, glad that the broad brim of his hat shielded his eyes from their view. He kept his mouth in a grim line and assumed a stiff, formal posture. In the corner of his eye, he saw Miss Folger approach, and his heart sank. He must not look at her, must not care what she thought of his coming decision. He must forget her, forget Father, forget Oliver, forget everything but the men in conflict before him.

*Lord, grant me wisdom as You have promised in the Holy Scriptures.*

"Mr. Baker, come forward." Frederick beckoned the pig's owner.

Shifting the sack holding the pig, the man snatched off his hat and then stepped up to the table beside the accused. "Yes, sir."

"This is your indentured servant, John Gilbert? And that is your pig?" Frederick pointed to the sack.

"Yes, sir."

Frederick noticed that Baker's expression held more worry than anger. Interesting. Did he hope for leniency or vengeance?

"Now, John, you have been accused of stealing this pig. Did you do it?"

Misery clouded the lad's blue eyes. "Aye, sir. 'Twas not just fer meself. Mr. Baker don't feed us aught but gruel. A man's gotta have meat now and then or he can't work the land."

Frederick saw color rush to Baker's cheeks. He did not deny the charge.

*Lord, grant me the wisdom of Solomon.* Frederick recalled that Governor Grant had required one man under judgment to hang his more blameworthy friends.

"Well, Mr. Baker, this man belongs to you to do with as you will. If you want him hanged, you will do it yourself." Frederick pointed his quill pen toward the noose hanging from the oak tree.

A great gasp and much murmuring rose from the crowd, some approving, some grumbling. Frederick would not permit himself to look at Miss Folger to see what her reaction might be.

"Now, Mr. Moberly, sir," Mr. Baker said, "if I hang him, I'm out a servant to work my land. I paid his fare to these shores, and he owes me six more years."

Frederick shrugged. "Then what do you consider a just punishment?"

Baker scratched his head. He glanced toward the stocks. "Forty lashes and a week in the stocks should teach 'im a lesson."

*And kill him in the process.* Frederick set down his quill and crossed his arms over his chest. "Three days in the stocks and ten lashes afterward. And you will scourge him yourself."

Baker's posture slumped, and he hung his head. After several moments, he gave John Gilbert a sidelong glance, then raised his eyes to Frederick. "That'll do justice. Thank you, sir."

The crowd burst into cheers and applause. John Gilbert slumped to the ground on his knees. "God bless ya, Mr. Moberly, sir. God bless ya."

Emotion flooded Frederick's chest, but he managed a gruff dismissal. "Are there other quarrels?"

With none coming forward, Frederick made notes in his ledger, blotted the ink, and closed the book. As the crowd dispersed, he cast a hasty glance at Miss Folger and barely contained a smile. Her head was tilted prettily, and a look of wonder filled her lovely face. Once again he swallowed a rush of emotion. Whether or not his judgment had been correct, her obvious approval was all he required.

\* \* \*

Rachel knew she must turn and walk away like the others, but her feet refused to move. To her relief, Mr. Moberly approached her. She struggled to think of a Scripture verse to relate to him in praise of his decision. But she could think only of some words from Shakespeare that nonetheless imparted an eternal truth: *The quality of mercy is not strained. It droppeth as the gentle rain from heaven upon the place beneath. It is twice blest: It blesseth him that gives and him that takes.*

"Miss Folger." Mr. Moberly gave her that boyish smile of his that belied his august position. "What brings you to the common on this lovely day?"

Unable to meet his gaze, she stared down at his well-polished black boots, now covered with sand. "Just a trip to the cobbler."

"Ah. And did Mr. Shoemaker serve you well?"

She looked up to see a twinkle in his gray eyes. "Indeed he did." At least with her shoe.

"Very good." He nodded his approval. "If I am not being too bold, may I escort you to your father's mercantile?"

Happiness swept through her. On the way, she could recite her Shakespeare to compliment his judgment. "That would be—"

"Moberly." Mr. Corwin approached them with a determined stride. He barely glanced at Rachel. "The tavern keeper had a visit from that rabble-rouser last evening. He can give us a description."

Mr. Moberly drew in his lips and shot a cross look at his friend. "I am certain he can wait for an hour."

Rachel's heart thumped wildly. The patriot was still at work.

"No, he cannot wait." Mr. Corwin's frown matched Mr. Moberly's. "He must meet his suppliers on the coast before nightfall."

Mr. Moberly blew out a cross sigh. "Miss Folger, will you forgive me?"

"Of course." A riot of confusion filled her mind. How could she long to become better acquainted with this gentleman when he represented everything she opposed?

For the briefest moment, she thought to delay him so he would miss learning more about the patriot. Or she could follow him and try to discern the man's identity herself. But both actions would be shocking improprieties. She would wait until next Saturday's party at Mr. Moberly's plantation. Surely there she would learn something useful to the revolution.

## Chapter Six

"Are you certain I should wear this one?" Frederick studied his reflection in the bedroom mirror while his manservant fussed with the turned back tails of the gray linen coat. "Why not the red brocade?"

"Sir, if you will permit me, the red most assuredly is your finest coat." Summerlin brushed lint from the gray garment's padded shoulders. "However, I despair that you would waste it on these rustics." His lip curled. "Should you not save it for the day when you are called once again to the capital of this wilderness?"

Frederick shot him a disapproving glance in the mirror, but Summerlin had shifted his attention to the lace at Frederick's cuffs. Never mind. He hated to scold the old fellow, who had been ordered by Frederick's father to leave the comforts of London and come to East Florida, a crushing change for a man in his fifties. Perhaps he was another spy like Oliver, sent to make certain Frederick brought no scandal upon the family, as his brothers had. But, white hair and stooped shoulders notwithstanding, Summerlin's talents as a valet could not be matched.

"Very well. I shall accept your choice of attire but not your attitude toward my guests." Frederick kept his tone soft.

"Some of these 'rustics' can be quite charming, not to mention intelligent and clever at business."

Summerlin straightened in his odd way and stared at Frederick. "Charming, sir? Oh, dear. Has some young lady caught my master's eye?" The clarity in his pale blue eyes and the half smile at the corner of his thin lips removed any doubts about where his loyalty lay. "Well, then, perhaps the red—"

"No, this will do." Frederick breathed in the orange and bergamot cologne Summerlin had concocted for him. "Now that I think of it, if I were to dress as for an audience with the governor, my clothing might intimidate my guests. Since my purpose is to ensure their loyalty to the Crown and foster a feeling of community, I should avoid strutting before them like a peacock."

"Ah, well said, young sir." Approval emanated from Summerlin's eyes such as Frederick had longed for in vain from his father. "Lady Bennington would be proud."

Summerlin's words further encouraged him. Indeed, Mother would understand his choice of clothes, despite her own exquisite wardrobe, for she always sought to make even the lowliest of her guests comfortable.

"Forgive me, sir, for disparaging your new friends." Summerlin glanced over his shoulder toward the closed bedroom door and bent toward Frederick with a confidential air. "I am your servant in all things."

Frederick mirrored his move. "Thank you. But there will be no trysts. The young lady will be courted properly." He caught Summerlin's gaze. "Only time will tell, of course, but I believe Miss Folger is all I could wish for in a wife."

Serene comprehension washed over Summerlin's face, softening his pale wrinkles. "As I said, sir, I am your servant in all things."

A sharp rap sounded on the door. "Moberly, your guests are arriving." Oliver's tone sounded almost jovial.

Summerlin's expression flickered with distaste for the briefest instant before giving way to his customary formal air. In that half second, Frederick knew without doubt that his devoted servant had purposely left Oliver's letter on his desk, and warmth filled his chest, as it had over Templeton's friendship.

Father would sneer at his idea of calling these lower-class men "friends," but Frederick could consider them nothing less. And how relieved he had been to discover that Templeton was not the agitator, as Corwin had suggested.

"Coming, Corwin." Frederick strode toward the door.

Summerlin hobbled close behind, brushing lint from Frederick's coat all the way. "Have a good evening, sir."

Visions of the lovely Miss Folger danced before Frederick's eyes as he grasped the door latch. "That I shall, my good man. That I shall."

The wagon rattled along the well-packed sand and seashell road beneath a canopy of oak, pine and cypress trees. Seated beside Papa on the driver's bench, Rachel held her poorly mended parasol overhead while the late afternoon sun blasted its heat through the tree branches. Perspiration had begun to wilt her freshly pressed gown, and her curls threatened to unwind. Nevertheless, excitement filled her as she anticipated the party. She would try to discover if the patriot was among the guests. And she hoped to find the opportunity to tell Mr. Moberly how much she admired his wisdom in the case of the stolen pig.

Savoring the fragrances of the tropical forests, she studied the undergrowth for evidence of panthers, bears or poisonous snakes. Papa had assured her that this road lay too far from water for them to chance upon an alligator, yet she watched for them, as well. Several times she thought to have seen one of those fearsome dragons only to realize the object was a fallen tree.

As they rounded a stand of palm trees and a large white building came into view, Papa pointed with his wagon whip and whistled. "Thar she blows. Now that's a house, if ever I saw one."

Rachel laughed at his understatement even as her own feelings swelled. The two-storied mansion sat elevated several feet off the ground on a coquina foundation. A broad wooden porch extended across the wide front, and four white Doric columns supported the porch roof. Eight tall front windows, four on each floor, suggested airy rooms inside.

The blue and red bunting Mr. Moberly had purchased from the store now hung around the columns in a festive display. Their crisscross pattern against the white background vaguely suggested the British flag, a nettling reminder to Rachel of who ruled this land. With some effort, she dismissed the unpleasant thought. Even if their host had deliberately hung them that way, he was after all an Englishman who no doubt loved his homeland.

On the left side of the main house, smoke curled from the kitchen house's chimney, and a warm breeze carried the aroma of roasting pork.

"That'll set a man's mouth to watering." Papa steered his two mules into the semicircular drive before the front entrance, where several liveried black grooms awaited.

As Papa pulled the reins, one groom grasped the harness, and another stood ready to take control of the equipage. Rachel saw Mr. Moberly hastening from the house, followed by a slave carrying a small white boxstep. At the sight of him, finely dressed but by no means haughty, her heart missed a beat.

Papa jumped to the ground and hobbled to her side of the wagon. But Mr. Moberly reached her first.

"Good evening. Welcome." Mr. Moberly shook Papa's hand. "Will you permit me to assist your daughter, Mr. Folger?"

"As ye will." Papa bowed.

"Put it here." Mr. Moberly motioned to the slave and indicated a spot on the ground. "Miss Folger, may I?" He held
out both white-gloved hands.

"Yes, thank you." She grasped them with pleasure, and her
face warmed as she climbed from the wagon. Never in her life
had she received such attention.

"Welcome to Bennington Plantation." Mr. Moberly offered
Rachel his arm. "Won't you please come inside?"

The entrance to the house was a welcoming red door with
an oval etched-glass window. Inside they were introduced to
Mr. Moberly's cousin, a tall, older woman.

"Do come in. We're pleased to have you." Mrs. Winthrop
wore a black linen gown, and her hair was pinned back in a
roll. A kind look lit her finely lined face, and her voice reso-
nated with sincerity.

Dr. Wellsey greeted the newcomers, and even Mr. Corwin
spoke pleasantly to them. They met a Reverend Johnson and
his wife, and the minister invited them to his church services.
To Rachel's surprise and delight, Papa accepted. Mrs.
Johnson, however, showed no interest in further conversation.

Several other couples were in attendance, and Rachel
studied each face upon introduction trying to discern if any
of them might be the patriot. Although everyone seemed
friendly, not one person lifted an eyebrow upon meeting the
Folgers from Boston. Had they not heard of the British
invasion and the battles of Lexington and Concord?

While servants passed trays of hors d'oeuvres and cups of
citrus punch, the men stood in a group and chatted about
crops and weather. Rachel passed by as one man mentioned
the "agitator" who frequented the taverns, and she glanced
about the group to see if anyone appeared nervous. Not one
expression informed her.

"The problem is," Mr. Moberly said, "his description does

not match anyone we know along the St. Johns River or in the settlement. So, if you see a stout fellow with a long red beard, do mention it to the nearest soldier."

While the other men accepted the charge without much concern, Rachel felt a tremor of delight. Now she had one description, but perhaps there were other patriots.

She joined the other ladies, who stood on the opposite side of the drawing room making polite conversation about the challenges of living in the wilderness. The youngest woman in the group, Rachel listened more than she spoke, as propriety demanded. But she prayed for an opportunity to mention the matter close to her heart. In Boston, all the talk had been of the revolution. Here, none of the women seemed aware that their counterparts up north were sewing uniforms for their soldier husbands and weeping for those who had died for freedom's sake a short two months ago.

"Miss Folger," Mrs. Winthrop said, "I understand your father's store has many wares we are generally deprived of here in East Florida."

"Yes, ma'am." An unexpected wave of pleasure swept through Rachel at being addressed so particularly by this kind, elegant lady. "We have been fortunate to import many useful items for sale, and my cousin will bring more from London."

The other women cooed their approval.

"Then I must come and see for myself," Mrs. Winthrop said, "for I am certain Mr. Moberly has not told me everything that would be of interest to ladies." A proper hostess, Mrs. Winthrop now turned her attention to another guest. Yet her comments put an approving stamp on both Rachel and Papa's business *and* their presence at this party.

Rachel cast a casual glance across the room and found Mr. Moberly staring at her. Her breath caught, and she hastily turned away. Her glance had also taken in the pleasant look

Mr. Corwin sent her. Heat filled her cheeks. Why would these high-born gentlemen thus regard her? She recalled her mother's cautions regarding men.

Outside the drawing room, a large commotion captured everyone's attention. Servants hurried past the doorway, and soon the stout black butler entered to announce "Lady Augusta and Major Brigham."

"Moberly." Lady Augusta marched into the room with both hands extended toward him. "How good of you to invite us."

While the vicar's wife, Mrs. Johnson, released a sigh suggesting envy, Rachel almost gasped at the newcomer's appearance. Perhaps ten years older than Rachel, Lady Augusta wore a tall, white-powdered wig and a green silk gown with broad panniers and a low-cut bodice. Her face, which seemed well-formed, bore a masklike covering of white. A single black dot, clearly not a blemish, had been placed to the right of her rouged lips, perhaps to suggest a dimple.

Rachel had seen a few ladies wear such a facade in Boston, but surely here in East Florida, the heat would melt that mask off of her face—if indeed the substance melted—before they sat down to dinner. And there stood her husband, dressed in his full regimental uniform, a glaring red banner of British pride emphasized by the haughty lift of his equine nose. Rachel shook away her distaste. She must do nothing to damage Papa's favor among these people.

Mr. Moberly did all the proper honors to welcome the two latecomers. Their rank demanded that other guests be presented to the couple, so the company filed past them. Major Brigham languidly studied every person up and down through his quizzing glass, as though trying to decide if each were some sort of miscreant. Not one guest elicited a smile or even a polite nod from the officer or his wife.

Instead, Lady Augusta looped an arm around Mr.

Moberly's. "Dear Moberly," she simpered, "you must show me your house. How clever of you to bring a bit of English country charm to this horrid jungle."

"Of course, my lady. Come along. All of us shall go." Mr. Moberly waved his free hand to take in the whole room.

Lady Augusta's arrogant expression soured into a frown. Rachel could not help but wonder whether the woman had wanted to be alone with Mr. Moberly.

He guided his guests through the house's ten rooms, each of which inspired Rachel's admiration. While elegant in all appointments, the rooms were not ostentatious or gaudy. She particularly liked the library and would have been happy to spend the rest of the evening perusing the many books there. Lingering by the gentleman's desk, she thought she spied a familiar pamphlet partially covered by a book. She longed to know what Mr. Moberly had been reading, but the party moved on, and propriety required her to follow them into the hallway.

"Shall we see the grounds?" Mr. Moberly addressed Lady Augusta, for everyone understood her approval alone would permit the expedition.

"Of course. I should not wish to miss anything."

Mr. Moberly offered his arm to Lady Augusta, and Rachel noticed with surprise that Papa also offered his arm to Mrs. Winthrop.

The party moved outside, where a cool breeze from the east gave some relief as they walked along the narrow pathways among the plantation's many trees. Mr. Moberly gave commentary as he showed them the sugar mill, the fields of sugar cane, cotton and indigo, and the fragrant, flourishing orange grove. He took them to the springhouse, a covered coquina cistern that caught water flowing from the earth's depths, where a house servant dipped in a pitcher and filled goblets for the guests. From there, they moved to Bennington Creek, across which lay vast rice paddies.

As the party wended its way back to the house, Rachel noticed countless slaves, both men and women, at work in the fields, and her heart sank. How she despised slavery, an evil that had been abolished in Nantucket in 1773. Did Mr. Moberly approve of it or merely tolerate it by necessity?

Ahead Mr. Moberly was assisting Lady Augusta up the front steps. How courteously he behaved toward her, and even toward Rachel and his other guests of lower rank. But how did he treat his slaves? The men and women in the fields did not wear chains, but iron bands on some slaves' ankles suggested they were chained at night. On the other hand, the black servants in the house seemed truly devoted to Mr. Moberly. In particular, Rachel had noticed the little slave girl who sat in the corner of the drawing room to wave the palm fans. The child had gazed at Mr. Moberly with clear adoration.

But despite Mr. Moberly's frequent friendly glances in Rachel's direction during the tour of his plantation, she came to know one thing. As proven by the ease with which he socialized with Lady Augusta, any kind attentions he gave Rachel were merely the actions of a gentleman displaying good manners. If she received them with any sort of expectation, she was nothing short of a fool.

In the dining room, they sat down to supper at a long, damask-covered oak table laden with exquisite bone china, delicate etched crystal and heavy silverware with an ornate floral pattern. A vast array of delicacies graced the board.

Rachel found herself seated between Señor Garcia and Reverend Johnson, neither of whom she could imagine to be the patriot. The Spaniard seemed to prefer eating to conversation, but the vicar made pleasant conversation.

"What do you think of the alligator, Miss Folger?"

"I find it surprisingly tasty, especially seasoned with these exotic herbs. And I should far rather eat alligator than for one to eat me. As we came by skiff from the coast, a large one bumped our vessel so hard I thought we would be swamped and devoured." The memory made her shudder.

"How dreadful. Thank the Lord you were spared."

Major Brigham and Lady Augusta, on either side of Mr. Moberly, spoke to no one but their host, although the officer seemed to take an inordinate number of opportunities to peruse the company through his quizzing glass. From his perpetual frown, Rachel guessed the haughty man might be having difficulty controlling his temper, but she heard and saw nothing to suggest why. When his stare fell on her, she stared back, and his frown deepened. But what did she care about the opinions of a rude British officer and his equally rude wife?

At the end of the meal, Mr. Moberly directed his guests to the drawing room, where rows of chairs faced the magnificent pianoforte in the corner. "Mrs. Winthrop, will you entertain us with your delightful playing?"

"Now, Mr. Moberly." The lady shook her head. "Surely someone else can play better than I." She gazed around the room. "Mrs. Johnson? Señora Garcia?"

All the ladies declined, denying any musical skill.

Standing beside Rachel, Papa looked down at her with a clear question in his eyes, but she warned him off with a frown. As much as she longed to play the beautiful instrument, she refused to put herself forward in this company, where Lady Augusta might ridicule her and who knew what Major Brigham might say.

"Very well, then." Mrs. Winthrop sat down to play, and the other guests took their places.

Rachel chose an armless brocade chair in the back row where her panniers would not poof out in front. When Mr. Moberly took the chair next to her, her pulse quickened. This was the first personal attention he had given her since helping her down from the wagon. Foolish hope assaulted her, and she had no weapon with which to defend herself.

"I do hope you're enjoying yourself, Miss Folger." His eyes beamed with kind intensity. "Did you find the meal satisfactory?"

Against her best efforts, Rachel's cheeks warmed. "Oh, yes, it was—"

"Moberly." Lady Augusta appeared beside him. "I must speak with you, and I fear the noise of your aunt's playing will drown me out. May we find a quiet corner?" She waved her silk fan languidly, and her eyes sent an invitation Rachel could not discern.

"Of course, my lady." Mr. Moberly glanced at Rachel and offered an apologetic smile. "Forgive me, Miss Folger. I shall return in a moment."

"Of course." Rachel echoed his words, working hard to keep the sarcasm from her tone.

Once again, certainty shouted within her. She was nothing more than a trifle in Mr. Moberly's eyes. He would always defer to those considered well-born. Why had she ever permitted herself to think otherwise?

But just as Papa claimed the empty seat beside her, another thought quickly replaced her disappointment. She stood and moved past him, determined to discover Mr. Moberly's true character. When Papa raised his bushy eyebrows to question her, she whispered "the necessary." Instead of searching for that room, she tiptoed down the hallway just as Mr. Moberly disappeared into his study. Rachel stopped outside the door, still ajar, leaned against the wall and, heart pounding, prayed no servant would discover her eavesdropping.

## Chapter Seven

"**D**ear Moberly, I congratulate you on a delightful supper."
Lady Augusta gazed into Frederick's eyes with a doelike expression, her own dark orbs encircled by dreadful black lines and her face covered with white lead ceruse. A despicable fashion, if ever he saw one, especially when the lady seemed not to have suffered the ravages of smallpox that required such a covering.

He shifted from one foot to the other and glanced beyond her toward the open door. Brigham could come down the hallway, see them poised close to one another, and misunderstand. Worse still, Miss Folger might do the same. Where was his watchdog Corwin when he needed him? Frederick stepped back from Lady Augusta to sit on the edge of his desk, glad to distance himself from her heavy rose perfume.

"Thank you, my lady." He crossed his arms. "I hope you did not find the wild boar too gamy."

"Not at all, silly boy." She tapped his arm with her closed fan and gave him a coquettish smile. "It was delicious."

"Excellent." He tugged at his cravat. "Well, then, was there something in particular you wished to say…to ask…to offer complaint about?" He grinned.

The brightness in Lady Augusta's eyes dimmed, and the coquette vanished. "I want…no, I *require* a favor from you." Her voice wavered, and she swayed lightly.

"My lady, you have but to name it." He uncrossed his arms, ready to catch her if she fainted.

She clutched her fan. "You must know my husband is the bravest man in His Majesty's service, so you must not think ill of him or tell him of my request."

Frederick leaned against the desk. "Madam, you may depend on me."

"Thank you." She exhaled a soft sob. "Will you write to Lord Bennington on my behalf? Ask your father to use his influence with His Majesty to keep Major Brigham in East Florida, say that you cannot do without him, that only he can manage the Indians, that—"

"Shh." Frederick lifted a finger to his lips. "My lady, your voice grows louder. Surely you do not wish Major Brigham to hear this unusual request." Nor did Frederick wish to hear it.

She sent a furtive glance toward the open door. "No, no. He must not know." She pulled a lace handkerchief from her sleeve and dabbed the corners of her eyes, smudging the black kohl. "I would never ask such a thing except for the rebellion in Boston. I cannot bear it if Brigham is sent there to fight."

Even as understanding welled up in Frederick's chest, another thought intruded. His brother Thomas, who served in His Majesty's navy, would be deeply shamed before the admiralty if his wife were to beg this favor.

"Oh, Moberly." She lifted her hands in supplication. "Say you will write the letter." She straightened, seeming to gain a measure of self-control. "In turn, I will write a letter to *my* father asking him to look with favor upon you."

"Me? I did not know Lord Chittenden knew of my existence, much less that I am out of favor with him."

"Oh, he doesn't, and you aren't. But I have four sisters, each of whom has her own small inheritance." Her voice lilted slightly. "I know how difficult it is for a younger son to find a bride among his peers."

"I, uh, that is—"

"With your successes here in East Florida, surely His Majesty will soon bestow a knighthood upon you. And, if I ask Father, he will receive you, and you may choose among my sisters for your wife." She opened her fan, once again the coquette. "They are beauties, one and all."

"My lady, I am honored, but—" A month ago, this proposal might have filled him with hope. Now he had a sudden urge to seek out Miss Folger and spend a pleasant hour in her company to clear his memory of this conversation.

"Please." Transparent honesty now emanated from Lady Augusta's eyes.

Frederick sighed his surrender. "You must permit me to write what I deem best."

"God bless you, Moberly. I shall never forget this." Her tears washed the ghastly black substance down the mask on her cheeks. Dabbing with her handkerchief, she seemed unaware of the mess she had made of herself.

"My lady, there is a looking glass in the necessary room."

She gave him a sheepish smile. "Yes, of course. Thank you." She walked toward the door, then turned back. "I believe Eleanor would suit you well. She is sweet-tempered and—"

"Please do not trouble yourself, Lady Augusta." If memory served, Lady Eleanor was one of the young ladies who had refused to speak to him at Lord Abingdon's party some four years ago.

"Or perhaps Margaret, the youngest." Her voice trailed off as she left the room.

Frederick leaned back on the desk and exhaled his relief. Hearing Cousin Lydie's music, he forced himself to recover, for he must return to the drawing room. Her arthritis might flare up if he left her playing the pianoforte for their guests too long.

As he stood, one hand brushed over an unfamiliar paper stuck halfway under a book. Lifting the pamphlet, he read its title, *A Declaration of Rights and Grievances.* A copy of the disgruntled colonists' complaints against King George! Frederick's heart leapt into his throat. Where had this come from? Who had placed it on his desk? He rubbed his forehead. This could bring him serious trouble if Brigham saw it when they toured the room. Perhaps that accounted for the man's ill humor during supper. Frederick started to tear it up and throw the pieces into the unlit hearth, but mad curiosity stayed his hand. He thrust it behind the books on one of his shelves and hurried to the drawing room.

While the other guests sat listening to Cousin Lydie's lovely music, Brigham and Corwin stood across the room in intense conversation. The officer gave Frederick a dark glare, and Frederick's pulse quickened. His father's influence with the king might not be sufficient to save him if he could not convince the major he knew nothing about the pamphlet.

He sensed Lady Augusta's presence beside him and gave her a quick glance—a mistake, for she gazed at him over her fan flirtatiously. Now Major Brigham's glare grew even darker. Did he suspect them of a tryst?

Seated again with Papa near the doorway, Rachel had difficulty not laughing. Lady Augusta's furtive rendezvous was the furthest thing from an assignation, and poor Mr. Moberly's discomfort had been apparent in his conciliatory tone of voice. He truly was an honorable gentleman.

Rachel turned her attention to Mrs. Winthrop, even as her own fingers itched to play the fine mahogany pianoforte. The lady's playing was adequate but uninspired, and she often hit a wrong key. But propriety forced everyone to sit with rapt admiration.

Guilt nudged at Rachel for such ungenerous thoughts. Throughout the evening, Mrs. Winthrop had shown her nothing but the kindest of attentions, and the dear lady exhibited modest awareness of her shortcomings at the instrument.

Footsteps behind them drew Rachel's attention to the doorway, where she saw Mr. Moberly enter the room. Against her will, she glanced behind him to see if Lady Augusta had followed. When the lady entered a moment later and gave Mr. Moberly an intimate look over her fan, Rachel again wanted to laugh. But Mr. Moberly wore a troubled frown as he looked toward the lady's husband.

The moment Lady Augusta sat down, her husband and Mr. Corwin crossed the room to Mr. Moberly, and the men stepped out into the hallway. With a casual air, Rachel leaned back to hear their conversation. Perhaps these men would say something useful to the revolution. She glanced at Papa, but his gaze was focused on Mrs. Winthrop, who now played a rousing tune at full volume.

"Now, see here, Moberly." Major Brigham's words came out in a low growl. "I'll not see my wife involved in a scandal."

Rachel smothered a gasp and forced herself to remain seated. But if necessary, she would tell that odious major that his wife was the one at fault.

"I will not have Lady Augusta disgraced in this manner." His voice low and menacing, Major Brigham placed one hand on the hilt of his ceremonial sword and waved the other fist at Frederick.

Frederick felt certain his heart had stopped. "But, my lord, I assure you—" He glanced toward the lady in question, who now sat listening to Cousin Lydie's concert, oblivious to his dilemma.

Brigham marched toward the front door and back again. Frederick sent a questioning grimace toward Corwin, who shrugged and shook his head.

"How dare you entice my wife off in some corner for who knows what?" Brigham's cheeks flamed, and his blue eyes sent out an icy glare. "I demand to know what you did."

Frederick swallowed hard, praying for the right answer. He forced himself to assume a relaxed pose. "She will be disappointed in my telling you, but since you insist…"

*Lord, give me an answer, please.*

"Well?" Brigham took a step closer, his hand still on his sword.

"Ah, very well, then." Frederick studied his fingernails and brushed them against his jacket shoulder. "She asked me to help her arrange a, um, surprise for you."

"What? A surprise, you say?" Brigham drew back, and his eyes widened. After several moments, his raging scowl melted into a slow smile. "I see. Well, then, I'll ask no more questions." He gazed at his wife tenderly, then frowned again. "But there is another matter which I will not so lightly dispense with."

Frederick had difficulty maintaining his composure. Was this a parlor game this couple played? "And whatever might that be?"

"The very idea," said Brigham in terse, quiet tones, "that you invited the daughter of an earl into company consisting of nothing more than shopkeepers, sailors and Spaniards, to sit at table with her as if they were her equals, why, it's preposterous. An affront not to be borne."

Frederick struggled to keep the sarcasm from his tone. "I beg your indulgence, sir. I thought it was clear when I invited you and Lady Augusta that you'd have no peer here. No one holds a rank equal to yours outside of St. Augustine, a bit far to go for a simple supper." He pasted on a smile that had often won over his older brothers in times of conflict.

Corwin coughed away a laugh.

Brigham glared at Frederick, and he blustered out a few huffing breaths, as though he was trying to maintain the intensity of his anger. "Humph. A poor excuse for forcing us to mingle with this rabble. Do you have any idea of the scandal it would bring upon my wife if anyone in her London circles found out about this? Why, she would be humiliated, pitied behind her back." As he looked in her direction, his threatening stance relaxed, and his dark frown softened into an expression of unmitigated affection.

Frederick also relaxed. After all, the man was merely a gallant knight defending his lady.

"If I may say so, sir, Lady Augusta appears to be enjoying herself." Frederick wished he could say the same for Miss Folger. Her posture stiffened noticeably during Brigham's tirade. He and Brigham spoke softly, but no doubt she heard every cruel word. Would that he could shield her as Brigham now attempted to shield his wife from perceived injury to her reputation.

"Perhaps she is. Yes, you may be right. The dear, brave girl has put up with much since I dragged her away from her friends and brought her to this beastly wilderness."

"And who would tell those friends about this evening's innocent gathering?" Frederick could see the man relenting. "Not I. Not Corwin here. Not Mrs. Winthrop."

Brigham turned a stern face to Corwin. "I suppose not. But—" He stood squarely in front of Frederick and studied him up and down through his quizzing glass, as if inspecting one of his insubordinate dragoons. "There is yet another matter that cannot be easily explained away."

"Indeed?" Frederick crossed his arms and tilted his head to feign interest. But in truth, this man was beginning to irritate him. Frederick was His Majesty's magistrate and, peerage notwithstanding, possessed more authority than Brigham in this part of East Florida.

"Indeed." Brigham's eyes took on a steely glint. "Corwin here tells me you have permitted an Indian village to remain in the southeast corner of your plantation. Is that right?" Again, his anger was too excessive for the matter at hand.

"Yes, of course. The Timucuan people know the land as no Englishman possibly could. They're peaceful, and fostering their friendship benefits all of us."

"I want them out." An order, not a request.

Frederick studied the major while countless responses warred within him. He saw Miss Folger watching over her shoulder, her face solemn. Suddenly he felt like a spineless toady.

"Major Brigham, I will be responsible for the people living within my domain." A strange thrill shot down his spine. "All of them."

Brigham lifted his chin and sneered. "Do you refuse my orders?"

How many times in his life had Frederick disarmed such animosity with a joke, a smile, a feigned surrender? But this man would not tell him what to do on his father's land. This time he would not give way, must not give way. Not in front of Miss Folger.

"Sir." He kept his voice low. "You do not have the authority to give me orders. If you have a grievance or question about the manner in which I manage my father's plantation or St. Johns Settlement, we can take the matter before Governor Tonyn in St. Augustine."

Brigham stared hard at him for several moments. "Very well, then. I shall inform His Excellency of your refusal to send those savages to Cuba, where the rest of their kind went when we took possession of these lands." He snorted. "If I did not know better, I would think you were one of those traitors, like the fools up north who are demanding *independence*." The last syllable sizzled with his distaste.

"Haven't we Englishmen always been fond of our independence?" Frederick relished the unfamiliar courage surging through him. "You know, the *Magna Carta*, and so forth?" A renegade grin forced its way to his lips.

Brigham's eyes narrowed. "Be careful, Moberly. Lord Bennington may have His Majesty's ear, but I have my own resources, including my esteemed father-in-law."

Frederick offered a genial shrug. "We should not be enemies, my lord. We have too much to gain through friendship."

Brigham drew himself up into a stern military stance, as if to forestall any attempt at alliance. "You will excuse Lady Augusta and me. I must take her away from this rabble and convey her safely home before complete darkness."

Frederick bowed slightly. "Of course."

Courtesy required him to see the couple to their carriage, where mounted, torch-bearing soldiers waited to guard their passage up the darkened road. Facing away from her husband, Lady Augusta gave Frederick a conspiratorial wink that made him shudder. He must keep his promise to her and plead for Brigham's continued posting in East Florida when his preference would be to see the man sent straightaway to the very location she feared.

As he walked back into the house, disappointment crowded out the pleasure he had felt over standing up to Major Brigham. He had planned this party to get better acquainted with the lovely Miss Folger but hadn't had but two separate moments to speak with her. Hardly the way to impress or interest her. But now he inhaled a deep, refreshing breath. He still had time to redeem the evening. He would seek out Miss Folger straightaway.

# Chapter Eight

While the other guests adjourned to the terrace for dessert, Rachel lingered behind at the pianoforte. She brushed her fingers over the surface of the keys, not making a sound but longing to bring forth music.

"Aha." Mr. Moberly appeared and pulled up a chair to sit close beside her. "You play, Miss Folger." His masculine citrus scent, perhaps his shaving balm, sent a wave of agreeable dizziness through her head.

"You have discovered me, sir." Her pulse quickening, Rachel rested her hands in her lap. "I am guilty."

He tilted his head. "Why did you not confess earlier? I'll warrant Cousin Lydie would have gladly surrendered the instrument to you."

She studied his well-formed face, and her pulse hammered in her ears. "Everyone enjoyed her playing."

"She does play well."

The soft light in his eyes proclaimed his affection for his cousin, a sentiment that clearly kept him from seeing her musical shortcomings. But then, Rachel thought it might be pleasant to be the object of Mr. Moberly's generous opinions.

As before, she forced herself to dismiss such foolish

thoughts. This gentleman treated everyone with kindness. She must protect her heart or risk the devastation of her soul. Still, her esteem for him grew due to his proper behavior with Lady Augusta and his courage in the face of the woman's terrible husband. What might it cost Mr. Moberly if Brigham became a true adversary?

"Well." He put on a severe expression. "I suppose I should pronounce sentence on you for failing to confess that you play."

Heat rushed to her face. "I am at your mercy, sir."

His unnerving smile reached all the way to his eyes, and she could not look away. The smile faded, and he seemed to move closer, focusing on her lips. Would he kiss her? Right here and now? She tingled in anticipation, even as she struggled against such impropriety. Yet she could not break free from his invisible hold on her.

"Rachel." Papa's distant voice broke through the fog in her mind.

Mr. Moberly inhaled sharply and moved back from her. "Forgive me, Miss Folger," he murmured. "That was most unseemly."

Rachel jumped up, knocking over the pianoforte stool.

"There ye are." Papa halted at the double doorway across the room. A quizzical look crossed his face, and he looked from Rachel to Mr. Moberly, who was righting the piano stool. He stared again at Rachel. "I wondered what become o' ye."

Rachel edged past her host. "At the piano, of course." Her voice wavered. "You told me I should offer to play, and now I'm sorry I didn't."

Mr. Moberly stayed her with a light touch on her hand. "Please say you'll forgive me," he whispered, his dark gray eyes exuding regret. "Although my actions were unforgivable."

"I am not without fault, sir." She kept her voice low. "But it will not happen again." She moved beyond Mr. Moberly and joined Papa. "Shall we go to the terrace? I need some of that coffee Mrs. Winthrop offered. I do hope it's strong."

They proceeded to the wide tabby terrace, where a refreshment table awaited. A servant handed her a delicate china cup, and she took a sip. "Mmm. Excellent coffee, Mr. Moberly. Don't you think so, Papa?" She could hear the strain in her voice. "Are you ready to go home?"

Papa turned to their host. "Ye'll excuse us, won't ye, sir? I've promised Reverend Johnson we'll attend services tomorrow, and Rachel'll need her rest."

"Of course." Mr. Moberly looked the picture of misery, with his forehead wrinkled in sorrow and his posture slouched. He crossed the terrace and reached out to Papa. "Mr. Folger, it has been my pleasure."

"And mine, sir." Papa pumped his hand with his usual enthusiasm.

While Papa drove back to town, once again with the musket across his lap, Rachel held a lantern and kept watch for predators. This time as she stared out into the darkness, she wrestled with thoughts very different from her earlier happy anticipations. Not only had she not found the patriot, but Mr. Moberly had behaved most disrespectfully toward her.

Did he think she was a strumpet to be kissed when they barely knew each other? Mother had warned her about certain types of men, wealthy ones in particular, who regarded less affluent girls as nothing more than casual entertainment.

Rachel had hoped for, yes, even longed for Mr. Moberly's attentions. But certainly not in the manner he had delivered them. All the way home, she chided herself for expecting more and for almost permitting the kiss. As the dimly lit inn came into sight, she resolved never to permit her heart to betray good sense, no matter what emotions Mr. Moberly might stir there.

What's more, her duty here in East Florida was not to seek a romance but to help Papa with his mercantile. And of course, to discover ways to help the revolution.

Frederick lounged across a settee in the darkened drawing room, staring at the ceiling and rubbing his forehead. What a muddle he'd made of this evening. Why had he even arranged the event? He'd antagonized Brigham, made a foolish promise to the man's wife and came far too close to kissing the young lady for whom he'd planned everything. After all his mistakes, he'd not even managed to have a true conversation with Miss Folger. Instead of being drawn by her thick blond curls, delicate lavender scent and those full pink lips, he should have sought to know her mind, her heart, her soul.

"Freddy?"

He glanced over the settee back and saw a dark form in the doorway.

"Come in, Cousin Lydie." Reassurance swept through him. Throughout his life, quiet, intimate moments with his older cousin had often soothed Frederick's worst anxieties. He sat up to make room for her.

Already in her dressing gown, with her hair bound in a long braid, Cousin Lydie settled beside him. "Could you not sleep?"

"No."

"Have you made your rounds?"

"Corwin offered to do it."

She hummed her approval. "Very good. You deserve a rest after your hosting duties."

"Thank you for playing tonight." He reached over to pat her dear, wrinkled hands, which often had chastened and more often calmed him in his boyhood. "I hope it did not cause you pain."

"Not excessively." She gently squeezed his fingers. "Mr. Folger says his daughter also plays, but modesty keeps her from asserting herself. I thought that was charming."

Frederick's pulse quickened. "You found her charming?"

"Why, yes, of course. Her modest dress and proper deportment are entirely pleasing. And one finds it more than a little surprising to see such refined table manners in a merchant's daughter living here in the wilderness." Cousin Lydie gasped softly. "Freddy, have you formed an attachment with the young lady?"

"No." He emitted an ironic laugh. His own foolishness had spoiled that effort. Yet he longed for an ally in his endeavors. Perhaps Cousin Lydie would help him. If not, at least she would never betray him to Corwin. "But I would like to."

"Oh, dear."

With his cousin's face shadowed, Frederick could only imagine her arched eyebrows and pinched-together lips.

But she grasped his hand. "Dear boy, have you counted the cost of such a decision?" Distress filled her voice. "Do you know how my entire life has been affected by one such choice I made at nineteen?"

Guilt shot through him. He'd never inquired about Cousin Lydie's life, even though she knew every detail of his. "You must tell me about it."

"Simply put, I fell in love with a man of no prospects, then compounded the offense by marrying him against my father's wishes."

Frederick's mind reeled. His cousin's loving heart had led to her impoverishment. "What happened to Mr. Winthrop?"

"A fever took him less than a year after our marriage."

Frederick would not ask her why she never remarried, for her tone conveyed sorrow even after these many years. How she must have loved him. Such constant love would be a treasure.

"But…" Her brightened tone, tinged with humor, startled him. "The wealthy man my father wanted me to marry was a dreadful beast who turned out to be dishonest. Father was most pleased not to be connected to him. Of course, he never confessed that to me."

He felt her lean against the settee back.

Soon she continued. "If given the opportunity, I would do exactly as I did, however short-lived my happiness."

For a moment, the meaning of her words lingered above him. When at last they flowed into his mind, he nearly sprang to his feet.

"Cousin Lydie, do you hear what you are saying? What you are suggesting? Do you know what that means to me?"

She sighed. "I fear I do. That is why I hesitated to tell you. But things will go well for you, dear boy."

"Only if you help me."

"I?" Her maternal laughter grew more musical. "Oh, what fun we shall have. Now, tell me what to do. Shall I write to Lady Bennington and ask her to influence your father?"

"There will be a time for that, but it's a bit too soon." Guilt once again gripped him. "I must tell you all that happened this evening." He related his encounters with Major Brigham and Lady Augusta. After a pause to gather his courage, he confessed to almost kissing Miss Folger.

"I cannot imagine what I was thinking," he said. "No, I wasn't thinking. That was the problem. After I'd suffered Major Brigham and Lady Augusta's nonsense, Miss Folger's presence was entirely refreshing, and thus I almost surrendered to unseemly emotions. I would say I could not help myself, but I should have. Were a man to treat my sister thus, I should have called him out."

"Oh, my, I can see we have some repair work to do. I have already promised the young lady I will visit her father's shop."

His enthusiasm renewed, Frederick gently squeezed her

hand. "Thank you, dear cousin. I shall arrange for Ben to drive you into the village on Monday."

"But I heard Mr. Folger say they would be at church tomorrow." Her tone turned conspiratorial. "That is not too soon to begin our strategy. Here is what I advise…"

"Think of it, Papa. Only one more breakfast in this place." Rachel glanced toward the tearoom door to be certain Sadie was not nearby. "On Tuesday, we will awaken in our own home to Inez's fine food." She took a bite of the greasy ham on her plate only because she needed sustenance.

"And good riddance, if ye ask me." Papa devoured a large slice of fresh-baked bread dripping with honey. "I'd sooner try to sleep through a storm at sea than in this rickety pile of wood with no decent foundation."

Rachel glanced at the broad boards beneath their feet and wondered why the innkeeper had not built on tabby or coquina. Perhaps he had been in a hurry to build it and begin his competition with the settlement's other tavern.

"If not for my promise to the reverend," Papa said, "we could move the last of the furniture in today." He puffed out an impatient sigh. "Church. Why did I ever agree to go?"

"We should have attended when we first arrived last month." Rachel tried to keep a rebuke from her tone. "Reverend Johnson seems to be a godly man. And perhaps his wife will demonstrate more courtesy in church than she did last evening."

"Ah, well." Papa dug into his porridge. "That was a motley gaggle of geese in Moberly's barnyard. More than one had no idea of how to comport himself."

Heat filled her face as she pushed her overcooked eggs around the plate. If Papa learned what happened with Mr. Moberly, she could not guess what he might do. "But, Papa, I noticed you had no trouble engaging the attention of Mrs. Winthrop."

Lifting his coffee cup, Papa washed down his last bite and seemed to focus on some distant point. "Aye, she's a true lady. All manners and all sincerity. The genuine article."

Rachel stared at him, her eyes wide with surprise.

"Why, captain, have ye formed an attachment with the lady?" She imitated Papa's inflections.

Papa shot her a guilty glance. "O'course not." He blustered and mumbled under his breath. "Can't a man compliment a lady without being accused of impropriety?"

"But it wouldn't be improper, Papa." Rachel had long hoped he would find a suitable companion. "You're both widowed. And if you're both agreeable to it, why not keep company?"

Papa set one elbow on the table and scratched his fresh-shaven chin. "Hmm. Well, now. I don't know. Perhaps 'twas mere courtesy that urged her to take my arm when I offered it. I'd not have ye ashamed of me for being an old fool."

"I'd never be ashamed of you." Rachel patted his hand. "You have my permission to call on Mrs. Winthrop." The instant she spoke, she wondered whether the genteel lady would consider herself above Papa. *Lord, please do not let me advise Papa amiss. Let my heart break, but not his— again.*

"Well, now, let's not be hasty." He fussed with his cup. "I s'pose I could see if Mrs. Winthrop treats us with the same courtesy today." He repositioned his napkin in his lap. "Well, now, if I go calling on her, ye must come with me. If I've misunderstood, she'll be none the wiser, for she'll think ye initiated the call and I'm only along to protect ye as ye travel."

"Oh." Rachel could not think of going back to the plantation, especially unannounced.

"What is it, girl?" Papa eyed her. "You disapprove? Say it right out."

"Nothing, Papa. Nothing at all."

"Well, then." Papa tossed his napkin on the table. "Let's be off." He stood and moved toward the hall. "Come along, now. We don't want to be late."

Delighted with his change of attitude about attending services, Rachel nonetheless followed him slowly. At the prospect of seeing Mr. Moberly again within the hour, she found her heart misbehaving once more, and she had no idea how to control it.

Walking beside Papa, she breathed in the fresh pine and sweet magnolia fragrances of the warm, rain-washed June morning. They skirted a few puddles spotting the road, but most of the previous night's showers had disappeared into the sandy soil or run down into the many creeks flowing through the hilly landscape.

The small rough-wood church had been built on a sturdy base of coquina, the same foundation supporting Mr. Moberly's plantation house. The granite quarries of Massachusetts offered no better foundation stone than this.

Rachel recalled the verses in Matthew that spoke of a wise man building his house upon a rock, and she sent up a silent prayer that Papa would begin to build his life on Jesus Christ this very morning. Old Reverend Johnson might have an unfriendly wife, but he seemed to possess a true concern for souls. Rachel had been pleased to see Papa talk so easily with him. If the vicar expounded a clear revelation of Christ's love and sacrifice, how could Papa resist?

At the church door, her heart began to race as she followed Papa inside. The half-filled sanctuary held an assortment of people. Soldiers and indentured servants sat behind the free white tradesmen, and black slaves stood in the galleries above. Instead of boxed family pews like those in Boston churches, the room was furnished with benches that held perhaps a hundred souls, far fewer than Rachel's home church. Yet the familiar peace she had always experienced when she entered a house of worship now filled her chest. Strangely, the peace intensified when she spied Mr. Moberly seated near the front with Mrs. Winthrop and Mr. Corwin.

Perhaps he sensed her gaze, for he turned, and a soft smile graced his lips. Now Rachel almost stopped breathing, and she turned her eyes toward the cross above the altar. She would not permit this man's presence to intrude upon her time of worship. But as she moved into the row behind Mr. Moberly and his companions, she feared that, instead of worshipping, her pious soul would spend the next two hours at war with her disobedient heart.

Soon Reverend Johnson entered, accompanied by other church leaders to assist him. Dressed in pale brown cotton cassocks with little ornamentation, the four men moved through the holy rites with the ease of those used to serving together.

Rachel followed the liturgy in her prayer book, holding it for Papa to read along. Yet her gaze kept straying toward Mr. Moberly, who never cast a second glance in her direction.

As Rachel had hoped, the vicar gave a brief but wisdom-filled homily concerning the simple path to salvation, summing up his discourse by reciting John 3:16. While he spoke, Rachel prayed Papa would comprehend the love of God. She could not bear to think of his perishing for want of faith, and promised the Lord she would endeavor to do everything to win his soul to Christ, though Papa rarely listened to her opinions.

When the last prayer had been spoken and Reverend Johnson had pronounced the benediction, her thoughts flew to the awkward situation sure to erupt when she and Mr. Moberly stepped out into the heat of the East Florida sun.

# Chapter Nine

"A fine message, Reverend Johnson." Frederick shook hands with the vicar while watching to see if he could reach Miss Folger and her father before they walked too far away. Running after her would be most unseemly for the settlement's magistrate, yet Frederick's legs ached to do just that. He forced himself to maintain propriety and bowed to the vicar's wife. "Mrs. Johnson, you look lovely, as always."

She beamed at him. "Thank you, Mr. Moberly. And thank you again for a delightful party last evening. Lady Augusta was the very picture of charm and elegance, and I was so delighted to be introduced to her. You simply must have another party because—"

"Mrs. Johnson, what a pretty bonnet." Cousin Lydie stepped to Frederick's side. "Do tell me the name of your London milliner. I shall ask Mr. Moberly to order something for me."

The younger woman blushed and fell into conversation with Cousin Lydie, apparently forgetting the wonders of Lady Augusta.

Frederick moved away, wishing he could kiss his dear cousin. Their talk last night had resulted in a plan to rectify his misdeed, but Mrs. Johnson almost ruined it.

To his relief, the Folgers had not wandered far from the church. They stood talking with the innkeeper and his family in the shade of an oak tree. Squinting in the morning sun, Frederick approached the group and waited for their conversation to conclude.

"'Tis the Lord's truth, miss." The innkeeper tipped his hat to Rachel. "Having you and the captain stayin' at me inn has been a blessin'." He bent his head toward Papa.

"Thank ye, sir," Papa said.

"Thank you, Mr. Crump." Rachel searched for some compliment to return. "Mrs. Crump, we are so grateful for the clean sheets every other week. That is a special kindness to your guests. You and Sadie have enough work."

The heavy, red-faced woman beamed. "'Twas a special kindness fer you, miss. Don't do that for ever'one."

"You have my gratitude." Rachel felt a sting of remorse for her heartless thoughts about this hardworking couple. In truth, they were the salt of the earth, the same sort that comprised the militia back home. She regarded the stout, red-haired innkeeper, but his clean-shaven face precluded his being the red-bearded patriot. Or perhaps not. Perhaps a disguise?

"Mr. Crump, I am curious." Rachel glanced at Papa but proceeded anyway. "Have you had any visits from that patriot, uh, the agitator who has been spreading news of the revolution taking place up north?"

"Rachel." Beside her, Papa exhaled a lengthy sigh.

"No, miss," Mr. Crump said. "He'd find no welcome at the Wild Boar, and no doubt he knows it." His cross frown and grumbling tone underlined his words.

Mrs. Crump put a plump hand on her hip. "He'd better keep his ideas to hisself, or I'll set on 'im with my rolling pin."

Mr. Crump looked beyond Rachel and jerked to attention.

"Well, Mrs. Crump, 'tis time to quit gabblin'. We've a meal to serve the boarders." He tipped his hat. "Cap'n Folger, good day t'ya. Miss Folger, you can be sure we'll miss yer kind face onc't ya've moved."

"Thank you, sir." Rachel gave a little wave of her hand while a familiar ache of disappointment filled her. She lifted a prayer that she could soon find just one person, any person, who agreed with her sentiments regarding the revolution.

She turned to find Mr. Moberly standing not two yards away, a frown on his handsome face. A strange shiver swept down her spine. Had he heard her question the Crumps?

"Good morning, Mr. Folger, Miss Folger." Mr. Moberly swept off his broad-brimmed hat and bowed, but still no smile touched his lips.

"Good morning, sir," Mr. Folger said in a hearty tone.

Miss Folger's curtsy looked unsteady, and she quickly stared down at her prayer book rather than meet his gaze. He wished he could address her in particular, wished he could give her a reassuring smile, but that would spoil the plan.

"Miss Folger." Cousin Lydie appeared beside Frederick. "How charming you look. I'm pleased to see you this morning. Did you enjoy the service?"

"Yes, indeed." Miss Folger bestowed a pretty smile on Cousin Lydie.

Frederick yearned to be the recipient of such radiance. He hoped his attempt to kiss her had not destroyed forever the chance that she might smile at him again.

"Mr. Folger," Cousin Lydie said, "may I borrow your daughter for a moment?"

"Aye, madam." His eyes wide, Mr. Folger nodded. "Of course."

She looped her arm in Miss Folger's. "My dear, you must see the garden behind the vicarage."

As the two ladies walked away, Frederick noticed Mr. Folger's gaze followed Cousin Lydie. Curious.

"Well, sir," Frederick said, "I suppose you miss Captain Templeton."

Mr. Folger seemed reluctant to turn his attention away from the ladies. "Aye, my nephew's more like a son to me." He now focused on Frederick. "And we thank ye for sendin' along the oranges and lemons with him. Scurvy can be a blight on any voyage, but we'll not worry about that striking the crew due to yer generosity."

Relief swept through Frederick. The young lady's father seemed unaware of his misstep the previous evening. "And I am grateful to the captain for taking letters to my family. They do not hear from me often enough to suit them, so they will be pleasantly surprised. So you see, we have done each other a favor." Especially if Templeton kept his promise to tell Father of Frederick's successes.

"As befits a budding partnership, do ye not think?"

"Yes, I agree. In these wilds, and troubled times, one can never have too many friends."

"True, true." Mr. Folger stared off toward the path the ladies had taken. "I think I'd like to see that garden. Do ye think the ladies'd mind me comin' alongside?"

"Surely not." Frederick shook his head. "In fact, I'll go with you." All according to plan.

Rachel reminded herself that Mr. Moberly had smiled at her in church, but just now he barely addressed her. Without doubt, he heard her speaking to the Crumps and caught her use of the word *patriot*. Surely that would bring to an end any interest he might have in her. She tried not to care. After all, he was an Englishman in authority. Hardly the right man to attract her interest. And yet…

She yielded to Mrs. Winthrop's gentle guidance as they

walked to the backyard of the vicarage. Mrs. Johnson's lush fenced garden bloomed with an abundance of vegetables and flowers.

"Reaping two garden harvests a year will always seem odd to me," Mrs. Winthrop said. "In most parts of England, we complete our single harvest by mid-October."

"Boston is much the same." Seeing the corn and squash, Rachel felt a pang of hunger. But dinner could wait. Mrs. Winthrop's interest in her filled an empty spot food could never satisfy. Beyond her own concerns, she thought of Papa and prayed he and the lady might establish a friendship. With Papa's lack of interest in the revolution, he would have no conflict of beliefs with an English lady.

They wandered arm in arm around the garden's border, peering over the fence to see tiny melons with withered blossoms still attached, string beans ready to harvest, and thumb-sized green tomatoes clinging to their vines.

"Ah, there ye are, ladies." Papa limped toward them across the grass, Mr. Moberly following a few steps behind. "We thought we'd like to take in the garden with ye."

Mr. Moberly's expression remained sober, and he bent over the squash plants with apparent interest. Rachel decided she must act as if nothing were amiss.

"Papa, we must have a garden like this behind the store."

"Indeed, daughter, many things bloom well here." Papa gazed not at the garden but at Mrs. Winthrop. He cleared his throat. "Mrs. Winthrop, will ye join us for a repast at the inn?"

Rachel winced, knowing what the effort cost him. She prayed he would not be rebuffed.

But like a flower blossoming in the rain, Mrs. Winthrop's whole face broke into a wide smile, and a delicate blush touched her ivory cheeks. "How kind of you to ask, sir. But I fear my duties at home demand my attention straightaway. Perhaps another time?"

Disappointment flickered briefly in his eyes. "Ye have but to name the day and time."

Now Rachel's spirits lifted. She glanced at Mr. Moberly to see his response. Although he continued to study the garden, she could see his smile in profile, and contentment filled her.

Soon he turned to face them. "Cousin Lydie, are you ready to go home?"

"Yes, dear." She did not remove her gaze from Papa.

"Then we must take our leave." Mr. Moberly bowed to Rachel. "Miss Folger. Mr. Folger." Mrs. Winthrop stepped over and squeezed Rachel's hand. "I shall see you soon."

Wondering at her remark, Rachel took Papa's arm and watched the two depart. Perhaps she had been wrong about Mr. Moberly hearing her remarks to Mr. Crump.

As she and Papa began their trek across the lawn, a long black snake slithered through the grass and almost ran over her shoe. She jumped back with a gasp. "Oh, my."

Papa gripped her hand. "Stand still till it's gone, daughter."

"Harmless, I assure you." Mr. Corwin walked around the corner of the vicarage, swinging a fine ebony cane. "They keep the garden free of rats and other pests. But they certainly can surprise a person."

Rachel willed away a shudder. "And of course, one must make certain they're not poisonous."

"Indeed." Mr. Corwin swished the grass with his cane. "I say, Mr. Folger, may I speak with your lovely daughter for a moment?"

Papa stared at Rachel, his eyes twinkling. "Well, daughter?"

Her face burning almost as much as her curiosity, she nodded. Papa limped away toward the road.

"Yes, Mr. Corwin?" The overhead sun burned through her bonnet, making Rachel dizzy, and she hoped this would not take long.

He lifted an eyebrow, and a wily expression crossed his handsome face. "I'd like to discuss Moberly's intentions toward you."

# Chapter Ten

Rachel stood aside as stocky Mr. Patch carried her trunk up the stairs, his shoulders bent to the task. The sweat pouring from him pushed her back, but her heart warmed toward this former member of Papa's whaling crew, who now helped with the store.

"Please put it in my room." She motioned toward the door.

"Aye, miss." He placed the heavy trunk on the floor with care. "That's the last of it."

After he left, she surveyed the boxes piled throughout the four rooms, and sadness filled her. Once she unpacked, once she set Mother's vase on the mantel and her porcelain tableware in the china cabinet, this would be home, whether she liked it or not. She had no energy to start the task. Life would soon become very dull, Mr. Corwin's daft remark notwithstanding. If Mr. Moberly were smitten with her, why had he barely spoken to her after church?

"Rachel, come quick, daughter." Papa's voice boomed up the stairs. "Ye're needed down here." The joviality in his tone eased her sadness.

"Coming, Papa." She glanced in the tiny mirror over her bureau, brushed back a few stray hairs, and hurried downstairs. "Yes, sir?" She stopped short. "Mrs. Winthrop."

The lady stood across the counter from Papa, but no wares had been laid out. Instead, she held a bouquet of fragrant white flowers.

"How nice to see you again so soon, ma'am." Rachel's face warmed.

"And it is a pleasure to see you, as well, Miss Folger. I hope you do not mind my calling at this early hour, but one does best to travel before the day's worst heat." She handed the flowers to Rachel. "From my garden."

"How lovely. Thank you." Rachel breathed in the large blossoms' sweet smell as she glanced at the empty counter again. This truly was a social call. "I am so pleased to see you." A nervous twinge tickled her insides. Did Mr. Moberly know his cousin had come here? She smelled the flowers again. "What pretty, sweet-scented flowers. What are they?"

"Gardenias. The bushes were recently imported from China. Isn't the fragrance lovely?" Mrs. Winthrop leaned close to Rachel. "Miss Folger, if I am not being too forward, I thought I might help you arrange your apartment."

Rachel could barely withhold a gasp. She could not think it proper for such an elegant lady to engage in such work. Yet turning her down would be an insult. "How kind, ma'am. I do not know how to thank you." She glanced at Papa, whose face radiated his delight. Rachel wondered how long they had chatted before he called her downstairs.

"No thanks are necessary, my dear. I would imagine the task will take some time, perhaps all day. Shall we get started?" Mrs. Winthrop laughed, a pleasing sound. "Forgive me. I do not intend to manage things, merely to help you."

"I am very grateful," Rachel said. "And I will appreciate every suggestion. Shall we go?" She turned toward the burlap-covered door to the back room, aware of the store's humble look compared to Mr. Moberly's grand house. A sudden longing filled her. How pleasant it would be to have a proper front door where she could greet her guests.

Mrs. Winthrop followed her up the rough wooden staircase and looked about the apartment with an appraising eye. "What excellent accommodations and what spacious rooms." Her maternal kindness radiated from her gray eyes. "Nothing invigorates me more than a scheme of this nature."

Her own energies renewed, Rachel found Mother's cutglass vase for the gardenias and set them on the maple dining table. Their scent filled the room with a fragrance as sweet and welcome as Mrs. Winthrop's offered friendship. Perhaps this new home would be happier than expected.

They spent the morning unpacking china and other small items. After a quick midday meal, they proceeded to the trunk in Rachel's room. In it, Mrs. Winthrop found a small framed drawing of Rachel's mother. "She was quite lovely."

Rachel gazed at the picture. "Yes, ma'am. But she did scold my sister for sketching her likeness, for she considered it a vanity." A soft chuckle escaped her.

"Ah, yes. But then, perhaps the Quakers are correct in their humility. There is far too much vanity and selfishness in this world."

"I agree. That is why your kind help means so much." Rachel bent over her trunk, and musty but pleasant ocean smells met her senses, stirring memories of her carefree childhood on Nantucket's windswept shores.

Mrs. Winthrop reached across to pat Rachel's hand. "It is my privilege."

The gentle expression in her gray eyes brought a lump to Rachel's throat. Were the lady not Mr. Moberly's kinswoman, Rachel would confide in her regarding him.

"What have we here?" Mrs. Winthrop unwrapped a carved whalebone fan and spread it open to reveal intricate lacelike filigree. "What delicate workmanship."

"Isn't it exquisite? Papa carved it for Mother on one of his whaling voyages."

Mrs. Winthrop tilted her head. "Indeed? Your father is a gifted artist." Her cheeks grew pink, and she waved the fan in front of her face. "How useful here in the tropics."

Rachel wanted to laugh. Instead of thinking about her own hopeless romantic interests, she should foster the romance right in front of her. "Papa has many talents."

"And a prodigious wit, as well."

"I'm pleased you think so." Rachel was smitten with playfulness. "A man who has been long at sea can forget his manners. But I have noticed that in your presence, he remembers them very well."

"Oh, my. Well, a true gentleman does not require much reminding." Mrs. Winthrop waved the fan with vigor. "Do you mind if I use this?" She glanced at her wrist. "Oh, I have my own." She set down the borrowed one and used her own. "My, this East Florida heat."

Rachel ignored the lady's chagrin. "Indeed, it can be quite oppressive."

Mrs. Winthrop lifted a drawing of Papa from the trunk. "It must be difficult for a man to lose his wife and be left with two young daughters, especially when his work takes him to sea." She held Mother's portrait side by side with Papa's. "Perhaps just as difficult as being left with three unruly sons but having to spend all of one's time in the king's service instead of seeing to their behavior."

A little twinge struck Rachel's heart. "Of whom do you speak, madam?" Mr. Moberly had mentioned being a younger son. Had he grown up without a mother's care?

"Lord Bennington, the proprietor of this settlement."

"Mr. Moberly's father?" Rachel risked another question. "What did Lord Bennington do about his sons?"

Mrs. Winthrop's eyebrows arched. "Why, he remarried, of

course, as soon as he could do so within propriety." She set the pictures on Rachel's desk. "To my cousin Maria, who presented him with two more children, young Frederick and his sister, Lady Marianne." She heaved a great sigh. "Alas, dear Maria could do nothing with those three older boys, rapscallions all. They grew up entirely untamed."

Rachel's mind spun with more questions. Mr. Moberly had a sister, a *titled* sister. Why did he not have a title?

"May I ask…" Mrs. Winthrop set a pewter vase on the desk. "How did your father see to your care?"

Rachel hesitated. Would Mrs. Winthrop think it scandalous? "He took me on his next whaling voyage."

Her eyebrows arched again. She appeared not quite shocked, but perhaps amazed and even a little amused. "Gracious, young lady! What an adventure you had. No wonder you are doing well here in East Florida. You are a hardy soul."

Relief filled Rachel's heart. "Thank you. I was eleven when Mother died, and Papa had difficulty deciding what to do with me. After the voyage, I went to live with my married sister in Boston." Curiosity prompted another question. "Did Mr. Moberly take after his older brothers?"

"Mercy, no. He and Lady Marianne have brought nothing but joy to their mother. Lady Bennington is a woman of great faith, and she personally saw to their catechisms." Seated beside the trunk once more, Mrs. Winthrop folded her hands in her lap. "She is also the soul of generosity. My Mr. Winthrop died not long before her marriage, and my sweet cousin insisted I come to live under Lord Bennington's protection." Tears glistened in her eyes. "She would have nothing else for her wedding gift from him."

Rachel struggled to stop her own sudden tears. "A true Christian."

"Yes." Mrs. Winthrop bowed her head. "My, I did not

intend to speak of such things." A frown crossed her brow, but it softened. "What I did intend to say was this. Mr. Moberly is a kindhearted soul like his mother. A true gentleman. And he is so utterly mortified by his behavior on Saturday evening that he has enlisted my assistance in ascertaining whether he has lost all hope in regard to…becoming your friend."

At first, the words seemed so implausible Rachel could not grasp them. Her throat constricted, preventing any response other than a tiny, silly squeak. To think he had confessed his misdeed to his kinswoman.

Mrs. Winthrop's eyes twinkled. "Miss Folger, your face is a study. May I assume you are amenable to friendship with Mr. Moberly?"

Rachel thought her head might explode. Friendship? He desired friendship with her? His coolness and strange responses had not been a snub or suspicion but, rather, continued mortification over his actions. She recalled Mr. Corwin's claim that Mr. Moberly was smitten with her, but she had not believed him. Nor had she accepted Mr. Corwin's offer to advise her as to how she might "snare" Mr. Moberly. Instead, she had politely thanked him, then walked away before he could further insult her. Now this kind lady had made a milder, yet just as startling claim. But could she, *should* she accept such a connection with him, knowing where it might lead? Knowing where it must not lead?

"Oh, dear lady." She stood and paced across the room. "How shall I respond?" Returning to kneel in front of Mrs. Winthrop, she grasped the lady's hands, breathing in the delicate gardenia fragrance clinging to her. "In your eyes, I see no deception, only goodness and truth. You must answer me truly. How can Mr. Moberly, an earl's son, seek a pure and proper friendship with a shopkeeper's daughter?" Until this moment, the attraction she felt for him had seemed a foolish fancy. Yet even if he felt an equal attraction to her, were they not mad to think a romance could follow? Every force of man and nature seemed against it.

Sadness flickered over Mrs. Winthrop's face. "I cannot promise you an easy path, my dear. But having loved deeply and without regret myself, I would not deny it to anyone else."

Rachel stared up into her kind gray eyes. "Then we each must count the cost before taking even the first step down that path."

Mrs. Winthrop caressed Rachel's cheek with her soft, smooth fingers. "You are wise for one so young."

Rachel shook her head. "Only time will reveal whether that is true or not."

"Then you will receive him?"

A giddy laugh bubbled up from within her.

"Yes, I will receive him."

Frederick paced the inn's taproom, his boot heels thumping noisily against the wooden floors. He ignored the nervous glances and murmuring of the off-duty soldiers lolling about the nearby tables. These men steered a wide berth around their magistrate and showed almost reverential respect when they did encounter him. Frederick supposed it worked to his advantage, for people had treated his father with a similar cautious respect, but even after more than two years, he had yet to become accustomed to it.

Would that Oliver held the same respect for him. Just this morning Frederick had discovered another betrayal. Clear discrepancies had appeared among Oliver's financial reports to Father, the books he kept for the plantation and the funds in Frederick's safe. Did Oliver think he would not be found out? Now Frederick must confront him, a task he dreaded almost as much as receiving another letter of censure from Father.

At every thought of Father, Frederick prayed that Captain Templeton would find favor with the old earl. Surely the man would make a good impression on Father, proving to him that Frederick possessed good judgment and an astute business sense. And Mr. Folger had made it clear he welcomed Frederick's patronage and partnership. Now if only he could receive the same welcome from Miss Folger, he would be more than satisfied.

The hot breeze blowing through the windows carried the smell of pigs and other barnyard creatures and made normal breathing a chore. The proprietor really should keep his animals farther from the inn. Frederick would speak to him in that regard.

What on earth was keeping Mrs. Winthrop? Surely it could not take long to unpack a few trinkets and trifles, have a bit of conversation—about him, of course—and have done with it.

Frederick sat down at a rough-hewn table. How foolish and selfish of him to think Cousin Lydie would be content with a pretense of helping Miss Folger. The old dear would have her elbows deep into the packing barrels. She might not want to leave until the entire project had been completed. Frederick would not have her any other way.

"Mr. Moberly, sir?" The innkeeper approached him. "Yer man Ben's out back. He asked me to tell ya the lady's ready to leave. Will ya have a drink afore you go, sir?"

"No." His pulse racing, Frederick dug a coin from his waistcoat and handed it to the man. "But I thank you for the message, my good man."

He hurried out the front door to meet Ben.

"Missus Winthrop's called for the rig, sir. I'll fetch it from the livery barn."

"Very good, Ben. I'll ride down and meet her."

His horse Essex quickly covered the half mile from the inn

to the mercantile, where Frederick peered in the window and
observed Mrs. Winthrop perusing the shop's wares with Miss
Folger. At the doorbell's jingle, the ladies turned to greet him.
Mrs. Winthrop gave him a triumphant smile. Miss Folger
blushed.

His pulse hammering, Frederick swept off his hat and
bowed. "Good afternoon, ladies. I hope the day has been pro-
ductive."

"Prodigiously so." Mrs. Winthrop donned her straw bonnet. "Shall I assume Ben is awaiting me outside?"

"Indeed he is." Frederick hoped his grin did not appear
foolish. "May I take you to your chariot, my lady?"

"No, no." She gave her head a little shake. "You need not
bother. Ben can assist me. I am certain you have other
business to attend to."

"Ah, very good."

"Good day, Miss Folger." Mrs. Winthrop passed by Frederick with a swish of her skirts and a hint of gardenia.

Frederick gazed at Miss Folger, and she returned the same.

"This is madness, you know." Her sober expression belied
the lilt in her voice. "You are mad, and so am I."

He chuckled, a strained and foolish sound in his own ears.
"But it is a merry madness, do you not agree?"

She looked down, as if trying to hide the smile spread
across her lovely face. A blond curl fell over her cheek, a mere
wisp, delicate like her.

He longed to brush it back, to lift her chin, to reclaim her
gaze. But he dared not risk another temptation to kiss her. So
he cleared his throat and glanced about the room, trying to
discover some safe topic of conversation. He settled at last
upon a bolt of blue gauze.

"Miss Folger, I admired your exquisite gown the other
evening." Perhaps not the best beginning, for he would not
wish her to recall his blunder. "Most ladies would hide the

bolt—" he pointed to it "—so no other lady could purchase the same material."

She glanced at the fabric, and the pensiveness in her eyes gave him pause. Had he spoken amiss? The air here in the shop, with its strange mix of cinnamon, lavender and new leather, was decidedly more pleasant than in the inn, but he still found it difficult to breathe.

"I must admit I was tempted to hide it." She gave a charming little shrug. "But gauze is hard to come by, and Papa will make a tidy sum on the remainder. I could not deny him that." Her melodious voice shook slightly.

"Ah. The dutiful daughter. I understand."

Her face took on a beguiling radiance. "I believe you do. And that brings up a matter that deeply concerns me. I would not have you disappoint your parents."

Frederick felt as if he had been struck in the chest. She had uncovered the core of his dilemma, for he did not yet know if he could surrender all his former dreams for the sake of marrying her. Could she help him reason it out? "But may a man not decide his own destiny? Must he always seek his parents' approval?"

Voices sounded on the street. Frederick hoped desperately the speakers would not enter the store. He felt tempted to lock the door, but that would reek of impropriety.

Her lips formed a pretty little bow, and her brow wrinkled, as if she were considering his question. "You must count the cost, Mr. Moberly. You have more to lose than I. No doubt your father will disown you or, at the very least, devise some form of discipline for you."

"Perhaps so. Perhaps not. But what of you? I would not have you suffer on my account."

"I risk only my heart, as women have done since time began."

He turned his hat in his hands. "If your heart suffered, I

would grieve being the cause of it." A memory surfaced. "Someone once told me that in America every man has the opportunity to earn his fortune and his place in society. As a younger son, I will inherit no part of my father's fortune, for it is entailed by law to my eldest brother. Perhaps it is time for me to earn my own."

If a man could snap his fingers and bring forth light, it might resemble the brilliance in Miss Folger's eyes, in her entire beautiful face.

"Why, then, sir, I believe our friendship might prosper, after all."

## Chapter Eleven

Rachel continued to study Mr. Moberly's handsome face, which reflected her own happiness.

"Shall I call for tea?" Her decision made to receive him, she relaxed at last. Until this moment, she had felt as if her feet were rooted into the floor, and all her senses seemed suspended. Now the fragrance of lavender wafted about her, and the day's heat felt like a cozy caress. "We can sit over there." She pointed toward the table and chairs in the corner.

"Alas, I must see to matters at home." A wry grimace claimed his handsome features. "Duty is a cruel master to tear me away just now, but unfortunately I must obey."

"Of course." Her mind churned with dozens of questions, for she longed to learn more about him without delay. "I understand."

"I fear that same duty will keep me at the plantation throughout the week. But perhaps on Sunday you and Mr. Folger will come for dinner?" His hopeful, eager expression soothed her disappointment.

"I shall ask Papa. He loves fine cooking, so I do not imagine he'll say no."

Mr. Moberly chuckled. "I do not exclude myself when I say that describes most men."

"Indeed? Then I shall return the invitation. Will you dine with us the following Sunday?" Rachel decided to offer a modest boast. "I would be pleased to discover if you like my mutton stew, a specialty my mother taught me to make when I was a child."

He stared at her for a moment, his mouth open slightly. "You cook?"

"Why, of course I cook." She laughed but quickly sobered, for earnest concern emanated from his eyes.

For the longest moment, they merely looked at each other. Rachel could think of nothing to say, and she could see from his slackened jaw that he was struggling to grasp her revelation. Her own memories added to her turmoil, for she recalled that the wealthy ladies in Boston disdained such common chores. Rachel would not ask if Lady Bennington or Lady Marianne prepared the family meals. For as surely as cooking had been a part of her training for womanhood, it just as surely would have been consigned to servants in the home in which Mr. Moberly had been reared. By confessing her skill, she no doubt reminded him of the stark differences between their classes.

This attempt at friendship was a mistake. Never mind that everyone required food to survive or that people of wealth demanded meals tasting nothing short of splendid. Ladies of his social rank simply did not cook.

"I say, Miss Folger." His face brightened. "No wonder your good father depends upon you. Is there anything you cannot do?"

Rachel turned away to hide a grin, while her sinking heart returned to its proper moorings.

"Did I speak amiss?" He touched her shoulder.

Startled, she spun around. He was so close she could smell his shaving balm, a heady bergamot scent.

He pulled back his hand as if burned. "Ah, forgive me."

"No, no, I am not offended." Not at all. In fact, his touch had bestowed further reassurance on her. "I thought perhaps you were…that you thought—"

"I would never think anything but the best of you, Miss Folger." He seized her hand. "I can only hope to be worthy of the same consideration in return." He bent forward and held her fingers to his lips for a half second beyond propriety. When he straightened, his gaze sent a wave of joy through her.

He released her hand and put on his hat. "I must go now." His voice was husky, but also a bit playful. Then he turned and strode toward the door, stopping there to glance over his shoulder. "Until Sunday, Miss Folger." Then he was gone.

"Until Sunday," she whispered. But her heart shouted with happiness.

A wild whoop burst from Frederick, unbidden and unbridled. He kicked his heels against Essex's sides and bent forward in the saddle as the stallion leaped into a gallop. People on the street—workmen, soldiers, servants on errands—gawked, but he shook off concern. Let them think their magistrate was mad, for he was. Mad with love.

Love? Was he ready to call this wild exhilaration *love*? Inner voices advised caution, the caution that had always saved his neck and kept him from getting into scrapes like his older brothers. But happiness clamored for preeminence, for mastery. And for once in his life, he would rip caution from his soul and cast it to the wind, as the roadway sand was dug out and tossed aside by Essex's hooves.

Another impulse seized him. He would find some rare gift to present to Miss Folger, something to delight her. But where could he find such a gift? Mrs. Winthrop would have to help him find something appropriate. Perhaps Captain Templeton would bring such a gift in his London cargo.

Laughter seized him. What an adventure this would be, this courtship. He'd seen merriment in the young lady's eyes and knew she was a cheerful soul. They would laugh together. Real laughter such as he had never known, except when he and Marianne had played about the manor house as children.

Dear Marianne. She would love Rachel. Perhaps he should write his sister and beg her support in this matter. Marianne was a romantic soul and determined to marry for love. Perhaps she would understand his plight and sway Father, who always gave her whatever she asked for.

Father. The thought of him sobered Frederick, and he tugged on Essex's reins. As the stallion slowed his pace, Frederick's pulse slowed, as well. For a brief half hour, if that long, he had managed to forget his father. Where he had savored the refreshing fragrance of magnolia blossoms, he now smelled his own sweat and that of his hard-run horse, pleasantness supplanted by reality. But he would not draw back. Some force perhaps even stronger than the fear of Father had gripped him, and he would not lightly dismiss it.

Yesterday during church, as the congregants repeated the general confession, Frederick had asked God's forgiveness for almost kissing Miss Folger. The assurance that filled him gave him confidence to ask the Lord's favor in pursuing the young lady. Today's events could be nothing less than proof of God's approval of that pursuit.

If only he did not have to confront Oliver this evening, he could have stayed for tea with Miss Folger. He had many questions to ask her. Did she like to read? If so, what sort of books? What did she think of the turmoil in the northern colonies? Would she be interested in traveling to Europe? He could imagine a wedding trip to his maternal grandfather's villa in Tuscany. Could see her dipping her toes into the Mediterranean Sea. Could hear her melodious voice squeal with delight over every new adventure. Would that these fantasies might be fulfilled.

But first he must contend with the reality of Oliver's betrayals.

Consumed with that objective, he could barely keep his peace during supper. He did not mind addressing the subject of the mismanagement of the books in front of Dr. Wellsey. In fact, he might need the good physician for support. But Cousin Lydie should not be subjected to such a conversation, especially if things turned out badly. Fortified by prayer, he plunged ahead with the distasteful task.

"Oliver." He used a sober tone. "I should like to see you in my study after supper."

A sneer curled Oliver's upper lip. "You sound like your father. Have I been a bad boy?"

Cousin Lydie gasped softly.

Dr. Wellsey gaped. "Now, really, Corwin."

Frederick sent the doctor a look, and tilted his head in the direction of the hallway, hoping the usually preoccupied man would understand. He was rewarded with a narrowing of the doctor's eyes and a slight nod.

Few words were spoken for the rest of the meal, and in short time, the men had gathered in Frederick's study. He sat behind his desk and indicated two chairs for the others.

"Oliver, I won't waste your time or mine. We have been friends since boyhood. My father thought well enough of you to send you to Florida as my companion." At Oliver's continued sneer, Frederick emitted an ironic laugh. "In truth, Lord Bennington felt that I needed your assistance in managing the plantation finances."

A flicker of some sort crossed Oliver's face. Apprehension? Guilt? But he sat back, arms crossed. "What of it? You've always been a spendthrift. Someone has to tighten the purse strings."

"Tighten them, perhaps. Not dip into that purse and help yourself." Without proof of theft, Frederick could only imply wrongdoing to see Oliver's reaction.

Eyes wide and mouth hanging open, Oliver appeared to be rendered mute. Yet the darting of his eyes told Frederick that the other man's mind was working. "Are you calling me a thief?"

Frederick shrugged. "If you are blameless, you won't mind my examining the discrepancies in my bookkeeping and yours." He casually repositioned his ink bottle and quill. "Further, we should discuss a certain letter to you from Lord Bennington that accidentally found its way to my desk. Oh, and I shall need to have your keys until this matter is fully examined."

Shaking with rage, Oliver stood and leaned over the desk. "My, my, aren't we getting bold. Little Freddy takes charge of the plantation."

Long accustomed to deflecting his brothers' taunts, Frederick nonetheless barely managed to keep his hands relaxed. He ached to stand and smash his fist into Oliver's scorn-filled face. Instead, he leaned forward with his forearms resting on the desk and stared up at his lifelong friend. "Yes, in fact, I am taking charge. Will you take these matters to heart? Or shall I simply send you home straightaway with a letter of dismissal?"

With a distasteful curse, Oliver retrieved his set of household keys from his jacket and slammed them down on the desk. "You will not take this position away from me. I will appeal to Lord Bennington, and then we shall see who prevails, especially when I tell him of your dalliance with a certain shopkeeper's daughter." He spun around and strode from the room. In a moment, the back door banged shut, jarring the paintings on the walls.

Dr. Wellsey stood and stared at Frederick. "I thought for

a moment I might have to step into the middle of a fight." He released an unsteady breath. "Thank the Lord for your cool head."

Frederick shook his not-so-cool head. "I don't know what's become of him. Perhaps he has always been this way but managed to hide it." He waved Dr. Wellsey back to his chair. "Can you think of any reason for his changes?"

Seated again, the physician pulled his lips into a thin line and gazed toward the night-darkened window. "Of course you know he suspects Lord Bennington of being his father."

Nausea leaped into Frederick's throat, and he rested his forehead on his hands. In all their years together, how had he failed to comprehend the source of Oliver's torment? Such a vile, wicked lie. Wasn't it? Mad doubts stretched across his mind, followed apace by the urgent need to defend Father's honor. "Preposterous. And I am certain we will have no difficulty proving it."

"Even if it were true, what has he to gain by discrediting you? Our English law prevents his inheriting anything."

"True." Frederick drummed his fingers on the desk. "But, should I be removed from my positions here, he could convince Father that he is the perfect replacement for me."

The back door slammed again, and soon Oliver raced into the room. "Fire! Fire in the settlement."

## Chapter Twelve

"Rachel!" Papa dashed up the stairs with energy that belied his age. "The inn's going up in a blaze."

Her heart racing, Rachel set aside her mending and sprung up from the settee.

Papa paused to gasp a few hurried breaths. "Shut the windows. The wind might shift our way, and the smoke'll ruin everything it touches."

"Yes, Papa." Rachel hastened to the front windows, catching the scent of smoke as she shoved the lower panes into place.

"I'm going now," he called from the top of the stairs.

"I'll come, too." Rachel started toward her room to change into an old dress.

"No. Stay here."

"But perhaps I can help."

"There'll be nothing for women to do." He spoke in his sharp captain's voice. "You'll get in the way." He ran down the steps, losing for a moment his limping gait.

Rachel clamped her lips together to keep from answering crossly. Of course she could help—somehow. After she closed the windows upstairs and down, she locked the shop door and hastened out into the night. After a quick glance into the empty kitchen house, she guessed Inez had already gone to help.

Her pulse pounding, she lifted her skirts and ran toward the inn. Even from a hundred yards away, she could see the bright orange glow that lit every front window and the tongues of fire that reached out from under the eaves to lick the shingled roof. Without doubt, the inn would soon be burned to the ground.

Rachel permitted herself a moment of relief that she and Papa had removed all their belongings. But poor Mr. Crump and his family would no doubt lose everything.

A throng of settlers—both men and women—hastened toward the conflagration. Most watched in horror, but Rachel saw a few brave men cautiously venture near enough to retrieve items of value: an oxen yoke, a harness, a wooden tray, a pewter pitcher. Screams and cries rose up in discord against the roaring crackle of the flames. Terrified animals shrieked as men released them from the livestock pens and herded them away.

Soldiers had cast off their red coats and formed a bucket line from the creek to the building. Papa joined them and, with powerful arms that had harpooned many a whale, flung the contents of the pails to quench the raging blaze.

Her own arms aching to help, Rachel searched for a useful task. The acrid smoke filled her lungs, and she moved upwind to the back of the building. There, she looked up in horror to see Sadie standing immobile inside an open window holding her baby.

"Sadie," Rachel cried, "come down. Oh, do come down." But even as she screamed out the words, she knew it would be impossible, for the stairs were surely on fire. "Jump, Sadie, jump!" Her heart twisted as she saw the flames behind the mother and infant.

"Sadie, girl!" A soldier appeared beside Rachel. "You've got to jump. Come on, now, be a brave lass. We're here to catch you."

"She's scared to move," another soldier said.

"Sadie, Sadie," the first man shouted. "Toss me the boy. Don't let him burn."

"She can't even hear you," the other soldier said.

"Bring a wagon, Henry," shouted the first soldier. "Bring something. I've gotta climb up."

"It can't be done, Bertie," Henry said. "There's no time. The whole place'll soon collapse."

With a dark scowl, Bertie grabbed his friend's shirt. "Will you look Rob in the eye and say you didn't try to save his wife and son?"

"All right, then. I'll get something." He dashed away.

"Sadie!" Rachel screamed out her name again. "Drop Robby down to us. Please, Sadie." A sob caught in her throat. *Dear God, please make her hear us.* She found a rock and threw it as hard as she could, but it fell far short of the window.

"Yes, that's the idea." Bertie also grabbed a rock and flung it, striking a glass pane with a loud whack.

Sadie jerked, then glanced back at the flames and screamed. "Mercy. Dear God, have mercy." She knelt by the open window's lower half. "Miss Folger, my baby!"

"Let him go, Sadie," Bertie called. "I'll catch him. I swear I will."

Weeping hysterically, Sadie pushed the terrified child out the window. He clawed for her as she held him at arm's length. With an agonizing cry, she shoved him away from the building but clutched at the air an instant after he left her fingers. "Robby!"

The screaming infant landed in Bertie's able arms. The soldier handed him to Rachel, then gripped her shoulders. "Take the boy to safety." He gave her a little shove toward the road.

"Yes, of course." With one last look at Sadie, one more prayer for her to be saved, too, Rachel clutched the wailing child and retreated from the roaring fire. Her heart screamed at the unfolding horror, but she forced herself to coo reassurances to Robby.

As she rounded the building, five soldiers bustled past, rolling a large shipping barrel, with Major Brigham in their wake. As they passed her, Rachel turned back to watch.

"Put the barrel against the wall," Brigham ordered in terse tones. "Banks, Carter, Smith, steady it." He stared up at Sadie, who now lay draped halfway out of the window. "Sims, Martin, climb up and bring her down." His stern expression bore not a hint of his former arrogance.

Henry and Bertie climbed on the barrel and braced their feet against their comrades' shoulders, forming a pyramid. Stretching their bodies upward beyond natural reach, they none too gently pulled Sadie through the window. As they lowered her to the ground, smoke billowed from her skirt and petticoats, and her leather shoes and long auburn hair smoldered.

Major Brigham pulled off his jacket and smothered the flames in her skirts, while another soldier found a bucket of water to douse her hair. The soldier named Bertie pulled off her ruined shoes and cast them aside.

"Move her away from the building." Brigham pointed toward the road.

The entire troop ran thirty yards to a place of relative safety, with Sadie bobbing limply in the arms of two soldiers.

Rachel followed and watched, praying all the while. With a whimpering babe in her arms, she could do no more. Unconscious, Sadie moaned and cried out.

A thunderous roar sounded behind them, followed by a blast of heat. A hundred terrified cries filled the air. Rachel fell to her knees, managing not to drop Robby, then turned back to see the crowds running from the collapsed building. Fed by splintered wood, the fire once again roared out its fury. All the people moved a safe distance away. There they inspected themselves and their neighbors for injury. Cries of pain pierced the night.

Blackened and breathing heavily, Papa stood among the other helpers watching the disaster play itself out. Inez emerged from the throng and hastened to Rachel and helped her up.

"Señorita Folger! Are you well?"

Rachel nodded. "Yes, but Sadie isn't." She glanced toward the girl. "We must take care of her, Inez."

"*Sí.* God would have us do this." Inez moved to where Bertie, Henry and Brigham still knelt beside Sadie. "Señors, you have done your job." Her grandmotherly tone held a hint of authority. "Now you take this *pobre madrecita,* the poor little mother, to my kitchen house where I can care for her."

"Indeed?" Brigham glared at Inez. He glanced at Rachel, and his sneer relaxed. "Miss Folger?"

"Yes, of course. We'll take responsibility for her." She glanced over her shoulder.

The bucket line reformed and made progress in dousing the outer edges of the blaze. Three soldiers who had helped with Sadie hurried to join them.

"Major Brigham." Rachel's eyes stung with tears and soot, and her lungs felt as if they might burst. "Do you know… where the Crumps are?"

A sad, almost kindly expression filled his eyes, and he shook his head.

Comprehending his meaning, Rachel groaned. But she shuddered away her feelings. Robby had fallen asleep in her arms, and she would not waken him by weeping for the deaths of his grandparents.

"Mr. Sims, Mr. Martin," she said to the soldiers. "You saved Sadie's and Robby's lives. You were very brave."

Bertie Martin shook his head. "No, miss, 'twas yourself. If we hadn't heard you cryin' out, we'd've never known she was still in there. We never saw her in the window when we checked around back."

"Well done, men," Major Brigham said. "Well done, Miss Folger. I shall write of your courageous actions in my reports to the magistrate and the governor." He started back to the fire. "You men carry the girl to Miss Folger's store and make haste to return."

The soldiers lifted Sadie and followed Rachel and Inez home. The smoke set all of them to coughing. But the wind had not shifted, and the small party soon moved beyond the worst of the choking air.

"Señorita Folger, will you let me carry the child?" Inez's slumped posture revealed her exhaustion.

"No, Inez, I can manage." In truth, Rachel could not bear to surrender her precious burden, though he seemed to grow heavier with each step she took.

"Ah!" Inez cried out, her eyes round and white in her soot-covered face. "Another fire."

"Miss Folger," one soldier shouted, "it's your store."

Frederick's stomach knotted as he rode hard toward the settlement, with Corwin and Dr. Wellsey close behind him. During the three-mile journey, he mentally checked off the list of orders he had given at the outset of Corwin's alarm. Mrs. Winthrop was to wake Cook and have her prepare food for those who would fight the fire. His overseer would assemble the male slaves least likely to run away to come help in the settlement. Frederick ordered Dr. Wellsey to bring his bag and tend the injured. But amidst it all, he had only one prayer: *Dear God, please don't let it be the Folgers' mercantile.*

Nearing town, Frederick saw flames above the distant trees

and gauged that the fire was far beyond the store. Relief swept through him. But the blaze rose so high that, even though the wind blew at his back, he smelled the stench of burning wood. He slowed his mount to a brisk trot as he tried to locate the tragedy somewhere beyond the trees. His companions followed suit.

"Oliver, check the church and vicarage." He pointed his riding crop toward a side street. "If all is well, come into town."

Without answering, Corwin rode away.

As they came around a giant oak tree, Dr. Wellsey reined his horse alongside Frederick. "The only buildings large enough to kindle such a fire are the store, the church and the inn."

"True." Frederick stared toward the darkened settlement, which seemed lit from behind by an eerie red glow. Muted shouts and cries met his ears. "You'll have many patients this night, doctor."

"Not what I would wish for, sir."

"There. Look."

A little more than a half mile away, red and orange flames blazed over the inn, and people darted about in a frenzy to save it. A great sudden roar filled the air as the building collapsed, sending people running in all directions. Their cries of fear rose in a crescendo above the bedlam. The flames diminished briefly. But fueled by the broken wood, they soon roared upward into the sky.

His eyes on the conflagration, Frederick cast a glance at the store as they rode by. A movement caught his attention, a dark form and a flicker of fire in the shrubbery next to the building. Fear for Miss Folger shot through him, and he pulled back on Essex's reins.

"Wait," he called to the doctor. "Here." He nudged Essex nearer just as a large bush burst into flames. The horse reared up and shrieked. Frederick nearly lost his seating. "Whoa, boy." He pulled to the side and jumped from the saddle, letting the reins fall free. "You there," he called to the fleeing man. "Stop."

The man ran into the forest behind the store, and Frederick charged after him.

"Sir," cried Wellsey. "It's starting to burn the building."

Frederick stopped short and spun about, racing back to the fire. He pulled off his coat and beat at the flames, but the linen fabric snagged on a branch and caught fire. He yanked it free and threw it in the sand where it could do no harm, then cast about for something to stop the blaze. A memory of something he had seen earlier in the day shot through his mind.

"Burlap. In the back room." Thankful the door was not locked, he dashed inside and grabbed several burlap bags. "Mr. Folger. Miss Folger," he called up the back stairs. When no one responded, he ran up the staircase to find an empty apartment, then hurried down the stairs and out the door. "The stream. Over there." Twenty feet from the store, a lazy spring ambled from beneath a limestone outcropping and wended its way toward the creek.

He and Wellsey plunged the bags into the water and ran to slap the drenched material against the burning wall. The battle raged for countless minutes. The flames seemed to die, but another spark ignited, and the dry bushes farther down the wall lit up the night.

Frederick and Wellsey alternated in their trips to the stream to rewet the burlap. Soon Frederick's arms and lungs ached. Wellsey seemed not to fare much better as he frequently stopped to gasp for breath. Just when Frederick thought he might fall to the ground in exhaustion, two men appeared beside him.

"Here, sir." A soldier grasped the damp bag and tugged it from Frederick's hands. "Let me take that."

His companion relieved Wellsey.

Frederick bent over, hands on his knees, and gulped in smoke-streaked air. After a violent bout of coughing, he rejoined the two new men.

Oliver appeared on the scene and set to work beside them. "The vicarage is unharmed. The vicar and his wife are safe at home."

Still struggling to breathe, Frederick shook his head. "Go back. I saw someone starting this fire, and I've no doubt they set the one at the inn. Watch over the Johnsons."

"Yes, sir." Oliver left without another word. No complaint about his assignment. No disputing Frederick's authority. Perhaps that was one fire quenched.

With the soldiers' help, they beat back the flames. One man found a hoe and chopped away all the vegetation near the building, removing it to the sandy area where Frederick lately had tossed his burned coat.

"Mr. Moberly."

A soft, shaky voice came from behind him. Frederick turned to see Miss Folger silhouetted against the glow of the still blazing inn. He hurried to her, longing to pull her into his arms, but stopped short at the sight of a sooty, ragged moppet in her arms.

"Are you well, dear lady?" He gently turned her to the light and found his reward: her fair face was blackened but unburned.

"I am well, sir." Her glistening tears caught the fire's red reflection and washed down her cheeks in black rivulets. "But poor Sadie is badly burned." She glanced beyond him. "You have saved our home." Sniffing, she wobbled where she stood but did not appear faint. "We shall be forever grateful." She gave her head a little shake. "We must see to Sadie. She's beside the road." She tilted her head. "Back there. Inez went for Papa."

He held her shoulders, then cupped her chin with one hand. "Carry the boy to the kitchen house. I'll bring Sadie." At her nod, he added, "Don't go into the store until I've made certain no live embers remain."

Again she nodded, but her eyes did not seem to focus.

"Wellsey, come see to Miss Folger."

As the good doctor led her away, Frederick sent up a prayer that she had not breathed in enough smoke to make her ill. At the thought of such a possibility, a nettling pain lodged in his chest. He must not lose her. *Must not.*

The urgency of his emotions startled him. His regard for her had deepened far beyond all previous contemplations, and he could do nothing to guarantee she would recover.

## Chapter Thirteen

After assuring Dr. Wellsey that she had suffered no injury, Rachel requested that he assist Frederick in bringing Sadie to the kitchen house. There, at the doctor's direction, Rachel and Inez inspected beneath Sadie's skirts and found blisters on her feet, ankles and lower legs. He gave Rachel a small tin of salve, the same vile-smelling medicine he had put on her injured hand, and instructed her to apply it liberally to the wounds.

"We can treat the external injuries," he said, "but I fear she inhaled a great amount of smoke. Only time will tell whether she will recover." He closed his bag and walked toward the door. "I'll come back once I've seen what's needed at the inn."

After he left, Inez sniffed the salve and wrinkled her nose. "Why ruin aloe with bear grease?" She snorted as she began to spread the medicine on Sadie's wounds. "The aloe works good alone. Many people in the islands use it since my *antepasados,* ancestors, bring it there."

While Inez administered the healing balm, Rachel leaned over and wiped Sadie's face with a damp cloth.

Sadie moaned, and her eyelids fluttered. "Robby. Save my Robby."

"Shh. Don't fret, Sadie." Rachel blinked back tears. "Robby is safe." She glanced across the kitchen house. Inez had made the baby a bed in an old crate, and there he slept soundly. Rachel released a weary, broken sigh.

Inez eyed her. "Señorita, you must rest. Go to your new house and sleep there. I will see to the señora and *su niño*."

"No, I should stay here. You're exhausted, too." Rachel slumped on a wooden bench. "Besides, Mr. Moberly wants to check the store to be certain the fire won't begin again." Fear gnawed at her. Why would someone want to burn down the inn and Papa's store?

"Miss Folger." Mr. Moberly stood in the doorway. "May I come in?"

"Please do." At the sight of his soot-covered hair and face and his singed shirt, a flurry of anguish and appreciation gripped her. He had risked his life to save the store.

"Oh, how will I, *we*, ever thank you?" The tears that had threatened for the past two hours now seized control. Choking sobs burst forth, and she covered her face in her hands.

His strong arms pulled her up into a comforting embrace. "Shh, there now. Everyone is safe." His gentle voice strummed a soothing chord in her soul, but she wept harder, gulping in air between sobs. After several moments, he gripped her upper arms and moved back a half step to look into her eyes. "Your father has returned from the fire."

She gasped. "Is he all right?"

"Believe me, Miss Folger, he is well." Mr. Moberly's even gaze conveyed the truth of his words. "He will come here after inspecting the store." He settled her back on the bench and sat beside her, draping an arm around her shoulders. "And you? Are you recovering?"

"Yes I believe so." Her words seemed to ease the tension in his face.

She leaned into his broad chest, discounting the impropriety and relishing the reassurance of his embrace.

"My overseer has brought workers from the plantation. They will sort through the debris at the inn and carry it away after the fire has been completely extinguished."

She nodded, but a nettling displeasure stung her conscience. When he said "workers," of course he meant slaves.

A cooling wind gusted in through the doorway, bringing a sprinkle of moisture.

Mr. Moberly bent down to capture Rachel's gaze. "Listen. Can you hear the rain? Would that it had come four hours ago."

His comment brought fresh tears to her eyes. "Yes. It might have saved Sadie's parents, if not the inn, too."

"Rachel. There ye are, my girl." Papa entered the kitchen house brushing raindrops from his filthy shirtsleeves.

"Papa." She stood and hurried to him. "Are you hurt? Burned? I saw your courage." She leaned into him, hoping for a hug. "You'll forgive me for disobeying, won't you? I had to help."

"I'm unharmed." Papa embraced her briefly, placing a quick kiss on her forehead. "And I do forgive ye. Mr. Moberly here told us how ye saved the girl and her babe. That's Nantucket courage, no mistake." The tenderness in his eyes belied his casual tone.

"Inez and I will take care of them." Rachel glanced at her servant, who nodded her agreement. "I knew you would wish it."

"Aye." Papa's scratchy voice revealed the fire's effects. "I'd be ashamed if ye didn't take on the task." He looked at Mr. Moberly. "I've checked all over the house and store. A few boards are needed to replace the scorched ones, but we're in no danger. Ye saved my property, and I thank ye for it."

"If you need lumber," Mr. Moberly said, "I can provide it from my sawmill."

Papa appeared flustered. "Indeed. That's more than generous. Thank ye, sir."

Rachel noticed the heightened color in Mr. Moberly's soot-streaked face, and her heart delighted to see such feeling in a man of his position.

"I must go now." Mr. Moberly brushed a hand through his hair, sending soot cascading down his shirtsleeves. "Major Brigham will want details about the man who started the fire. He's ordered the entire garrison to patrol the settlement until the man is caught." He took Rachel's hand and kissed it with more feeling than a mere courtesy. "Good night, Miss Folger, Mr. Folger."

He walked out into the growing rainstorm, and Rachel followed, stopping at the doorway to watch him mount his horse. As he rode out of sight, she ached to ride away with him, far away from the disaster.

Stinging rain pelted Frederick's head and back, but he ignored the discomfort, for the events of this night had secured more than one matter in his life. That Miss Folger's fondness and respect for him were growing, he felt more than hopeful. That he could manage Corwin and his dishonesty, he felt likewise sanguine. But the fire had tested him to a greater degree than any previous event in his life, and he had emerged triumphant. At the outset, he had known what to order, what to do. By God's mercy, he had seen the fire at the store and sent the culprit running. And never once had he surrendered to his fear.

How he longed to report the whole of it to Father, like a child seeking praise for well-formed letters or clever computations—anything to discredit Oliver's evil reports. But Father would dismiss it all if Frederick boasted. Best to make an objective list of events, leaving out his concerns for Miss Folger, of course, and point Father to the community's collective efforts. Perhaps Brigham would lend a note of praise, and Frederick would dispatch the same in return. He had yet to ascertain how to win the fellow over. Perhaps this event would seal that matter, as well.

When he reached the garrison, the guards recognized him and gave him entrance. One man led his horse away for grooming and oats. At the commander's house, a servant greeted him and offered a change of clothes.

"No, thank you, my good man. I won't be here long, and it's not cold."

The man brought towels to sop up moisture from his dripping shirt. Some of the soot had washed off in the rain, so he would not do too much damage to the commander's house.

"Mr. Moberly." Lady Augusta joined him in the small, elegant drawing room. She wore a modest dressing gown. And without her dreadful makeup, she seemed younger, prettier and decidedly more pleasant.

"Forgive me, madam, for my frightful appearance. Major Brigham asked me to come, but I shan't stay for long." He offered a lighthearted chuckle. "I promise I shall not sit down."

Her soft laughter sounded free of intrigue. "Thank you, sir, for then I should be required to have my chair recovered at your expense."

"As tired as I am, I should sit and pay the consequences. This night has brought its challenges."

At her second laugh, he relaxed further, but the memory of their last private meeting still cautioned him.

"You must know, madam, that your husband performed brilliantly tonight. In the thick of the fire, he executed his duty with unflinching courage." Frederick had not seen Brigham's performance, but others had praised the officer's valor.

A blush touched her cheeks. "Yes, I am certain of it." She glanced at the closed door behind her, then turned back to him with pleading eyes. "Will you temper your praise when you report the incident? Please?"

Frederick drew in a breath. "No, madam. That I cannot do."

"But our bargain—"

He glanced at Major Brigham's portrait above the fireplace. Dressed in uniform, he appeared the perfect British officer. "A fine picture. Gainsborough, if I'm not mistaken."

"Mr. Moberly."

He turned back and stared hard at her. "Madam." He leaned toward her and spoke softly lest Brigham enter the room and hear him. "Are you unaware that a man like your husband would rather die than face dishonor?"

Tears sprang to her eyes, and her jaw jutted forward. "Yes," she hissed. "And if forced to make such a choice, I would rather he be dishonored than die."

"Surely you do not mean that."

Her defiant expression answered him.

"Moberly." Brigham entered with a hand extended, but his stern look shot back and forth between Frederick and Lady Augusta.

"Brigham." Frederick shook his hand heartily, determined to ignore the suspicious stare. "What are your plans? I should like to accompany you as you pursue the culprit."

Brigham shook his head. "A man would be mad to order troops out in this weather. You've experienced an East Florida hurricane. This storm shows every sign of becoming one. If it diminishes tomorrow, we can decide about pursuit then."

"By then all tracks will have washed away, as they no doubt already have." Frederick grunted. "But you're right, of course."

"Will you have some tea, Mr. Moberly?" Lady Augusta asked.

He shook his head. "Thank you, madam, but no. I should like to be at home before the storm worsens."

Essex met the challenge of carrying Frederick through the blinding rain on the road back to the plantation. Along the way, Frederick bent into the headwind, wishing for his hat, which had blown off on the ride into town.

Just as the rain battered his head, Lady Augusta's request beat against his conscience. He had written the requested letter and came close to sending it with the latest mail delivery going to Father, but something had held him back. The letter sat in his desk, and now he would destroy it. Brigham was a brave man, the kind of soldier needed to help quash the rebellion up north. He would be shamed to know of his wife's machinations, seemingly on his account. And he would blame Frederick for his part in it.

What did a woman know of men's matters? Of a man's need to succeed in the world? Clearly, Frederick would have to choose between keeping his promise to Lady Augusta and honoring her courageous husband.

# Chapter Fourteen

After a two-day storm, Frederick surveyed the damage to the plantation and gave orders for cleanup and repairs. Although the storm had prevented travel and all but the most necessary outdoor work, it was nothing like the previous year's hurricane. This time the overflowing creeks did not reach severe flood levels and had already receded to their natural banks. Branches littered the ground, but no trees had been blown down. And the slave quarters had escaped serious loss due to Frederick's recent orders to reinforce the structures to make them as sturdy as his other outbuildings.

Frederick had more reasons to be encouraged. During the fire, Oliver had obeyed orders without complaint. He had also displayed exceptional valor in rescuing plantation animals in the storm. Perhaps his letters to Father had been written out of frustration over his future. While Frederick faced the challenges of a younger son, Oliver's illegitimacy presented a far more formidable barrier to advancement. No doubt he had been tortured all his life by not knowing his paternity, and Father's generosity must have seemed like the actions of a guilt-ridden parent. Oliver's courage called for extending another chance to work out their conflicts.

The air smelled fresh and clean, and the fragrance of pine wafted on the breeze. But the sun returned from its two-day absence eager to make up for lost time. It beat down smartly on Frederick's back as he rode toward town along the leaf-strewn road. Yet he would endure a fiery furnace to reach the mercantile and discover whether the Folgers had suffered any loss from the hurricane. With Mr. Folger there, Frederick had some assurance that the man who started the fires could not cause any further mischief. But until he saw Miss Folger himself, he would feel no peace.

At the edge of town, he encountered Major Brigham on horseback overseeing the removal of a fallen oak tree lying across the road. The officer hailed him.

"Moberly, how fares your plantation?" His military demeanor bore not a hint of his former arrogance.

"Very well, sir. A few repairs are needed, but nothing to complain of. And the garrison?"

"Likewise." Brigham reined his horse closer. "You will want to know we have a suspect in the matter of the fires."

"Indeed?" Frederick felt an odd mix of disappointment and satisfaction. He would gladly have caught the man himself and seen to his punishment. "Did you apprehend him?"

"No." Brigham shook his head. "As we surmised, he fled into the wilderness. But we are confident of his identity. You recall of course the innkeeper's dead goose."

"Buckner." Frederick spat out the name and felt a mad desire to hunt the man down forthwith.

"He is the only man unaccounted for in the regiment, and we assume he's deserted." Brigham snorted. "Sims reported that Buckner carried a great deal of resentment after the goose incident. He vowed to make everyone pay dearly for his demotion. Vile coward."

"And a murderer."

"Too bad the man cannot be hanged twice."

"Beggin' yer pardon, sir." A soldier carrying an ax approached Brigham.

"Yes, sergeant."

"We're goin' ta need a winch to haul this tree off the road, sir." The man brushed sweat from his face. "It's too big to chop apart so we can clear the road in a timely way."

"Very well. See to it." Brigham turned back to Frederick. "If you're in agreement, I'll write letters to the commanders of other garrisons around East Florida to watch for Buckner."

Surprised, Frederick took a moment to consider the proposal and the manner in which it was delivered. Brigham had changed much in a short time.

"Yes, of course. Your signature will carry as much weight as mine in this matter." Frederick saluted Brigham with his riding crop. "If you need a winch, send someone to the plantation, and Corwin will make mine available."

"Thank you, sir." Brigham nodded his appreciation. "I'll do that."

Frederick took his leave, anxious to tell Miss Folger about Buckner. If the man dared to return to the settlement, she would need protection.

He left Essex in the shade of an oak tree and walked through a maze of puddles to the store, giving the building a cursory inspection before he stepped up on the narrow wooden porch. Inside, he found the object of his concern and immediately cast aside all worries. Serenity floated on the air with the scent of lavender.

As lovely as ever, Miss Folger stood behind the counter measuring a length of linen for the customer who stood on the other side. Frederick recognized the woman as a servant indentured to an upriver planter.

Miss Folger glanced up, and her face brightened. "Good morning, Mr. Moberly. I shall be with you in a moment."

The slender servant gasped. "Oh, no, miss. You must help the magistrate. I can wait."

"Not at all," Frederick said. "I'm in no hurry. Complete your transaction."

"Thank you, sir." Miss Folger turned back to the customer.

The other woman bent near her and muttered something in urgent tones.

Miss Folger shook her head. "Be at ease, Esther. Unlike other British aristocrats, Mr. Moberly does not insist that the waters should part before him."

The woman cocked her head and then glanced at Frederick. "If you're sure, miss."

Miss Folger folded and wrapped the linen. "There. Two dress lengths of brown, one dress length of white and thread to match. Will there be anything else for Mrs. Allen?"

"No, miss." The woman gathered her mistress's purchases and hurried out, but not before casting a nervous glance Frederick's way.

Struggling not to laugh, he sauntered to the counter. "So you do not find me an ogre—like most aristocrats?"

"I've not yet made up my mind." Miss Folger returned a box of snuff to the display case. "It is difficult to change an opinion one has held for a lifetime."

He leaned his arms on a small cask on the counter and tilted his head. "And such a terribly long lifetime, too." Emotion flooded him such as he had never felt for any young lady, but what to name it, he did not know. Surely his face must proclaim his feelings for her, for she blushed and her hands shook as she rewrapped the bolt of linen. He gently gripped them, enjoying the silken feel of her skin. "It is good to see you well and unharmed by the storm."

She pulled one hand loose and placed it on top of his. "And you, as well, dear friend." Her soft rush of words revealed feeling that seemed to match the depth of his own.

The jingle of the doorbells shattered the sweet moment. Miss Folger quickly freed her hands, but Frederick leaned against the counter and crossed his arms in a tranquil pose. He would not be ashamed of their friendship, even if Father himself should walk through the door.

Still, he did not wish for anyone to misunderstand his lingering presence. He straightened and sauntered toward the gun display to peruse the small selection. But his gaze frequently turned toward Miss Folger.

"Good morning, John," she said to her customer, the settlement's new wheelwright. "May I help you?"

Like the woman before him, the young man glanced at Frederick and asked whether he should not be served first.

"The magistrate is still considering his purchases." Miss Folger gave the man a reassuring smile. "John, am I correct in assuming congratulations are in order?"

"Yes, miss." John grinned broadly. "'Tis our first, a fine, healthy boy."

"Do you have a name for him?" Her lovely dark eyes exuded genuine kindness, a rare quality that Frederick found endearing.

"'Twill be William, if I have my way," John said. "George, if she has hers."

Miss Folger's merry laugh echoed in Frederick's heart. "Knowing Mary, I think you will be calling him George."

John's laugh held somewhat less mirth. "'Tis true, miss. But I love 'er all the same, and I'd like to buy her some small gift. Can you suggest anything?"

"Indeed, I can." She pulled a tray from beneath the counter. "We have several whalebone items carved by our Mr. Patch. Thimbles, combs, a candlestick and the like."

While John hunched over the tray and consulted with Miss Folger, Frederick found himself captured by the scene. This lovely young lady had a grace about her that entirely enchanted him. Like Mother, she did not hold herself above the common man, but treated the wheelwright with the same courtesy she had shown the more prominent guests at Frederick's party. No arrogance, no hauteur, nothing artificial. Except for his own sister, he had never known a young lady with such a generous demeanor—and good humor, as well.

While John argued for the practicality of a thimble, Miss Folger insisted his wife deserved nothing less than a pretty comb. In the end, Miss Folger won, but John seemed as pleased as she when he left the store with his purchase.

Frederick set his elbows on a tall display, rested his chin on his fists and gazed across the room at her. He recalled the tender emotion that had filled him as this delightful creature leaned into his embrace after the fire, thus revealing her trust in him. Now, deep sentiments for her stirred within him, feelings so strong he wondered if he could speak to her again without declaring his love. But no, he must wait. Must not play her false. Must examine his emotions to be certain of their depth and nature…and ensure that they would last forever.

Rachel's hands shook as she arranged the whalebone carvings in their tray. In the corner of her eye, she saw Mr. Moberly staring at her with twinkling eyes and a half smile, his admiration clear. With her own emotions in such a muddle, she feared even to speak to him again.

While waiting on John, she had wanted to ask the wheelwright's opinion of the revolution, but Mr. Moberly's presence prevented that. Yet she did not want the gentleman to leave. Indeed, recalling how much she had enjoyed his comforting embrace after the fire, she would not have him leave at all. Ever.

But with all their differences, could they ever truly be friends…or more? *Lord, let me not mistake Your leading in this.*

She sent a tentative glance in his direction. "Did you find something of interest, Mr. Moberly?"

"Indeed, I have found something of interest, Miss Folger. But the price is very dear—far beyond that of rubies."

Rachel could think of no response, for doubtless he would indeed pay dearly if they proceeded. Yet neither of them seemed to possess the power to stop. As he approached, she saw the ruddy color in his face was heightened, as hers must be.

He set one hand on the tray of wares, preventing her from moving it below the counter. "May I look at these? Ah, what fine craftsmanship. You must commend your Mr. Patch for me."

"I shall do that." Inhaling a deep breath, Rachel forced her racing pulse to slow. "Perhaps you would like to purchase something for dear Mrs. Winthrop."

He raised his eyebrows. "What an excellent idea. What do you suggest?"

"This candlestick is quite exquisite, do you not think?" Holding up the round article with a two-masted ship carved on its side, Rachel risked a glance into his dark gray eyes. Her pulse raced again.

"Perfect." He took it in hand, brushing her fingers with his, and a pleasant shiver shot up her arm and tickled her neck. "I will take it."

While Rachel wrapped the gift, Mr. Moberly stared at her again, while a teasing grin played across his lips.

She tried to tie twine around the package, but it slipped. "If you expect me to accomplish this, you must stop staring at me."

"Never." He stuck his finger against the string while she completed the task.

"Thank you." Rachel continued to stare at the package and prayed for some objective matter to discuss. A memory sparked in her mind, and her prayer became thanks. "For some time, I have wanted to tell you how much I admired your decision about the indentured man who stole the pig."

He straightened, and a frown swept over his fine features. "Truly? I still wonder about it."

Rachel's heart reached out to him. He seemed so young to hold the fate of hapless souls in his hands. "You must set your mind at ease. You displayed the wisdom of Solomon, and shame forced the owner to relinquish his demands for punishment, since he could not bear to administer it himself. You were guided by mercy, as our heavenly Father is merciful."

His countenance lightened, and he breathed out a long sigh. "Miss Folger, your words have dispelled my anguish. I am grateful."

Now she could gaze at him without shyness. In fact, she felt infused with courage. "'Tis nearly noon. Will you join us for our midday meal?"

"I should like to very much, but duty calls. I must ensure that the rest of the settlement has survived the storm." He claimed his hat from a nearby display. "And I must examine the ruins of the inn."

"Yes, of course." At the memory of the tragedy, Rachel's heart hitched. "Dr. Wellsey came to see Sadie early this morning. He suggests that she is not yet well enough to be told of her parents' deaths."

"I am grieved for her." He glanced away with a grimace. "After our pleasant chat, I despair of telling you this, but I must. Major Brigham has informed me that the culprit is none other than Private Buckner, who sought to steal the Crumps' goose."

"Oh, my." Rachel shuddered at the memory of the brutal soldier.

"He fled into the wilderness, and with the weather improved, the entire garrison will search for him. You may rest assured that he will be apprehended. But we all must keep watch for him and prevent him from doing more harm." Mr. Moberly touched her hand. "I do not think you need to fear."

"I promise to be vigilant."

But as he walked out the door, Rachel sorted through another muddle of emotions, as her delightful memories of Mr. Moberly's visit vied with her fear of the murderer who had yet to be apprehended.

## Chapter Fifteen

"Reverend Johnson's homily certainly suited our town's recent trials," Mrs. Winthrop said. "Do you not agree, Mr. Folger?" Seated across from Rachel and Papa in Mr. Moberly's fine carriage, the lady appeared the picture of serenity.

"Aye, madam." Papa's voice rang with enthusiasm. "The vicar's passage from the Book of James expresses the thinking that's guided my life for fifty-two years."

Rachel glanced sideways at him, working to keep shock from her expression. In vain she had tried these many years to extract a claim to faith from Papa. Yet Mrs. Winthrop had drawn out his deepest thoughts with a simple question.

"How so, sir?" Mrs. Winthrop's lined face seemed smoother as she gazed at him.

Papa scratched his chin, which lately he had kept clean-shaven, no doubt on Mrs. Winthrop's account. "As we saw last week and, I'm sure ye'd agree, ofttimes in our years on this earth, our lives truly are vapors that appear for a short time and then vanish away. A man'd be a fool to presume his own plan to buy and sell and get gain was equal to divine will."

While he and Mrs. Winthrop turned their conversation

from the sermon to other matters, Rachel eased back into her seat and looked ahead, where Mr. Moberly and Mr. Corwin rode horseback side by side, leading the way to the plantation. Papa's response had not been what she had hoped for, but it did reveal something new. At least he believed God existed. She offered up a silent prayer that Mrs. Winthrop would draw him closer to the Almighty.

Traces of delightful aromas—baked chicken and peach pie—met them as they came around the familiar stand of palm trees, and Rachel's stomach rumbled softly. Smoke from the kitchen house sent a gauzy curtain over their view, but a breeze from the east soon unveiled the elegant white mansion. Today, the front columns wore no festive bunting, and no slaves worked the distant fields. Rachel did, however, see uniformed black servants out front awaiting the arrival of their master and his party.

Did Mr. Moberly provide church services for those who worked his fields and cooked his meals? Did he grant them at least part of each Sunday as a Sabbath rest, according to Scripture as Papa did for Inez? Now her heart rumbled in rhythm with her stomach, and her mind churned with more questions, especially regarding overseers and chains. If Mr. Moberly could not answer them to her satisfaction, she must find a way to silence forever the siren call of…*friendship* that sang both night and day in her heart.

Oh, why was she using that word? What she felt for dear Mr. Moberly was far more than friendship. It was nothing less than the painful pangs of love.

Yet as she stepped from the carriage, climbed the front steps, and walked through the mansion's red front door on Mr. Moberly's arm, she felt as if she were coming home—a bewildering sensation.

Inside, familiar servants stood ready to attend to every need of their master's guests. The same sweet little slave girl sat in the dining room corner waving a large palm branch to direct the indifferent breeze drifting in through two tall windows.

Seated with the others at the dining room table, Rachel surrendered to her appetite and enjoyed the many courses the servants set before her. She noticed with interest that no trace of fear or unhappiness could be found on any of their faces, a credit to their master. Did they yearn for freedom beneath their placid smiles? Uncovering their true opinions would be difficult.

After many light pleasantries, Papa eyed Mr. Moberly. "Tell me, sir, have ye discovered the identity of the man who's trying to stir up trouble in the tavern?"

Rachel choked on her rice. Should Papa discover the patriot, surely he would not betray the man, despite his indifference to the cause.

"Unfortunately, no." Mr. Moberly buttered a piece of bread. "But we continue to get reports of his appearances at the oddest times and places."

"Well," Papa said, "I've been keeping an eye out for him amongst my customers, but no stout, red-bearded man's come in the store."

"We are grateful for your vigilance," Mr. Moberly said. "But in truth, I do not believe he has found any sympathizers for the rebels' cause."

"True, true." Papa savored a bite of chicken. "We shouldn't have to contend with the likes of him when we've got renegade soldiers starting fires."

"Mr. Folger," Mrs. Winthrop said, "you and your daughter have been so kind to take in Sadie and her son." Her eyes soft with sympathy, she turned to Rachel. "Who is caring for them today?"

"Our servant, Inez." Rachel served herself a second helping of greens from the bowl held by a liveried slave.

"She's very good with both mother and child and willingly gave up her Sunday morning off to attend to their needs."

"What a comfort." Mrs. Winthrop looked at Mr. Moberly. "What is to be done with the little boy if Sadie does not recover?"

"Can you not guess, madam?" Papa set down his food-laden fork. "Rachel and I will care for the lad."

Mrs. Winthrop's face seemed to glow with beatific beauty. "Why, sir, that is more than generous."

"Indeed, it is." Mr. Moberly gave Rachel a merry grin. "He's an active little scamp. Do you not tire of chasing him?" His well-formed lips gave way to a teasing grin.

"You may be surprised to learn that Papa keeps little Robby out of mischief more than I do and enjoys every minute of it."

"'Tis no more tiring than gamboling with my eldest daughter's little ones." Papa grinned broadly, then sobered. "Too many years was I out to sea chasing whales while my daughters grew up without me. Should need arise, I'll be a father to the boy and rear him, as I did Captain Templeton." Papa's eyes shone with feeling, and Rachel knew he missed Jamie. But she acknowledged sweet surprise at hearing of his regrets over missing much of her childhood.

"Then the boy will be well reared, sir." Mr. Moberly gave Papa an approving nod. "I must tell you, however, I asked Major Brigham to send word to Sadie's husband about the tragedy. With the insurrection in the northern colonies, it may be some time before he replies to advise us about any relatives in England. Until then, we must pray God's mercy for this family, that they might not suffer another loss."

"Amen," Papa said.

Rachel pursed her lips and concentrated on eating the aromatic, spicy greens on her plate. Perhaps her prayers had been answered. Perhaps the fire had changed Papa's thoughts

about trusting the Lord. As for Mr. Moberly's encourage-
ment to pray, how could it mean anything other than that he
was a Christian who sought to do God's will?

After dinner, the party stepped outside for an afternoon
stroll. Papa and Mrs. Winthrop lagged behind while Rachel
took Mr. Moberly's offered arm with gratitude, for many
roots and rocks covered the unfamiliar ground.

The East Florida skies were filled with wispy, meandering clouds and not a hint of rain. The scent of oranges filled
the air, and the oyster-shell pathways crunched beneath their
feet. Beside the unpainted shacks in the slave quarters, men,
women and children tended private gardens or hung laundry
they had washed in the stream. Around many of the humble
homes, youthful slaves swept the sandy brown earth into tidy
patterns with pine bows. Here and there, pansies and mari-
golds flourished in broken crockery or little wooden boxes.

As Rachel and Mr. Moberly walked past the humble
homes, the slaves stopped their work to offer a respectful
greeting. To each one, Mr. Moberly responded kindly and by
name, the latter of which Rachel regarded as a remarkable ac-
complishment. She clasped his arm more firmly, a gesture that
must have pleased him, for he set his hand over hers as they
continued their walk.

"Shall we visit the springhouse?" He pointed toward a
pathway meandering through the pine forest. Overhead, tree
branches met to shield them from the harsh summer heat.

"Yes. I would like that." Rachel glanced behind to see
Papa and Mrs. Winthrop walking arm in arm, their heads
tilted toward one another as if they were old friends.

"They will follow." Mr. Moberly squeezed her hand. "Mrs.
Winthrop is exacting in matters of propriety. She'll not permit
us to go unchaperoned." He glanced behind them. "And I'm
sure your father is of the same mind."

Rachel nodded her agreement. Papa had come close to

calling Charles out—with a harpoon, no less—when he began courting her sister Susanna. But he had never mentioned Mr. Moberly's attention toward her. Surely after today, Papa would perceive the depth of their mutual interest.

When they reached the springhouse, Mr. Moberly led Rachel to a little arbor woven of tender oak branches. She sat on a cushioned cast-iron bench while he fetched cups of water. After the first tasty sip, she inhaled a deep breath, knowing she could no longer put off the inevitable conversation. She considered several ways to begin but found none satisfactory.

"Is it all right?" Mr. Moberly lifted his own cup. "Seems good. The servants are instructed to keep leaves and other debris from the cistern."

Rachel's heart leapt. A perfect opening. "Why, yes, it's every bit as delicious as before. But forgive me, sir. Do you not mean 'slaves' instead of 'servants'?"

Seated beside her, he blinked in the most charming way, and she could not help but notice how his black eyelashes enhanced the appeal of his dark gray eyes.

"What an interesting question." He placed one finger against his chin in a thoughtful pose.

The pleasant fragrance of his shaving balm threatened to undo her senses. She detected the scent of bergamot and perhaps a bit of petitgrain. "Had you never considered it?" she managed to ask.

"Cannot say I ever have. But that is not to say I should not." He sat back against the arbor wall, extended his legs and crossed his arms. With a winsome grin, he added, "I shall consider anything you wish, dear lady."

Heat rushed to her face, as much from annoyance as from the pleasantness of his being close to her.

"Thank you. For I have many questions to ask you."

"Many?" His eyebrows arched. "Then let us begin."

She bit her lip to keep from smiling. "I am in earnest, Mr. Moberly."

Amusement disappeared from his face. "Forgive me. Please proceed."

She gazed beyond the bower opening to see Papa and Mrs. Winthrop seated on the cistern's wide coquina wall. From his broad gestures, she could tell Papa was relating one of his whaling adventures. The two of them spoke together easily. Perhaps that came with age, for they certainly had not known one another long enough for familiarity to have engendered such harmony. Or perhaps it was because neither of them demonstrated a passion as strong as Rachel's for matters that ate at her soul.

With a quick breath, she stared up at Mr. Moberly, noting against her will how his softened expression enhanced his handsome features. "Sir, I despise slavery of any sort. When my Quaker ancestors settled on Nantucket Island, they vowed before God that they would never enslave a person of any race or gender or age. While some of us have left the Society of Friends, we have not lost our hatred of slavery."

"Ah." He uncrossed his arms and placed his hands on his knees, while understanding filled his eyes. "I see. And so, of course, you are concerned about the slaves who work my plantation."

"Yes." Her answer came out in a breathless rush.

He seemed not to notice but, rather, studied the ground at his feet as if thinking over her words. "It may surprise you to know my mother shares your sentiments." He looked away and broke off a green twig from the arbor's latticed wall. "Father, of course, remains detached from all his New World enterprises so long as they are prosperous."

Hope surged through Rachel. "But how do you regard the matter?"

"I am my father's agent, Miss Folger. I must do his will

just as my servants...*slaves* must do mine. That is, if we are
to make this plantation a success." His firm tone conveyed no
displeasure, only that to him his statements were simple facts.

Rachel's pulse pounded. Could he hear it? "Success means
much to you, then?"

He sat up, and his eyes widened. "Why, of course. What
man worth his daily bread does not seek to succeed?" His lips
twitched with merriment, and her pulse increased. "Perhaps
you are aware that in England younger sons do not inherit any
portion of entailed estates, as my father's is. Therefore, we
must make our own way in the world."

"Yes, you mentioned something to that effect the day we
met."

"I am honored you recall my words."

Rachel gave him a sly look. "'Twas merely good business.
You were a new customer and an important one. I took care
to remember." Someday she would confess she had disliked
him that day simply for being English.

"Ah." He chuckled. "A commendable habit if one wishes
to—dare I say it?—*succeed*."

"Humph." She could not quite pucker away her smile. "I
was merely tending to my father's interests."

"Of course," he murmured. "That is something I fully
understand."

Somehow she must turn the conversation back to the
slaves. But before she could begin, he inhaled as if about to
speak, and so she waited.

"Lately, I have felt an even stronger desire than before to
prove myself." He seized another twig and twirled it between
his thumb and forefinger. "May I tell you why?"

"Certainly. I shall keep your secret."

"Can you not guess, Miss Folger? If I continue to do well
for my father, he can have fewer objections to our...oh,
bother, I'm weary of calling this a 'friendship' when to me it

is nothing short of a courtship." He sat back as if disconcerted, and his face was flushed, as if he were embarrassed. "There." He tossed the twig to the ground. "I've laid my heart bare before you. Do with it as you will."

Compassion filled her, along with the desire to reveal her own heart. But caution swept unbidden into her mind. "Sir, I shall always regard your heart as worthy of the tenderest care."

He stared at the ground and frowned, his disappointment evident. "I have spoken too hastily. Forgive me."

"Not at all." Rachel set her hand on his forearm. "I would but remind you there are differences in our opinions on certain essential matters. Such disparities do not make tranquil marriages. Did we not agree to discuss these things?"

His brow furrowed. "Yes, we did. Again, forgive me." He ran his hand through his hair, loosening several black strands from his queue. He brushed them back behind his ear. The ever-present stray curl graced his noble brow and enhanced his charm. "Tell me what concerns you. The slavery issue, of course. What else?"

"The revolution."

"The—? Ah, yes. The revolution." He stared out of the arbor with a dark frown. But he sent her a playful glance. "Now, really, Miss Folger. Do not tell me you are the red-bearded agitator trying to incite rebellion in our midst."

She smirked. "If only I could be." She dismissed her levity. "We…that is, the thirteen northern colonies mean to have their independence from England." She swallowed. "And had I not been forced to come here with Papa, I would be in Boston doing everything in my power to help their grand cause."

Dismay filled his eyes for a moment, and he gave her a sad smile. "I would expect nothing less from you, brave lady that you are. And so we have much to consider, do we not?"

Rachel bent her head in agreement, but a knot filled her chest at the thought of losing his regard because of their differences. Would it truly come to that?

## Chapter Sixteen

He had not meant to declare himself to her. What had incited him to such an extreme? Her eyes, of course. Those dark questioning eyes that made him turn to soft butter inside. Those inviting lips, which had tempted him nearly to distraction as he sat close to her in the arbor. That pert little nose, which wiggled in the most charming way when she spoke with passion about her interests. The scent of her lavender perfume, the modest cut of her gown that nonetheless enhanced her feminine form.

Frederick exhaled a happy sigh at the memory of her seated later at the pianoforte, enchanting the entire household with her exquisite playing. Despite months away from an instrument, she had quickly regained her skills. What an accomplished young lady.

He sat in his library with both feet propped on the desk, a pose that had earned him more than one scolding from Father. But somehow the earl's specter seemed less ominous than before. Now Miss Folger's image pervaded his every thought, his every feeling. His desire for her approval had begun to weigh more heavily upon him. While not quite supplanting Father, she had nearly attained preeminence. But pleasing her might turn out to be every whit as difficult.

Managing the plantation without slaves was a preposterous notion, of course, but somehow he must convince her of his kindly intentions toward his workers. Perhaps he could convince her of the good she herself could do for the slaves as the plantation's mistress, much like Mother's ministrations to the villagers near Bennington Manor.

As for the foolish rebellion up north, he had no doubt that would soon be quashed. A farmers' militia had no chance against trained British forces, and the colonists had no navy to fight His Majesty's unparalleled fleet. Frederick had not meant to deceive Miss Folger in regard to his opinions about the conflict, merely to diffuse her concerns about his feelings. Of course, he could never say so, but soon enough their differences would be settled by the course of history. He only hoped her friends up north wouldn't suffer for their participation in that rebellious cause.

With her departure, he felt the ache of missing her presence mingled with hope that they could soon resolve everything. If only he could comprehend her thinking and satisfy her concerns.

"Ah! Of course," he exclaimed.

Frederick rose from his desk and strode to the bookshelf. From behind John Milton's *Paradise Lost,* he retrieved *A Declaration of Rights and Grievances.* His fingers touched the pamphlet, and he had to force himself back to the desk rather than to the fireplace to burn the seditious paper. He read it over in a few minutes and wondered about its implications.

Everyone had known for some time of the difficulties in the dissenting colonies. Father would rant about it from time to time, especially after a session of Parliament. Undoubtedly, the earl had been one of those who had voted in favor of the choking restrictions placed on Massachusetts Bay. But now that Frederick had settled in the New World, he found the punishments leveled against the colonists to be harsh in the extreme, despite their throwing a shipload of tea into the Boston Harbor in '73. Many times he himself had longed to lodge a protest against the taxes on the plantation's produce, but Father would permit no complaints against His Majesty.

"Interesting reading?" Oliver appeared in the doorway, and his gaze shot to the pamphlet. He sauntered across the eight feet from door to desk as Frederick struggled to fold it with nonchalance.

"Merely passing the time." Frederick opened the desk drawer, put the document inside and then casually closed the drawer. Later he would place it where Oliver would never find it.

Oliver sat down and lounged in a wingback chair in front of the desk. He leveled a smug look at Frederick. "So you've fallen for the little Nantucket wench."

Rage shot through Frederick. Leaning forward, he clenched his fists on the desk and glared at Oliver. "If you use that word to describe her again, I shall call you out."

Oliver blinked and frowned. "Now, now, Freddy, no need for anger. I'll call her whatever you wish." He studied his fingernails, then stared at the ceiling. "Except Mrs. Moberly."

Frederick sat back, grasping for the appearance of calm while his emotions stormed within. "Suit yourself. There will be no need for any form of addressing her when you've returned to London." The quaver in his voice betrayed him.

Oliver's face flamed red clear up to his ears. "When my letter reaches Lord Bennington, *you* will be the one who returns to London."

Frederick went cold for the briefest moment. But the warmth returning to his chest was not anger, rather, an odd reassurance. So Oliver had indeed written the letter, and Father would soon know about Miss Folger. So be it. Let the dice fall as they would. He had not yet crossed the Rubicon, but the bridge was in sight.

"Why did you come in here, Ollie?" Frederick used the name he had called this former friend in childhood. Alas, when had they ceased to be friends?

Oliver smirked. "I thought you should know that I have written to Lord Bennington about your *courtship*." Sarcasm laced his tone.

Frederick drummed his fingers on the desk. "Oh, my friend, what makes you think I have not sent a letter to Father, as well? Did you think I would let him continue to regard me as a wastrel when in truth I have discovered proof of your dipping into plantation funds?" Despising the tremor of anger in his voice, he focused on his quill pen and raised his gaze only when he could speak in a tranquil tone. "My father is no fool. He will quickly discern your purpose in accusing me of impropriety."

"Do you think he will believe you, since you have showed such poor judgment in regard to other matters?" With a snort, Oliver stood and walked to the window, from whence he sent a sneering grin over his shoulder. "Besides, it is not as if I have absconded with the money. I have merely held it in trust for you against the day when you overspend and have need of it."

"Ha!" The tension in Frederick's chest burst free. "If that is true, then return it to me with a full accounting of your expenditures."

Oliver stared out the window. "And if I do not?"

Once again, Frederick drummed his fingers on the desk. "I do not wish to discredit you to my father. However, you have already betrayed me, and I think it only fair—"

"I have not 'betrayed' you…yet."

"But your letter?" Hope sprang up once more.

"Awaiting the next shipment to Lord Bennington." Oliver coughed out a mirthless laugh. "Surely you don't think I would be fool enough to entrust it to just any merchant vessel, do you?"

"Ah. I see. So no harm has truly been done." Frederick permitted a wave of jubilation to flow through him. "Oliver, let us put aside all this foolish rancor between us. There is no reason we cannot help each other achieve our desired goals." He offered him a genial grin. "Give me the money and the letter, and I shall help you devise a satisfactory future for yourself."

Oliver crossed his arms and clenched his teeth. "I suppose you mean away from St. Johns Settlement."

"Do you not agree that would be best?"

Oliver puffed out a mild snort. "I shall give it some thought." But as he left the room, the sly narrowing of his eyes did nothing to reassure Frederick.


Rachel stood inside the kitchen house door. "How is Sadie?"

"Shh. We must speak softly." Inez tilted her head toward the cot where Robby lay asleep. "She slept well through the night. I think the lemonade made this possible."

"I'm glad. Mr. Moberly sent a generous portion, for Dr. Wellsey is convinced that lemon can heal fever." Rachel lifted Sadie's sheet to inspect her injuries, but shuddered at the blackened, peeling skin visible at the edges of the fresh bandages.

"Ah. Mr. Moberly." Inez gave Rachel a sidelong look. "A very kind man, *sí?*"

"Yes." Rachel covered Sadie's feet. "And I know you want to hear all about my conversation with him yesterday."

"*Sí.*" Inez leaned close. "You must tell me everything."

Rachel glanced out the door. "I have to help Papa in the store soon, but I can tell you this. I lay awake long into the night considering what we discussed." She motioned for Inez to sit with her on the raised edge of the brick hearth, where a cast-iron pot hung above the embers keeping warm the cinnamon-flavored oat porridge. The room had a cozy atmosphere, with garlic, onions and dried peppers hanging from the low rafters, and the fragrance of other spices blending into an aromatic stew for the senses.

"Mr. Moberly says he can no longer refer to us as mere friends." Rachel enjoyed the grin creasing Inez's angular face. "Instead, he insists we are courting."

Inez's whole body shook as she clearly tried to contain her mirth. "Did I not tell you?"

Rachel struggled to mute her own laughter, but truth soon seized her. Soberly, she gave Inez the details of the previous day. "How can I receive his courtship until we resolve our differences over slavery and the revolution?" Her heart aching, she studied the maternal concern in Inez's expression.

"Mistress, this thing I have heard of *el patrón*. He is a kind master." She held her hands in a prayerful pose, and her eyes moistened. "If a man must live in *la esclavitud,* enslavement, then he must pray to belong to such a one as Mr. Moberly."

The intensity of her words brought tears to Rachel's eyes. "But why must anyone, man or woman, be enslaved?"

Inez took Rachel's hands in her soft grasp. "This I do not know. It is *simplemente* the way of this world." Her brow furrowed. "Mistress, I know how this matter troubles you, but I cannot advise you. Only *Dios* can."

As they rose from the hearth, Rachel embraced Inez. "I know. But you can pray for me."

"*Sí*, señorita, that I always do."

Rachel left the kitchen house and hurried across the patchy grass yard to the store's back door. She wished for more time with Inez, for no one else could be trusted to keep her deepest secrets. Inez possessed a true servant's heart, such as the apostles exhorted Christians to have. Rachel could not imag-

ine her friend ever rebelling against her servanthood. Nor, for
that matter, could Rachel picture her encouraging the revolution. Although the Spanish woman had seen much injustice
in her long life, she accepted it with grace that could come
only from God. Yet surely there was a time when one should
and must stand up against the forces of evil domination,
whether by a slave master or a wicked king.

Once inside the back room, she heard Papa's cheerful
banter, and curiosity propelled her through the burlap curtain
and into the shop. At the sight of Major Brigham, she almost
withdrew. Before she could retreat, both Papa and the officer
turned and saw her.

"Here she is." Papa beckoned to her. "Come, daughter.
Hear the good major's news."

Her face burning, Rachel forced a curtsy. "Good morning,
sir." Her feet seemed reluctant to obey as she forced herself
across the floor. True, just one week ago, she and this man
had helped to save Sadie and Robby. But though Major
Brigham and Lady Augusta had attended services yesterday,
they had left the church immediately afterward, speaking to
no one. If Lady Augusta had pointed her aristocratic nose any
higher, she would have fallen over backward wearing that ridiculous wig and enormous bonnet.

"Miss Folger." Major Brigham nodded briefly, but he also
smiled. Rachel was not the fainting sort, else she might have
required smelling salts at receiving such courtesy from the man.
"I bring you and your father good tidings from Governor
Tonyn."

"The governor?" Rachel grasped for an air of nonchalance, but her squeaking voice no doubt gave her away.

If the officer noticed, he gave no sign of it. "Indeed. You
are both invited to the capital for the governor's ball." He
seemed proud of himself for bestowing such news.

Her jaw slack, Rachel looked at her father, whose chest

was puffed out as though he had harpooned a particularly large whale.

"Say something, child." Papa's tone chided her. "Do ye not wish to know what brings us such honor?"

Rachel's belly clenched. Her proud father, once one of Nantucket's most respected whaling captains, now in obeisance to this officer in that despicable King George's army.

"Forgive me, Papa. I fear I am stunned into silence."

"Of course." Major Brigham smirked. "It is stunning news, after all. But as His Majesty's representative, the governor endeavors to do everything to make our colonists happy in this vast wilderness."

Rachel nearly bit her tongue to keep from adding *and no doubt to avoid the troubles King George has caused with the northern colonists.* "But why invite us?"

"Ah, well." Major Brigham fingered a nearby bolt of lace and inspected it through his quizzing glass. "I sent word of the fire to His Eminence immediately after the storm. My messenger returned last evening with the news that the governor insists upon rewarding the community's efforts to extinguish the fire before it destroyed the entire settlement."

"The storm would have put it out even if we had not lifted a hand."

"Rachel." Papa glared at her, fury riding on his brow.

Major Brigham turned his quizzing glass toward Rachel and looked at her up and down. "Perhaps so. Perhaps not. But on the battlefield, the soldier who acquits himself with courage receives his reward, no matter how the battle is won."

"Well said, sir." Papa's stormy frown forbade Rachel to deny it.

"In any event, the governor asked me to choose appropriate representatives, for we cannot have the entire populace sail down to St. Augustine, now can we?" He inspected his glass, blew on it and then brushed it against his red coat. "I could think of no better choice than you and your courageous father. And of course, Mr. Moberly, if he can get away."

A pleasant shiver swept through Rachel. This changed everything. "Pray tell, sir, exactly when is the ball to take place? For I must have a new gown." She sent Papa a sweet smile and batted her eyelashes.

Major Brigham snickered at Papa. "The ladies always require a new gown, do they not?"

Papa grimaced, but if he truly resisted the expenditure, Rachel would remind him that Lady Augusta had already seen her blue gown.

"July eighth, two weeks from this Saturday, Miss Folger. You should have plenty of time to prepare."

As the major left, several customers entered in his wake, casting cautious, curious glances at the officer as they bustled into the store. Taking care of the newcomers' needs, Rachel and Papa had no chance to talk until Mr. Patch came in to tend the store while they ate their noon meal upstairs. When they sat at the table, she waited in vain for him to address the subject, for he seemed lost in thought as he ate.

"Papa, how can you sit there and devour your dinner when you know I am anxious to hear all Major Brigham said before I entered the shop."

He looked at her with surprise. "Are ye, then? 'Twasn't much. Same as he said to ye." He shoved a spoonful of bean soup into his mouth.

Rachel tapped her foot under the table. There was more, she felt sure of it.

"Come to think…" Papa took a large chunk of bread and dipped it in his broth. "The major also mentioned that some loyalists from South Carolina will no doubt be there. With all the rumpus going on up north, they're feeling a mite fretful about the dangers to wives and children." He shrugged. "Not unlike me bringin' ye down here afore ye got yerself in trouble with those addlepated plans to spy on General Gage."

She stared down at her plate, her appetite gone. This old argument never solved anything.

"Seems to me," he said, "ye'd do yerself some good by makin' friends with some of these English. Where d'ye think yer people came from? England, that's where."

Rachel sent a sly look in his direction. "Do you not think your friendship with Mrs. Winthrop is enough fraternizing with the enemy for both of us?"

"Well, now, if ye recall, ye gave yer approval—" A glint lit his dark brown eyes, and a smug smile formed on his lips. "And I s'pose ye think I've not noticed yer moon eyes over Mr. Moberly, nor his lovesick stares in yer direction."

Heat filled Rachel's face that had nothing to do with the day's warmth. "Well. Good. I am glad you noticed. At last."

To her shock, Papa's expression sobered and he narrowed his eyes. "Aye. I've noticed from the first day he walked into the store that he was smitten with ye. And why wouldn't he be?" He frowned. "And ye, girl, *ye* be the one fraternizing with the *enemy.*" He stood and tossed his napkin to the table. "Finish yer meal. I'll be downstairs."

She couldn't read his expression as he left the room, and her heart ached with confusion. Did he approve or disapprove of Mr. Moberly?

But another thought interrupted her musings. If she did become friends with the English in St. Augustine, perhaps she could learn something of value for the patriot cause. Surely all the ladies would not be snobbish like Lady Augusta, at least not the ones from South Carolina, whose ancestors had settled there long after the Folgers had made Nantucket their home. But, if those ladies had taken on airs, Rachel would simply have to resort to eavesdropping. For was that not the quintessence of spying?

# Chapter Seventeen

"An excellent plan, sir." Frederick leaned against the indigo vat and dabbed sweat from his forehead with a linen handkerchief. "A trip to St. Augustine will be exhilarating."

Brigham also used his handkerchief, heavy with perfume, but he held it in front of his nose, no doubt to deflect the indigo's stench. "Of course you understand this will be more than a ball to please the ladies."

Frederick gave him a slight nod. "Understood." A weight sat heavy on his chest. Governor Tonyn would be ascertaining the loyalty of East Florida settlers, something that would not have bothered him before he met Miss Folger. Or before he read that vexing pamphlet.

"With John Stuart in the capital, we can expect a full appraisal of his talks with the Choctaw." Brigham wore a sober expression. "The Indians trust him, and Governor Tonyn will want to spread that influence to all the settlements."

"Does this mean they're concerned the Indians will cause trouble here?" Frederick would not inquire whether Brigham had changed his views on the Timucua, who still dwelled in the southeast corner of Bennington Plantation, lest the officer repeat his order for them to leave.

"I suppose His Excellency simply wishes to ensure their loyalty. With traitorous militias active in Georgia and South Carolina, we could use a buffer if they turn their sights southward."

Frederick grunted his agreement.

At the approach of several slaves leading a horse-drawn wagon filled with linen bags for drying the indigo, he stepped away from the vat. "May I offer you some refreshment?" He waved his hand toward the path to the house.

"Certainly." As they walked, Brigham continued to fan his handkerchief in front of his nose. "How do you bear it? I would rather smell a stable in need of cleaning than indigo being processed."

"Ah, well, the king's navy must have its blue." Frederick inhaled a hint of magnolia on the fresh easterly breeze and blew out the bad smell from his lungs. Long ago he had resigned himself to the unpleasant elements of managing the plantation.

"Well said, sir." Brigham eyed him. "In the future, I shall endeavor to more fully appreciate those of you who must do such distasteful work for king and country." His light tone and easy candor seemed sincere and quite different from his previous arrogance.

Encouraged by his friendliness, Frederick ventured a request. "Milord, I would be remiss if I did not request an invitation to the governor's ball for my cousin. That is, if you do not consider me out of order."

"Not at all. I had intended to include Mrs. Winthrop in my invitation. I know Lady Augusta will appreciate her company. My gallant little wife has endured much. She will be put out in the extreme when she learns the shopkeeper and his daughter will be along."

"Indeed?" Frederick coughed to hide his excitement. "Why would they be invited?"

"Ostensibly to honor them for their courage during the fire. But of course, Tonyn will be interested in learning of their loyalties. His letter conveyed his desire to meet strong leaders in the community, men like Folger with experience in leadership, the type who might foment rebellion such as happened in Boston." His eyes gleamed with sudden feeling. "Boston. Now that's the place to be. What I wouldn't give to be on the front lines instead of in this remote wilderness. In fact, before I even arrived here, I requested a transfer to Massachusetts. And I have every intention of asking the governor to use his influence to make that happen." He shrugged. "Of course, Lady Augusta will be disappointed."

As they passed the slave quarters, relief settled into Frederick over his decision not to keep his promise to the lady. If Brigham was determined to serve where the action occurred, so be it. Frederick would support his choice.

"In fact," Brigham said, "I think it best to send her back to London. She will be happier there. I cannot tell her until I receive my orders, of course." He tilted his head and lowered an eyebrow, inviting confidentiality.

"Of course. I'll not mention it to anyone."

They reached the house, and when Caddy pulled open the front door, Frederick followed his guest inside and called for refreshment.

Brigham's relaxed posture revealed that he felt comfortable here, but in his eyes Frederick read the longing for a future in another place. Pity. Now that the man had become more sociable, he might have proven to be a good friend. As for Lady Augusta, no doubt she would be glad to leave this wilderness, even though it would mean separating from her husband. And, in time she would be grateful for her husband's anticipated elevation. Then she could sail through the finest London drawing rooms with her head held high, deferring to no one and never having to socialize with those whom she considered rustics.

For his part, Frederick regarded their marriage as a good one, worthy of emulation, despite the couple's differences. Perhaps on the excursion to St. Augustine, he could observe how Brigham planned to sway his wife to his views, for that might prove useful in Frederick's own marriage some day. A marriage that might come about later rather than sooner if he and Miss Folger found their opinions too conflicting.

But then, Mother and Father often held different opinions, and their deep affection for one another was obvious to any who would see it. Yes, that was it. Couples must expect to have differences. It was the duty of the man to set the course for the marriage and the duty of the wife to follow him. As long as their love was constant, Frederick need not be troubled by Miss Folger's disagreements with him regarding the futile rebellion or the necessity of slave-holding. Nor need he feel forced to reveal all to her. As he'd seen with Major Brigham and Lady Augusta, there were some things women could not comprehend and therefore did not need to know.

"Señorita Rachel." Inez's voice held a note of humor. "If you do not stop lifting the lid, the lamb will never cook."

"Yes, I know." Rachel replaced the lid, then removed her apron and hung it on a wall peg. "You know when to add the vegetables." She counted tasks on her fingers. "The pies and bread are baked, the butter fresh-churned, the tea and lemonade are—"

"Please, señorita." Inez took her arm and gently tugged her toward the door. "I have cooked much food in my life, and no one complains about its taste." She tucked a loose strand of hair into Rachel's coiffure. "See, you are going to ruin my hard work."

Rachel squeezed Inez's hand. "Thank you for giving up another Sunday morning."

Inez's eyes shone. "It is my gift to *Dios*. Now, go to church. Pray for us. And we will pray for your nice dinner for *el patrón*."

With a laugh, Rachel hurried across the yard just as Papa emerged from the back door.

"Papa, you look quite handsome. Mrs. Winthrop will be impressed." Mischief got the better of her. "That is, if you mind your manners and do not slurp your stew."

"Is that how you show respect, girl?" With his chin lifted and his broad-brimmed felt hat cocked at a rakish angle, he put his fists at his waist as a breeze caught his coat and blew it wide like a cape.

Rachel's breath caught. How truly handsome he looked— as grand as when he had stood on the quarterdeck of his ship shouting orders to his whaling crew above the roar of ocean waves. How she longed to throw her arms around him and kiss his fresh-shaven cheek. But he would only tell her to belay such foolishness.

"Is this better?" She gave him an exaggerated curtsy.

"My lady, may I be so bold?" He offered his arm, and the glint in his eyes revealed his merry disposition.

"Yes, good sir, you may." She set her hand on his arm, feeling the strength that had propelled countless thousands of harpoons. "Papa, I am pleased you and Mrs. Winthrop have formed a friendship. Today Mr. Moberly and I will be discussing our friendship further." She dared not say *courtship*. "Will you give your approval?"

"Ye know yer mind, Rachel. I'll not deny ye yer happiness, even as I never denied Susanna hers."

"But the other day, you seemed concerned about it. You said I was making friends with the enemy. You, who care nothing for the revolution."

She felt him stiffen for the briefest moment.

"I would not have yer heart be broken, child." His tone was

soothing but sad. "Do not give it away too freely. But when ye do, give it entirely."

Happy tears stung her eyes. That sounded very near a blessing to her.

As the church came into sight and parishioners gathered from around the settlement, two thoughts struck her. First, Papa, always so straightforward before, had not answered her question about making friends with the enemy. And second, with no time to question him, she must set aside her concerns and prepare her heart for worship.

Visiting this humble church for the third Sunday in a row, Rachel felt at home. She nodded or spoke soft greetings to other parishioners as she and Papa found their pew. Even though the pews were not bought or assigned, everyone seemed to sit in the same place they had before, like well-mannered children taking their seats around a large family dinner table. The Father's table.

Seated beside Papa, Rachel offered up her customary prayer that he would understand the message of salvation. Soon peace swept into her soul, but she could not be certain whether it was an assurance from the Lord or because Mr. Moberly and his party moved into the pew in front of her.

Reaching his accustomed spot, Mr. Moberly turned. "Good morning, Miss Folger, Mr. Folger." His dark gray eyes communicated good humor, and his soft voice rumbled in a rich baritone against Reverend Johnson's opening intonations.

Although she managed to return his smile and nod to Mrs. Winthrop, Rachel's knees went weak. *Lord, forgive me. This is our time to worship You.* But once again, for the next two hours, she required much self-control to remember Whom this service was about.

## Chapter Eighteen

"I ate entirely too much of your excellent stew, Miss Folger."
Mr. Moberly patted his stomach.

"Indeed," said Mrs. Winthrop. "I do not imagine anything
we will be served in St. Augustine could be any finer. The
taste of your tender lamb took me back to Warwickshire."

"Thank you." Rachel's cheeks warmed. "But I would guess
Governor Tonyn will serve the best of everything to his
guests." She still could not grasp that she and Papa would have
such a grand adventure with Mr. Moberly and Mrs. Winthrop.

"Ye've got yer mother's touch, daughter." Papa beamed.
"Now, about that pie."

"Yes, of course." Rachel started to ring for Inez.

"Ah, dessert." Mr. Moberly's voice sounded reserved.
"Where to put it? Perhaps we should take a stroll before our
pie. I've not been in town for over a week, and I would like
to see if the workmen have satisfactorily cleared away the
ruins of the inn." He turned to Papa. "That is, with your permission, sir."

Papa nodded. "A brisk walk is good for the health, I always
say. Mrs. Winthrop, will you join us?"

From the opposite end of the table, Rachel glared at him,

willing him to understand that she and Mr. Moberly would not need a chaperone, in fact, must not have one if they were to freely discuss important matters.

"Why, yes, I should like a stroll." Mrs. Winthrop regarded Papa. "However, I wonder if you and I might walk back toward the church. Mrs. Johnson has promised to give me some of her daffodil bulbs, and I would like to collect them. We did not have time after the service."

"Ah, a fine idea." Papa's jovial tone soothed Rachel's concerns.

Out in the blazing, late-June heat, as Papa and Mrs. Winthrop walked in the opposite direction, Rachel cast an envious glance toward the lady's parasol, plain and black though it was. She could not think of bringing out her old patched one and hoped she would not suffer too much for her pride. Instead, she pulled her wide straw hat low and prayed the East Florida sun would not reflect off the white sand-and-seashell road to redden her face. At least her white gloves would protect her hands from burning.

"Is everything well with you, Miss Folger?" Walking beside her, Mr. Moberly wore a round, broad-brimmed brown hat to top off his skirted brown linen coat and blue breeches. With his tanned complexion, he bore the look of a handsome country gentleman.

"Everything is very well, sir." Rachel's pulse quickened. Here they were at last, and all she could do was fret about the sun. "Well, there is one small matter of complaint."

"Ah, that will not do. Tell me what it is, and I shall do all within my power to amend it."

A dog cart driven by a young slave boy rattled past, stirring up sand and dust. Mr. Moberly took Rachel's arm and moved her away from the onslaught. At his touch, she felt a pleasant shiver run up her arm.

"Will you call me Rachel?" Her heart pounding at her

audacity, she tilted her head and glanced at him from beneath her hat brim.

His charming smile dispelled her anxiety. "Only if you will call me Frederick."

"Agreed."

A few people wandered about town, some strolling and others going about necessary business such as tending animals, as befitted the Sabbath day. In the shallow inlet, great white cranes poked their long golden beaks into the water and pulled out frogs, insects or small fish, then lifted their heads to swallow. On the other side, gauzy Spanish moss hung on the nearby oak trees, swaying in the summer breeze like the gray hair of an old crone. The last magnolia blossoms spread over their giant leaves as if loath to end their season.

"Rachel." Mr. Moberly swung his riding crop at a fly. "What a lovely, biblical name."

"Yes. On Nantucket Island, most children received scriptural names."

"Ah. What a strong testimony to their faith."

"Truly, it is a fine heritage to have." Rachel felt her heart flood with joy. Their conversation was proceeding naturally. Surely that signified good things to come.

The tanner shouted his greeting from his front door, and Frederick responded with a majestic nod. Several mounted soldiers gave friendly, informal salutes as they rode past, and indentured servants stopped to bow or curtsy to Frederick. Rachel felt a measure of modest pride and pleasure for being seen in his company.

They reached the scene of the tragedy and found only a large charred patch to mark the ground where the two-story building had stood. Despite the rains that had washed over the site, the stench of the tragic fire remained. Some distance beyond, the stable had survived, as had the various animals

Mr. Crump had kept for feeding his guests. The creatures now resided at Bennington Plantation.

"You were kind to purchase Sadie's livestock," Rachel said as they walked toward the stable. "The money will be more than enough to meet her needs."

Frederick shrugged. "No other course would have been acceptable." He studied the stable. "Do you mind if I look inside?"

"Not at all." Rachel stood by the empty stockyard. "I shall wait here."

His quizzical look was charming. "Would you not like some relief from the sun?"

"Indeed I would." She located a nearby giant oak across the road. "And that fine tree will provide it."

He grimaced and shook his head. "Forgive me. I wasn't thinking. I need not inspect this place. I shall send Oliver tomorrow."

Rachel sent up a silent prayer of thanks that Frederick understood why they must remain in plain sight of the townspeople enjoying this Sunday afternoon.

They found a seat on one of the ancient tree's arching branches that lay across the ground, extending some thirty feet perpendicular to the main trunk.

Toying with a tender stem beside her, Rachel decided not to waste time, for Papa had granted them only one hour. "Have you considered the matters we discussed last Sunday?"

Frederick did not meet her gaze, and a frown replaced his smile. "Yes."

Fear crept into her mind. "And?"

He reached over to take her gloved hand. "Dear Rachel, what can I say? How can I argue against your concerns? For they come from a pure Christian heart."

Her hand felt so right in his. So safe. So protected. His eyes exuded nothing but kindness and concern. And, perhaps, even love.

"Then you agree with me?" Surprised to feel the sting of tears, Rachel blinked and sent them splashing down her cheeks.

His gaze seemed almost paternal. "Dear one, many of these matters are beyond our human comprehension."

Pain stabbed into her deepest sensibilities. "No, they are not beyond our comprehension. If men are evil and do evil, it is easy to comprehend that they must be stopped." She pulled her hand away and immediately felt adrift.

He released a long sigh, and she turned to study his face. How she ached to reach out and touch his cheek, to reclaim those strong hands. But to do so would be a betrayal of her most cherished beliefs.

"Frederick…" How she loved the feel of his name on her tongue, in spite of their differences. "This is the essence of who I am. If you cannot accept the things I hold dearest to my heart, then you cannot love me."

His gaze grew intense, burning into her. "Do not tell me I cannot love you, Rachel." His voice resounded with feeling. "I have loved you almost from the moment I met you. And it has cost me…*will* cost me everything, yet I count it nothing for the love I have for you." He grasped both of her hands this time. "Do you understand? I love you."

She could not breathe. Could not think. Could only feel.

"And I love you."

Frederick gazed into her eyes, barely able to breathe. She loved him in return! With all his being, he longed to kiss her. Longed to rush back to the church to marry her this day. After much inner struggle, he settled for brushing his hand across her tear-stained cheek and giving her what he hoped was a reassuring smile.

"Are you well, Rachel?"

The smile she returned was radiant. "I am well, Frederick."

As if in silent agreement, they released each other's hands, a concurrence that could only portend future harmony between them.

"Will you free your slaves and pay wages to those who want to stay and work for you?" The innocence in Rachel's eyes and the tenderness in her tone stirred his soul.

"Would that I could. But they are not my property. They belong to my father. To set them free would be nothing less than thievery." Even as he said the words, they sounded hollow.

"I see." Rachel waved at a little brown boy walking past on the road. "You must know that I will never own a slave."

Frederick gazed off beyond the stable and across the marshy inlet where a myriad of birds, great and small, foraged for sustenance. "I would not ask it of you. But will you grant me what I must do for my father?" He grunted, considering the question's irony. "That is, for as long as he permits me to continue as his agent."

Rachel's eyes widened, and she stood and walked several feet from the tree. Hoping she did not intend to leave him, Frederick stood, ready to pursue her. But she turned back, and her lips were drawn in a decisive line.

"Perhaps the Lord will provide you with another occupation, one that does not require slaves."

Frederick stared at the ground and nudged an old seashell with the toe of his riding boot. Just when he felt he had succeeded beyond Father's expectations—with God's blessing—she wanted him to leave the work he loved. Again, his soul wrenched over this absurdity. Must he lose one dream to gain another?

But a sudden insight took him by surprise. He had not the slightest doubt Father would disown him for choosing to love and marry Rachel. He would be forced to find another occupation. That being true, he could seek one for which slave labor was not required.

He looked up to see Rachel staring at him, doubt and hope at war in her expression. He walked to her and reclaimed her hand. To his relief, she did not pull away.

"We must depend upon the Lord to show us what He would have us do."

Her little gasp of delight sent a strange mix of optimism and trepidation down his spine.

"Oh, Frederick, God will bless you for this. And should your earthly father reject you, your heavenly Father will take you up in His arms."

Nothing could have encouraged him more. She believed in him, and that was enough.

Glancing up at the sun's position, Frederick felt certain an hour had passed since they had left the store. "I must take you home. If I am to remain in your father's good graces, I must keep my word to him."

"Yes." She looped her arm in his as they once again took to the road. "But you know there is another matter we must discuss."

"Ah, yes. The rebellion." Frederick hardly had to concern himself with it. Like the certainty of Father's disowning him, he had no doubt the uprising would fail.

*"Revolution."*

"Very well. Revolution." What difference did a word make? The color of the sky seemed richer, deeper to him today, as if a vat of indigo had splashed across the fields where woolly cloud sheep frolicked. Below, pine trees waved their good wishes to any who walked by.

"Well?" There was a slight tug on his arm.

Frederick glanced down into the dark brown eyes of an Inquisitor. But he could not be cross with her. "I recently read an interesting pamphlet called *A Declaration of Rights and Grievances.*" He enjoyed her wide-eyed shock. "I am convinced that the cause of the thirteen rebelling colonies is not without merit."

"Truly?"

"Truly. But you must give me more time to consider it."

"Oh, I shall. But we should discuss it, too."

"Certainly." Frederick sent up a prayer that all conflict would be over before he was forced to tell her of his sworn loyalty to the king, a pledge he felt no urging to abandon.

For the present, her contentment revealed itself in her light steps beside him. He felt a little like a playful colt himself. Yet they managed to keep a respectable pace as they strolled along the sandy road. The townspeople now greeted them with open stares and knowing winks, as if privy to a delightful secret. Let them look, then. Let them talk. For he had crossed the Rubicon, and he would not go back.

## Chapter Nineteen

Early Friday morning, Rachel and Papa made their way to the plantation. At Bennington Creek, twenty-foot flatboats waited in boat slips to carry them on the first leg of their journey. The boats' red and yellow canvas awnings flapped in the soft breeze like birds taking flight, reflecting Rachel's soaring excitement.

Already awaiting the company's departure, Lady Augusta whispered to her husband in urgent tones. Major Brigham shook his head and assisted his wife across the wooden planks into the boat. Lady Augusta sent an angry glare toward Rachel before plopping into her seat and staring off into the distance.

Rachel's merry mood plummeted. But what had she expected from the pompous aristocrat? At least Lady Augusta had the good sense not to wear her hideous wig and makeup for this outing. In the dim morning light, she appeared at least ten years younger, and her dark brown hair framed a truly pretty face, marred only by her arrogant scowl.

In contrast, Frederick shook Papa's hand as if greeting an old friend, then placed a kiss on Rachel's fingers as the pleasant scent of bergamot wafted into her sphere. She must ask him about that enchanting fragrance one day.

"Let me assist you, Miss Folger." Frederick's formal address bespoke their agreement to keep their declarations of love a secret, but his gentlemanly manners restored her bruised feelings. "I ordered these cushions for comfort and the awning for shade."

"How lovely. Thank you." Rachel took his arm and stepped into the boat. With the boatman's help, she settled into a down-filled canvas cushion at the opposite end from Major Brigham and Lady Augusta. Soon Papa and Mrs. Winthrop joined them.

"A lovely day for an excursion, my lady," Mrs. Winthrop said to Lady Augusta. "Do you not think so?"

Chin lifted, Lady Augusta snapped her head toward her. As her gaze settled on the older woman, she offered a slight smile, one that enhanced her natural beauty. "Yes. Quite." Again she peered out across the marsh.

In short time, the boatmen shoved the flatboat from the slip and steered it northward into shallow Bennington Creek, rowing toward the St. Johns River. A second boat conveyed the servants and baggage, with a small squad of soldiers divided between the two vessels. Each red-coated soldier clutched a loaded musket. Rachel felt a mixture of relief for their protection from present dangers and distaste for the offenses of their fellow soldiers up north.

She saw that Lady Augusta had brought two trunks, her lady's maid and a slave girl. Mrs. Winthrop had packed a small trunk and also brought her housemaid. Rachel had one valise, which held her new pink gauze gown, her blue dress, a dressing gown and a night rail. She was used to dressing herself, but her hair was another matter. Inez had given careful instructions on how to create a stylish coiffure, but Rachel had little practice doing it.

The sun rose higher, and the ladies lifted their parasols for additional shade. Even though Rachel feared her old black one would embarrass Frederick, she'd decided she must use it. Last Sunday's walk had reddened her face, and she could not bear to further spoil her complexion.

Lady Augusta took one brief look at the tattered apparatus and rolled her eyes, even emitted a ladylike "humph" before lifting her own delicate lace parasol. Rachel cast a quick glance at Frederick, but he had engaged Papa in a discussion about fishing. Mrs. Winthrop reached over to squeeze Rachel's hand. With that bit of reassurance, Rachel reclined against the cushions to enjoy the passing scenery. She would not let the haughty aristocrat ruin this rare expedition for her.

She had forgotten the beauties of the river—the many varieties of trees, bright red and purple flowers she couldn't name, and myriads of birds calling to their own kind in a cacophonous symphony. Peeking over the boat's side, she could see fish large and small—bass with their gaping mouths, sword-nosed gar, giant spiny sturgeon. Occasionally one would leap into the air to devour an unfortunate insect before splashing back into the water. It seemed to her that a thousand streams fed the vast, shallow waterway, and numerous islands divided it along the way. How easy it would be to get lost without experienced boatmen navigating their course.

Yet always in the back of Rachel's mind was the memory of the alligator nearly as long as this boat that had noiselessly approached through the tall river grasses and slammed into their vessel upon their arrival those long weeks ago. Even now groups of the great hideous dragons sunned themselves on the river banks or slithered into the water in their ominous way.

She noticed Lady Augusta's hand draped over the boat's side and trailing in the water, and thought to offer a warning. Her husband doubtless saw the danger, too, for he spoke to her, and she snatched back the endangered appendage. Rachel shuddered.

"Are you well, Miss Folger?" Frederick leaned toward her, gentle concern in his eyes.

"I am well, Mr. Moberly." Warmth that had nothing to do with the sweltering heat rushed to her face. She would never tire of his loving gazes.

When the sun reached its meridian, Mrs. Winthrop ordered a basket brought forth, from which she dispensed bread and cheese to the hungry travelers. Lemonade, made from spring-water and kept cool in an earthen crock, slaked everyone's thirst.

Shortly after their meal, the party reached Mayport, where the two-masted sailing ship *Mingo* lay anchored and crewmen bustled about, ready to welcome them aboard.

There the travelers joined an Amelia Island plantation owner, Mr. Avery Middlebrook, along with his wife and two daughters, and an agent of Dr. Fothergill of London, Mr. Bertram, a naturalist who was writing a book about the flora and fauna of both East and West Florida.

Once aboard the brigantine, the Middlebrook women flocked to Lady Augusta like clucking hens, and she basked in their adoration, deigning to speak a generous word to each. Then, as the time drew near for departure, the ladies sought shelter from the sun in the stateroom. When their conversation offered no useful information, Rachel grew restless and joined the gentlemen on the foredeck.

Hiding under her parasol, Rachel stood between Papa and Frederick, eager to experience the delight of wind and salt spray on her face once again. The brigantine soon dropped its mooring lines, hoisted sails and then charged across the pounding waves into the Atlantic Ocean.

"See now," Papa said, "how strange this St. Johns River is. Not only does the water run north, but see how its lethargic outflow is nearly overpowered by the ocean's waves. What should carry us out to sea with ease puts up no fight against the breakers."

"Ah, yes." Frederick wore an amused expression. "But that lethargy works to our advantage on the return trip. If the tides are right, the boatman will have little trouble rowing us back home."

"Ha. I'll grant ye that, sir," Papa said. "I've heard tell sharks and other sea life can be found inland far beyond the cow ford."

"'Tis a wonder of nature, one must agree." Rachel copied his Nantucket dialect as she stood on tiptoe and peeked over the rail. From the safety of the merchant ship, she could regard the creatures below without trepidation.

"Do you like to sail, Miss Folger?" Mr. Bertram brushed gray hairs from his sweat-covered forehead.

"Indeed I do, sir." In fact, she had found her footing as well as Papa, while the other men clutched the rail. The smell of wood and tar and the slapping of lines against the mast reminded her of pleasant days aboard Papa's whaler.

"Remarkable young lady." Looking a little green, Mr. Bertram pulled a folded piece of paper and a pencil from his coat pocket and made notes. "Remarkable." He hurried away, but whether from seasickness or inspiration, Rachel could not tell.

Once beyond the reef, the vessel caught the wind in its sails and headed southward. While Frederick, Mr. Middlebrook and Papa discussed the weather and fishing, Rachel strolled about the deck. Seeing Captain Newman at the wheel, she climbed to the quarterdeck.

"A fine day for sailing, sir."

Coming closer, she noticed that the whiskered, fair-haired officer was younger than her first estimation. Of medium height and well formed, he had a handsome, ready smile.

"Yes, miss." He tipped his tricorn hat and gave her a little bow. "The current is mild. Would you like to take the helm?" Still gripping the wheel, he stepped aside and beckoned with his free hand.

"Oh, yes." Rachel tucked her parasol into the lines, then took hold of the wheel with one hand and a spoke with the other. How good it felt to direct the vessel, even if only to keep it on course with the captain's help. Waves surged beneath them, rolling the ship from side to side as it moved through the water parallel to land.

"Steady as she goes." He reached around her and gripped the wheel with both hands, pressing close to her back. "You're doing well."

A blend of sweat, wool and sea salt met her nostrils, and breathing became difficult, and she could feel the captain's hot breath on her neck. Maybe this wasn't a good idea, after all.

"There you are, Miss Folger." Frederick bounded up the steps to the quarterdeck, albeit a little unsteadily, and a glower rode on his brow. "I hoped we might take a turn around the deck."

"Why, of course, Mr. Moberly. Captain, will you excuse me?" Cheeks aflame, Rachel ducked under his arm, almost ripping her bonnet off. "Thank you for letting me steer."

"Of course." He gave her a crooked grin. "You may take the wheel again at your pleasure."

Tugging her bonnet back into place, Rachel whipped around and quickly descended to the main deck. What must Frederick think of her? How could she explain? She heard his booted steps behind her and hurried to a deserted place at the rail. She must confess her foolishness and ask his forgiveness.

"I saw the whole thing." Frederick stood beside her, staring out to sea, his arm grazing hers. "What a blackguard."

"What? But I—"

Frederick faced her now and grasped the rail as the ship dipped into an unexpected trough, sending a light, foamy spray across them. "Rachel, you did nothing wrong. One of your most admirable traits is your adventurous spirit. Of course you would like to steer a ship when the captain invites you." He gave her a gentle smile. "I wish I could have a portrait of your expression as you held the wheel. I have no greater wish than to secure such happiness for you." His frown returned, and he reached out to complete the job of straightening her bonnet, brushing her face in the process with a featherlike touch. "Captain Newman, however, stared at you as if he might devour you on the spot."

Rachel gasped. "Oh, my." Had she known, she would have slapped the man.

Now the salt spray had begun to sting, and she swiped a hand across one damp cheek.

"There, now, don't cry." Frederick pulled her hand up and gave it a lingering kiss. "I'll watch over you."

"But, I—"

"And to ensure that nothing of this sort happens again, I will make it clear to everyone that you and I are courting. That is, with your permission."

His bright eyes and tender smile dissolved her protest, and she nodded. One day, when they had been married many years, she would explain she had not been weeping at all. For now, she would bask in Frederick's adoring gaze and forget the ungentlemanly captain and the unfriendly ladies below.

The fragrance of Rachel's hair wafted up to enchant Frederick at the same moment he decided to call the captain out, thus thwarting that plan. What was the matter with the man? Could he not see her innocence? She even tried to take responsibility for the man's evil intent. That very moment, Frederick knew he could no longer act as if she were merely an acquaintance, a denizen of his father's settlement. He must let everyone from pompous Lady Augusta to scoundrels like Newman know that Rachel Folger, merchant's daughter, formerly of Boston and Nantucket, was his own true love, the woman he would marry and love for the rest of his life.

He glanced beyond her to see Mr. Folger eyeing them, a frown shadowing his leathery face. In another time, Frederick might have wilted under such a glare. But Rachel's sweet and trusting gaze emboldened him.

"I must speak to your father."

She peeked over her shoulder. "Now?"

"Yes, now." Frederick shot a quick look at the ship's captain. Another crew member stood by, perhaps to take the helm, leaving him free to approach Rachel while Frederick was engaged elsewhere. "I want you to join the other ladies below. This might take some time."

Rachel's eyes twinkled. "I have no doubt it will. Do not let him intimidate you."

"No, of course not. Your father and I are friends." Frederick swallowed hard and sent up a quick prayer that they would still be friends at their conversation's end.

After escorting Rachel to the safety of the ladies' stateroom, he returned to the foredeck, where Mr. Folger stood at the rail, an inscrutable expression on his age-lined face.

Frederick's knees felt as if they might buckle, much like the times when he had been called before his father for a lecture. Until just minutes ago, he had not considered that Mr. Folger might deny his request for Rachel's hand. How foolish, how arrogant to presuppose his superior rank would guarantee this man's acceptance. That assumption disappeared when he caught something in the old gentleman's glare that cast doubt on his success, a truly humbling thought. In London, Frederick never had to consider how to approach anyone's father, for the young ladies had been thoroughly schooled in rejecting younger sons all on their own. But then, none of them ever found their way into his heart, as Rachel had, and he could not think of losing her. Thus, he must face Mr. Folger whether the man planned to accept or reject him.

In their previous conversations, Folger had demonstrated a refreshing affability, a temperament Frederick himself always strove to project. For him, it was often a matter of survival, but this former whaling captain feared no one. Nor did he seek to strike fear into anyone else, at least never in Frederick's presence. Until now. Until he looked at Frederick with an expression that reflected Frederick's own anger at Newman for his improper behavior toward Rachel. But surely after all this time, Mr. Folger believed in Frederick's integrity.

Heart pounding, Frederick turned to face him.

"Captain Folger, it will come as no surprise to you to hear that I am devoted to Rachel. I have come to ask your permission to propose marriage to her."

There. The words were out. But the inner trembling did not cease. *Lord, what a coward I am, using his former title to gain approval.*

Mr. Folger's jaw muscles worked, and he breathed like an angry bull. Still staring out to sea, he gripped the rail until his knuckles turned white beneath a permanent tan.

Above them, seagulls called to one another. A pelican swept down to scoop up its dinner. The canvas sails captured the wind with a majestic *whoomp*. The ship's bow cut through the waves, and salt-scented foam dampened everything on deck, including his hopes.

Frederick tried to shake off bitter childhood memories and his drowning sense of inadequacy. Why did Mr. Folger not answer? Why should he not answer, if for nothing more than courtesy's sake? Frederick had done nothing to offend him, had done all to advance his business in both St. Johns Settlement and London.

As for Father, Frederick longed to face him this day and

show him how the failing plantation had been rescued by his efforts. How his kind treatment of the slaves encouraged energetic productivity. How the crops flourished so prodigiously that his indigo shipments would soon rival those of Lord Egmount. With bold determination, he had succeeded despite his father's doubts, despite his brothers' taunts, despite Oliver's lies, even beyond his mother's generous expectations. For Rachel, he would take that same determination into his marriage. For himself, he would never again wilt under the fear of every threat, real or imagined.

*I will care for Rachel as if my life depended upon it. Her happiness is my only purpose for living.*

"Aye. I can see that." Mr. Folger cast a sidelong glance his way. "No need to shout it."

"Ah." A little breathless, Frederick could not believe he had spoken aloud his heartfelt declaration. But it sounded good in his ears, felt good on his tongue. Felt good clear down to the depths of his soul. And yet—

"You are not pleased, sir. I entreat you to tell me why."

Mr. Folger turned halfway and stared hard into Frederick's eyes. "I'll grant ye love her, lad. Ye wear it all over yer face. But do ye *know* her? Do ye know what stirs her soul? Do ye care about those matters?"

Frederick started to assure him that he did know of her concerns over the useless skirmishes up north *and* for the slaves. But somehow the words would not come forth, for he knew nothing of Folger's thoughts on either subject and thus could plot no strategy to avoid potential conflict. *Coward.* Again his conscience accused him. He would not so quickly fall back into his old ways.

"We have discussed our deepest interests, sir, and have resolved our differences." Not quite true. "I should say, we have found ways to compromise."

"Hmm." Mr. Folger's stare softened. "I've no doubt ye'll

be the one who finds ways to compromise. For a while. Until the wedding's rosy bloom is off yer cheeks."

Frederick laughed, and the weight in his chest lightened. Those words sounded like approval.

"Well, then, take her to wife." Mr. Folger's shoulders slumped, as if in surrender. "And may the Almighty bless ye both."

"Thank you, sir." Relief flooded Frederick's chest.

Contrarily, sorrow and surrender—neither of which Frederick could comprehend—emanated from Mr. Folger's eyes. He set a callused hand on Frederick's shoulder and gave him a little shake. He chuckled, but no smile lit his eyes. "No reason it should not go well for ye, as it did for my wife and me."

"Thank you, sir," Frederick repeated. Although Mr. Folger clearly felt some reservations, kindness filled his voice, another sign that he had granted his blessing to the union. To honor that, Frederick vowed he would stay by Rachel's side and love her, no matter what forces sought to divide them. As attested to by both her parents and his own, a happy marriage was the greatest success, the greatest happiness of all.

Seated on a stool beside Mrs. Winthrop's cot, Rachel fanned the sleeping woman and brushed damp strands of gray hair from her face. This morning, the poor dear had confided to Rachel her aversion to sea travel, but with her cheery disposition, she made no complaints, not even about the smells of mold and putrid bilge water filling this cabin. Rachel hoped she would remain asleep for the rest of the voyage and be revived by the time they reached St. Augustine.

The Middlebrook women sat or reclined nearby as Lady Augusta held court, expounding on what had been fashionable in London when she left six months ago. Earlier, when Rachel entered the stuffy stateroom, no one acknowledged her. But she refused to be wounded.

Poor Frederick. Rachel prayed he would be able to face Papa without too much apprehension. She recalled how Papa had struck fear into Charles when he courted her sister Susanna. Perhaps every father felt the need to frighten his daughter's suitors. No doubt it served some purpose, though she could not imagine what that might be. At the completion of the dreaded discussion, Papa would grant his permission and then Frederick would be free to propose marriage. At the thought of it, Rachel's heart nearly sprang from her chest.

As for these silly women, she would simply ignore them as they ignored her. Frederick's love was all she required for happiness.

"*Rachel.*"

Lady Augusta's sharp tone shattered her thoughts, and Rachel jumped.

"What?" She would not call this woman "my lady."

The Middlebrooks seemed to gasp in one collective breath, and their eyes widened until they resembled three owls preparing to descend on a mouse. Lady Augusta arched her eyebrows and glared down her nose at Rachel.

"Do come fan me, Rachel. I'll wager Mrs. Winthrop has no notion of your ministrations."

Rachel noticed the elegant lace fan at Lady Augusta's wrist. She saw in the corner of her eye the gaping stares of the servants seated along the bulkhead. Comprehension filled her. This woman meant to cast her as a servant, a lower being, rather than someone whom the governor had invited to his ball on equal footing with his other guests, including aristocrats. Indignation filled Rachel. Or was it something else?

*Lord, help me. Must I bow to her? Is this Your way of subduing my pride?*

Warm certainty swept through her. Like the patriots of Boston, she must not submit to English oppression.

"Well, what are you waiting for?" Lady Augusta's voice cut through the tension-thick air like a newly sharpened razor.

Rachel stood and walked toward the hatch. "If you are overly warm, perhaps you should join me on the deck. The sea breeze is delightfully stimulating."

More gasps and much murmuring trailed behind her as she climbed the narrow steps and emerged into the fresh air. Try though she might, she could not dismiss the sick feeling in her stomach. No doubt Lady Augusta would seek reprisal for such defiance. Once the woman learned of her engagement to Frederick, she might seek to harm him, too. But just as the northern colonists had cried "Enough!" regarding British rule, she would never bow to such despotism. Like the brave patriots at Lexington and Concord, she had fired her cannon in self-defense and would not back down, no matter what revenge that woman devised.

"Rachel." Frederick hurried forward with his hand extended. "Come, my dear. We're sailing into St. Augustine. Let us go forward and watch."

The love in his eyes and excitement in his voice told her everything she needed to know. Frederick loved her. Papa had said yes. Why should she bother with any other matter?

As they stood at the bow watching the pilot boat tow the *Mingo* safely past the barrier islands and into Matanzas Bay, Frederick placed one hand at her waist, almost but not quite embracing her, as propriety demanded. She rested against him and let his lean strength soothe her soul. Soon the other guests joined them, exclaiming over the beauties of the century-old Spanish fort guarding the harbor.

Major Brigham and Lady Augusta stood several yards away. The officer bent to speak in his wife's ear, and she swung her gaze toward Rachel and Frederick. Major Brigham nodded to them, approval evident in his good-natured expression. Lady Augusta blanched, and her mouth gaped for an instant before a red rage marred her pretty countenance.

Rachel glanced up at Frederick, whose attention was focused on the fort. Clearly, he had no idea of Lady Augusta's outrage. Feeling slightly wicked, Rachel gave the woman a sidelong look and the sweetest smile she could muster. An uncontrollable giggle erupted from deep within her. This ball promised to be more enjoyable than anything she'd ever experienced.

# *Chapter Twenty*

Lulled by the comfort of the goose-down mattress, Rachel tried not to awaken, tried to continue the sweet dreams of her beloved Frederick. But the early morning breeze blew in through the open windows and brushed over her like a feather, inviting her to rise. The cool air carried the fragrance of some sweet flower she could not identify, along with the aroma of baking bread. On the guest room bed beside her, Mrs. Winthrop's soft, even breathing indicated she had rested well and recovered from yesterday's short voyage.

Rachel stretched out her limbs ready to greet the new day, but murmuring came from across the room. She lay still and strained to listen to the Middlebrook women.

"And Mr. Middlebrook said our contact wants all the information we can gather without risking exposure." Mrs. Middlebrook's alto whisper carried across the large chamber. "Fort Ticonderoga was a smashing success, and even after the defeat at Breed's Hill, our militia is more determined than ever. We must discover how much support they may count on in East Florida."

A shiver of astonishment ran through Rachel. These ladies supported the patriots' cause? She never would have guessed it. The two locations Mrs. Middlebrook mentioned must have been the battle sites. Oh, how Rachel longed to learn what was happening in her old home city. Why, Breed's Hill was right across the Charles River from Boston, visible from the upper floor of her brother-in-law's mercantile shop. Had the militia suffered great losses?

"Did you learn anything from Lady Augusta?" That was the unmistakable nasal voice of Ida Baldwin. That meant their hostess was also a sympathizer.

"Humph." Mrs. Middlebrook spoke again. "She cares for nothing but fashion and position." A pause. "We must play our parts well. We don't yet know whom to trust, nor do we know who our contact is. Take care. Trust no one."

As they continued to talk in low tones, Rachel felt a small measure of shame for thinking so little of them. But after their fawning over Lady Augusta, she could not be faulted for assuming they were loyal to King George. Should she tell them of her own sympathies for the revolution? A sense of caution filled her. None of these people knew her. Even at their introduction, no one had mentioned she came from Boston. Best to keep her own counsel. Why, they did not even know the name of their contact.

Yet if Rachel could discover who that person was, perhaps she could let him know she too was a patriot. Perhaps he would give her an assignment, as he had these ladies. She would befriend them, at least as much as they would permit her, and try to learn all she could.

She inhaled a noisy yawn and rolled over to stretch. The women abruptly stopped speaking and stared at her as if she were an intruder.

"Good morning." Sleep filled her voice, and she rubbed her eyes.

They murmured their greetings in return.

"I'll send the servants with hot water." Mrs. Baldwin left the room.

"Oh, Mother," Elsie Middlebrook simpered. "Do you think that handsome Mr. Moberly will ask me to dance at the ball?"

"If he asks either of us to dance, I should be the one," Leta said. "After all, I'm the oldest."

Rachel buried her face in the pillow to hide her mirth. They had resumed their roles as silly girls, and she would do nothing to interrupt their performance. As for Frederick, she would make certain he had no opportunity to ask either of them to dance, for she planned to fully occupy his time during the ball.

After morning ablutions and dressing, the ladies gathered in the breakfast room. Mrs. Baldwin announced that the men had eaten earlier and had then gone hunting. Rachel missed Frederick, even though she had not expected to see him here. As befitted their stations, he and the Brighams had spent the night at the governor's mansion. And although Mrs. Winthrop treated Rachel with kindness, the others still seemed uncertain how to place her in their social hierarchy. She could stave off loneliness only by thinking ahead to when she would see Frederick.

With all the exuberance of a woman who loved her city, Mrs. Baldwin gave the ladies a tour of St. Augustine, especially King George Street's many shops. Rachel's interest was piqued at the two rival mercantile stores. She would be certain to inform Papa about their displays of fabric, sewing supplies, spices and other wares. Like their own store, one mercantile bore the fragrance of lavender, while the other did not. She surmised that the scent must encourage customers to linger and perhaps make more purchases. The millinery shop also attracted her attention with its many broad-brimmed hat styles, for the fiery sun blasted down upon the women of St. Johns Settlement, as it did upon their counterparts in East Florida's capital.

As the ladies emerged from the milliner's, the Middlebrook daughters stared off across the sandy stretch of ground toward the fort.

"Mrs. Baldwin," said Leta Middlebrook, "may we not visit Fort St. Marks? I should love to see all the renovations and the grand new cannons."

"Renovations? Cannons?" Her sister Elsie giggled. "It's the soldiers you want to see."

Leta put on a pout. "And I suppose you don't wish to see a certain handsome lieutenant posted there."

While Mrs. Baldwin assured them that a tour of the regimental headquarters had been arranged for later in the day, Rachel studied the two sisters with interest. Beneath their bickering lay an affection she had never known with Susanna, whose nine year seniority had made her more mother than sister, especially after their mother died. But these two had another bond to incite Rachel's envy. United in the colonists' cause, they no doubt wanted to tour the fort to garner information for their father's patriot contact. Rachel would try to do that, too.

After a midday meal of bread, cheese and fruit, the ladies retired to the guest room. Rachel pretended to sleep, hoping the Middlebrooks would once again talk of spying. But they all lay quiet. Soon hazy, happy dreams of Frederick fogged her mind, and in no time she felt herself being shaken.

"Wake up, my dear." Mrs. Winthrop gently shook her. "Mr. Moberly has come calling."

With a gasp of delight, Rachel jumped out of bed. "He's here? Oh, my!" While hurrying to freshen up and put on her blue dress, she cast a nervous glance toward the other beds, but the Middlebrook ladies were no longer there. "How do I look?"

"Hmm." Mrs. Winthrop studied her up and down, then led her to the dressing table. "Let me see what I can do to help."

She brushed Rachel's long, thick hair into a smooth roll at her neck and used a tortoiseshell comb to keep it in place. "And now the hat." She secured Rachel's straw bonnet with a long hatpin. "Lovely. Now go and enjoy your tour. And take this." She held out her own parasol.

Rachel's face warmed. "Thank you. But won't you be going on the tour?"

Mrs. Winthrop's eyes twinkled. "Why, yes." From her small trunk, she removed a wide-brimmed hat that sported silk flowers and a large fluffy feather, which she gently shook back into its natural shape. "Mr. Folger is escorting me."

Rachel grasped Mrs. Winthrop's hands. "I am well pleased, madam. Very well pleased." She placed a quick kiss on the lady's cheek. "Enjoy your afternoon."

She descended the marble stairway and found Frederick alone in the large airy drawing room, staring up at a painting of King George III above the mantel. Her pulse raced. How handsome Frederick looked in his brown waistcoat and fawn breeches. With difficulty, she suppressed the desire to hasten across the tile floor and embrace him.

"Good afternoon, Mr. Moberly."

He turned, his eyes aglow with affection. "Rachel." With long, quick strides he reached her and enfolded her in his arms.

She rested against him and let every concern flow away like water after a rain.

After a few sweet moments, he moved back. "Come sit with me." He waved one hand toward the carved mahogany settee in front of the hearth.

"Are we not going to the fort?" Her words rushed out on a quivering breath. "I mean, if you wish to talk instead, I've no objections, but—"

"Yes, I do want to take you there. But first we must settle a matter." Frederick sounded a bit breathless, too.

"Oh." Every nerve seemed to dance within her. "Very well. What is it?"

"Would you not like to sit?" A mixture of happiness and confusion skipped across his brow. He took her hand and tugged her to the settee.

Working hard not to laugh with excitement, Rachel surrendered to his lead. He sat beside her and folded both of her hands in his.

"Rachel, I—" He blinked. "No, that will not do." Still grasping her hands, he slid down on one knee before her and cleared his throat. "Rachel, we have not known each other long, but, that is…"

Bursting with happiness, her heart nevertheless ached for his discomfort. "Yes, I will."

Again he blinked. "You will?"

"Must I say it again? Yes, I will."

A sheepish grin crept across his whole face. "I feel foolish." He moved to sit beside her. "Thank you for making it easy for me."

Rachel reached up and stroked the dark midday stubble on his unlined cheek. "Please set your mind at ease, dear Frederick. I would not have you feel foolish with me."

His expression relaxed into sublimity. "Nor would I have you anything but happy, my dear."

They gazed at each other in silence for some time, enjoying the moment. But soon, Rachel felt a twinge of impatience.

"You may kiss me now."

To her surprise, Frederick frowned. In fact, he stood and walked to the hearth. "I don't know, Rachel. I promised Captain Templeton I would never do anything improper regarding you."

"Jamie? What does he have to do with us?" She jumped up and strode to his side, gripping his arm to turn him around. Another grin played at one corner of his lips, and mischief beamed from his eyes. Rachel laughed. "Oh, I will scold him thoroughly when he returns. As for you, Mr. Moberly, I am certain it's perfectly proper to seal an engagement with a kiss, and it is nothing short of nonsense to wait any longer."

Just as she stood on tiptoes and tilted her head to kiss him, he bent down, and their lips met with a painful bump.

"Ouch." She touched her burning lips and wondered if her front teeth had been knocked loose.

"Unh." He touched his lips and wiggled his jaw. "Well, I must say that was not what I was expecting." Clearly trying to recover, he began to chortle. "Our first kiss, and I make a muddle of it."

Rachel joined him in laughing. "I did my part to spoil it, too." She turned towards the door. "Shall we go to the fort now?"

He caught her and spun her back, pulling her into his arms. "Do you not want to try that kiss again?"

Her breath caught at his gentle assertiveness. "Perhaps one not so painful."

"Very well, then. Hold still." His gray eyes twinkled.

She tilted her face upward and closed her eyes. At the gentle touch of his soft lips on hers, a rush of joy and certainty filled her heart. She loved him. He loved her. Whatever the coming days brought their way, they could work out their differences and face the future together.

## Chapter Twenty-One

As Frederick escorted Rachel to the fort, he thought he might burst with happiness. Tonight at the ball, he would ask Governor Tonyn to announce their betrothal. And if Rachel agreed, they would marry as soon as they returned to St. Johns Settlement. Although Frederick would like to marry her this very day, Reverend Johnson would appreciate the honor of performing the ceremony. And of course, Mrs. Winthrop would insist that they post the banns.

Rachel placed a dainty hand on Frederick's arm, and he covered it with his. She glanced up from time to time, giving him smiles he felt from his chest to his toes. The sparkle in her dark brown eyes revealed that her joy equaled his.

Now and forever, he would do everything in his power to ensure she remained happy, as Father had always endeavored to please Mother. Only now had he begun to appreciate Father's better side. No matter how much Lord Bennington disapproved of his youngest son, he had always been a tender, generous husband, an example Frederick aspired to follow with all diligence. With sweet Rachel as his bride, he would find the task easy.

Rachel seemed particularly interested in exploring the fort, and Frederick would use his influence to see her every wish was granted. His dear little dissenter might feel some sympathy for the northern rebellion, but nothing in St. Augustine should stir her concern. This morning during their hunt, the governor informed the men that the situation was firmly in hand. Despite the presence of a few dissidents in the colony, no strong rebel leaders had arisen to bring the mounting conflict this far south. Loyalist militias had formed in many areas. And with the able help of Mr. Stuart, the Choctaw Indians had been persuaded to help guard the border between East Florida and Georgia. That should settle the matter.

"Look, Frederick." Rachel nodded toward the couple some fifteen yards ahead. "Do you not think it dear that Papa and Mrs. Winthrop have become friends?"

"I do." Frederick watched his elegant kinswoman, graceful even as she walked along the rough, sandy path on Mr. Folger's arm. "I wish them to be as happy as we are."

Rachel repositioned her hand, looping her arm through his. "Surely no one could be happier."

"Surely not." He forced his gaze away from her tempting lips. Of course he would not demonstrate his affection for her in full sight of others. But more than the heat of the day brought warmth surging up to his face. Both their first disastrous kiss and the sweet one that followed had only increased his love for her. They must marry soon. Until then, he would direct his thoughts toward learning more of her interests.

At the fort's wooden drawbridge, guards stood at attention with their muskets shouldered, while the corporal in charge saluted and waved them beneath the raised iron gate. Beside him, Rachel shuddered. "Are you well?" Frederick asked.

Her pretty little nose wrinkled as if she smelled something foul. "Yes, thank you."

She sent him a quick smile that did nothing to reassure

him. But as they walked through the shadowed passageway leading to the fort's open courtyard, Frederick took in the odor of the unwashed soldiers who stood on either side. Their crimson uniforms might have the look of courage, but surely something lighter than wool would be more appropriate for this tropical climate. He would make inquiries in his next letter home. For now, he would try to shield Rachel from the stench that seemed to displease her.

Many other guests had already assembled in the courtyard and divided into smaller groups. A slender young officer approached Frederick and Rachel and bowed.

"Mr. Moberly, I am Lieutenant Cobb, sir. I'll be your guide." He pointed toward a wide stone staircase. "Shall we begin with the upper gun deck?"

They ascended the steps and emerged onto the wide bastion where a row of cannons jutted toward the sea through the battlement openings. Guard towers stood sentinel at each arrow-shaped corner of the fort. Above them, the red, white and blue Union Jack snapped proudly in the breeze, lifting Frederick's soul with love of country and king and life itself.

He noticed that Rachel's gaze swept over the impressive guns and nearby powder kegs as if she were counting them.

"Tell me, lieutenant," she said, "if a ship fires a cannon from the harbor, can it blow a hole in this wall?"

The officer chuckled. "No, miss. You've no need to fear. There's not a cannon made that can break through it. Even if a vessel sailed close enough without our navy blasting her out of the water, the cannonballs would bounce off the coquina and barely make a dent. The Spanish were right smart to use the natural stone to build this fort." He pointed across Matanzas Bay to a sandy promontory that guarded the inlet. "They quarried it from that island."

"Ah, I see." She brushed her gloved hand across the low

wall. "Then how did the British, I mean, how did we gain control of it? Was there a battle?"

Frederick noticed her word change with satisfaction. She had already begun to consider herself a British subject.

"No, miss, we had no need for a battle. The Treaty of Paris in '63 gave all of Florida to the Crown. The Spanish packed up and left, and in we marched." The lieutenant seemed to enjoy his own discourse. "Since early this year, we've been making the repairs you see in progress, including building a second floor beneath these battlements to hold more troops and supplies. We are prepared for anything the rebels might attempt." He waved his arm to take in the entire fort. "We're now the regimental headquarters, something you no doubt already know. The well has been cleaned out, and we can safely drink the water, which is particularly helpful in this hot weather, and the prison's been reinforced. Just in time, too, as we have a few rebels there who need a place to sit and behave themselves until things settle down up north."

Rachel shuddered, and her lips began to quiver. "You have pat…r-rebels right here in this fort?"

"Shh." Frederick put his arm around her. "I'm sure it's all right."

She looked up at him with a forlorn expression. "But—"

"Please permit me to assure you, miss." Lieutenant Cobb stepped closer, a solicitous frown on his brow. "They cannot escape. You are safe."

Rachel still stared at Frederick, her eyes wide. "Will they be e-executed?"

The lieutenant glanced at Frederick, questioning him with a grimace. Frederick shook his head. Rachel's tender concern for the prisoners was admirable and understandable, but she need not know the worst.

"No, miss, the commander has no orders to execute them, for they have not been accused of treason…or spying. Those would be the hanging offenses." He shrugged. "I'm not certain what the charges will be, or if there will be any charges. All I know is they were speaking in favor of the rebellion and stirring up local rabble in the taverns, and Governor Tonyn thought it best to keep them here so they could do no more mischief."

Again Rachel shuddered. But then she squared her shoulders and faced the officer. "May we see where they're being held?"

The lieutenant winced. "I'm not certain that's wise, miss."

"But we must know who they are." She looked at Frederick. "In case they manage to escape and come our way."

Frederick swiped his hand across his forehead. He wanted to please her, but this certainly was an unusual request. Still, it could do no harm. "Lieutenant Cobb, Miss Folger wishes to see the prisoners. Please take us there."

The lieutenant straightened. "As you wish, sir. This way, please."

Frederick offered Rachel his arm and squeezed her hand. "Your compassion for the prisoners is admirable, but please do not be overly concerned. I shall inquire of the governor regarding their treatment. You may trust me in this regard."

As they descended the broad stairway and crossed the courtyard, Rachel wondered how her trembling legs managed to carry her. She clutched Frederick's arm, but his encouraging words and agreement to her request revealed his misunderstanding of what had distressed her.

Spying was a hanging offense. She had never considered such a cost. And surely they would regard it as treason if she tried to help the imprisoned patriots to escape. Yet she must try to help them, must try to get information to help the revolution—somehow.

Lieutenant Cobb led them to the guardroom just inside the

fort's entrance. They passed through a chamber where a raised platform held beds for off-duty guards. One of the two sleeping guards snored loudly.

In a second room—a dank, smelly chamber—Papa stood before a wooden door chatting with a prisoner on the other side. *Chatting*, as if talking with Frederick or Jamie, as if communing with an old friend. Only a tiny window in the door made their conversation possible.

At the same time, a quick survey of the room revealed she would not be able to likewise speak with the patriots, for she could hear from their murmuring that they were imprisoned in the windowless black room beyond the door.

In the dim candlelight, Rachel could barely make out the features of the man with whom Papa spoke. His complexion appeared swarthy, and the collar of his once-white linen shirt bore stains of sweat and dirt. She could not determine how tall he was. Yet, in spite of his imprisonment, he spoke in jovial tones thick with an accent Rachel did not know.

"I will take your advice, my friend." He stuck one hand through the small opening. "You have my promise."

Papa grasped it in both of his. "A good plan, sir. And ye may be certain I shall keep my end of the bargain." He chortled in his good-humored way.

Nearby, guards with muskets watched the exchange. But rather than appearing concerned, they seemed amused. Rachel wondered what Papa could have said to entertain them.

Frederick bent to whisper in her ear. "Your father makes friends wherever he goes. Perhaps he has extracted a promise from this Greek to mend his ways."

"Greek?" Rachel quizzed him with a look. "Do you know that from his speech?"

"Yes. No doubt he's from New Smyrna south of here. Dr. Turnbull brought Greeks and Minorcans to settle the area, but they've always complained about broken promises and ill treatment. In fact, I resolved to avoid Turnbull's mistakes in managing St. Johns Settlement."

From his whimsical look, Rachel guessed he wished for her approval. "You've certainly succeeded. Your diligence in your duties is one of your many admirable traits."

Playfulness lit his handsome face. "Shall I list all I admire about you?"

"Perhaps another time." She tilted her head toward the nearby guards.

"Yes, of course." Frederick looked toward the inner door. "Lieutenant, that room is black as night. How many men are in there?"

"Twenty-seven at present, sir."

"So many in such a small, dark space." Rachel shuddered at the thought of being thus locked away from friends and sunshine.

"Would it ease your mind," Frederick asked her, "if I inquired about sending oranges and other provisions for them?"

"Oh, how good of you." Even as gratitude flooded her, Rachel's heart twisted at the thought of her failure to explain matters to him. Why, it was nothing short of deception. As for the Greek whom Papa had befriended, he could hardly be interested in the revolution. But if Frederick sent the patriots some nourishing food, her ploy had a useful purpose, after all.

And, perhaps, the episode had one additional benefit. Despite her shaking knees, despite being frightened for her life, she had walked into this prison filled with determination. Now she knew beyond any doubt she would willingly die for the patriot cause. And now that Frederick's sympathies had been stirred, she would do all in her power to complete the work of turning his opinions toward freedom for the colonies.

\* \* \*

Standing beside Frederick, Rachel took in the sights and smells of the large ballroom in the government house, an exquisite leftover from the days when Spain owned East Florida. The roses in her hair held secure, thanks to the skill of Mrs. Winthrop's maid.

Garlands of flowers vied with guests' perfumes for sensory preeminence. Some ladies wore tall powdered wigs like Lady Augusta's, but even she did not apply that horrid ceruse face covering she had worn at Frederick's dinner party. The ladies' low-cut gowns had wide panniers and a beautiful array of colors, from pink to green to blue, some with a lovely mixture of tones. Rachel decided she must be a little bolder in her color schemes. As for the gentlemen, most were dressed in embroidered coats and breeches, but none were as handsome as Frederick in his red brocade waistcoat and white satin breeches.

At the end of the large ballroom, a string ensemble sat on a raised platform and played music, and guests danced in the center of the room. At the other end, punch and cakes provided sustenance to last until dinner was announced.

Rachel glanced up at Frederick. He seemed somewhat distracted and kept looking about the room as if searching for someone.

"The music is lovely," she said. "I could listen to it for hours."

Frederick looked toward the musicians as if surprised to see them. "Yes, very nice. Forgive me, Rachel. Would you care to dance another set?"

"No. Two country dances are enough for me." She looked across the room at the musicians, trying to memorize the tunes so that she could play them on Frederick's pianoforte, soon to be *her* pianoforte. She exhaled a happy sigh in anticipation of that day.

Frederick took her hand. "The governor is approaching. Are you prepared for our announcement?"

A nervous flutter teased her stomach, but she nodded.

"Ah, there you are, Moberly." Governor Tonyn joined them, his wife on his arm. "As you requested, we will make the announcement at the end of this set."

"My dear, I wish you much happiness." Mrs. Tonyn squeezed Rachel's hands and took her place beside them.

"Thank you, madam."

As the music played on, Rachel located Papa and Mrs. Winthrop across the room. Papa was having a grand time, as he always did. After this evening, he would be able to remember the name and occupation of every person he met. Rachel had seen some guests snub him, but he forged on as if oblivious to the slights. One time she noticed Lady Augusta looking at Papa and whispering behind her fan to another lady, and both laughed. If Papa cared for their opinions, Rachel might have felt bad for him. But nothing ever seemed to hurt him. The joy in his face soothed away her anxieties on his behalf.

Deeper still, she admitted his bringing her to East Florida had been God's will for both of them. Loving Frederick and being loved by him was the fulfillment of her dreams. Papa's business was a success, and his feelings for Mrs. Winthrop made life in the wilderness even sweeter. And after Rachel and Frederick married, she could continue to look for ways to help the revolution among the few sympathizers who lived in the colony. With those happy thoughts, Rachel opened her heart to embrace her new life at last.

Papa and Mrs. Winthrop wended their way around the edge of the room to join Rachel and the others just as the music ended. The director bowed toward the governor, who straightened his gold waistcoat and cleared his throat.

"Good friends, it is always a privilege to announce happy

tidings, and this evening is no exception. Please permit me to present to you Mr. Frederick Moberly and his betrothed, Miss Rachel Folger."

Silence followed. Then several people gasped. Some ladies murmured behind fans. The deep tones of several men carried across the room, filled with anything but approval. Rachel looked at Frederick, and he gave her a smile no doubt meant to reassure her. But chagrin pinched his cheeks and darkened his eyes.

## Chapter Twenty-Two

How long the room buzzed with shock and censure, Rachel could not guess. Then Mrs. Pilot, a plump, merry and influential matron whose husband was a regimental officer, hurried from the crowd to Rachel and embraced her. "Oh, my dear, how wonderful. I wish you much, much happiness." Her high voice rang across the room like a call to an assembly.

In her wake, dozens of other ladies and gentlemen surged forward to offer congratulations. Rachel noticed Papa's eyes had narrowed, as they did when he felt some strong emotion. How she wished she could discover his true feelings toward her betrothal. But he was a closed book, her only bit of sorrow in the midst of her joy.

Here she stood among all these Loyalists, who no doubt assumed she and Frederick could be counted in their ranks. While trading pleasantries with them, she thought of her loved ones in Boston who bore the revolution's weight. And, encouraged by Frederick's behavior as they toured the fort earlier in the day, she decided tonight would be her only chance to tell Mrs. Middlebrook of where her true loyalties lay.

Yet later, after Frederick had returned her to the Baldwins' drawing room and she had whispered her thoughts to Mrs. Middlebrook, the other woman lifted her chin haughtily.

"I have no idea of what you are saying, Miss Folger." The woman's smile was tight, and her gaze did not meet Rachel's. "You must have had a dream. And of course, you were filled with romantic thoughts concerning your betrothal." She fanned herself with an ornate red-and-black fan. "Gracious, this heat."

Rachel glanced over her shoulder to make certain Mrs. Winthrop was still talking with their hostess on the other side of the room. The Middlebrook girls had already retired to the guest bedchamber.

"No, madam, I was not dreaming. I heard—"

"You heard nothing." Mrs. Middlebrook snapped her fan shut. "You are a silly girl. And, as if it were not enough that you, the daughter of a mere shopkeeper, have managed to ensnare a gentleman, the son of an earl, now you wish to stir up trouble in our peaceful colony. How dare you accuse me of…why, it is nothing less than treason."

Rachel's face flamed, just as it had earlier that evening when the governor's announcement had shocked the ballroom into silence. Never in her life had anyone spoken to her in this manner.

Mrs. Middlebrook leaned over her with a glare. "Your sort is reason enough not to mix the classes. Many of us will never forgive Mrs. Pilot for coming to your rescue this evening. To think that the wife of a noted regimental officer would rush to your side and countenance your betrothal, forcing us all to offer felicitations to Mr. Moberly, when all we felt for him was pity. Poor Mr. Moberly. To be shackled to a silly little gossip." She spun away and sauntered toward the other ladies, fanning herself once again. "Dearest Ida," she said to Mrs. Baldwin. "I am utterly wilted. Will you forgive me if I retire?"

Gulping back a sob of mortification, Rachel waved her own fan furiously to cool her blazing face. What a foolish mistake she had made. Of course Mrs. Middlebrook didn't trust her. A true patriot would not marry a loyal British subject. And Rachel could not, would not betray Frederick's sympathies for the cause. In truth, he had not yet voiced those sympathies to her. But his solicitous demeanor could mean nothing less than an agreement with her. They simply had not found the chance to talk about it.

Walking toward the tall, slatted veranda doors, she moved on legs rendered wooden by embarrassment. How could she redeem this situation? Never mind the shame of Mrs. Middlebrook's scathing rejection. If no one trusted her, she couldn't pass on information. Perhaps she wouldn't even be able to learn anything useful.

Outside, deep in the shadows of palm trees and fragrant geraniums, Rachel sat on a cast-iron bench and gazed up at the starlit sky through stinging tears. This should be the happiest night of her life, but her failure to find a contact spoiled it. Tomorrow morning after an early church service, their party would be returning to St. Johns Settlement. But what would she do at home? Nothing, simply nothing ever happened there that could help the revolution.

"Lord," she whispered, "please show me a way to serve the cause I hold dear." Conviction filled her. She must amend her prayer. "Please give me a way to serve Your righteous cause."

She leaned against the bench back and let the night breeze cool her face and soothe her bruised soul. After uncounted minutes, she grew drowsy and started to go inside, although she hated to think of facing Mrs. Middlebrook in the bedchamber. Before she could stand, something rustled among the palmetto bushes nearby. Fear clogged her throat. She never should have come out here alone.

"Did Odysseus give you the cylinder?" The hushed tones of a man's voice met her ears.

"Yes, I have it here." A second man answered in a low, gravelly voice. "All is well. They will put everything into place. We have only to get the cylinder to Perseus."

"You can do this?"

"Zeus will deliver it to Hermes. He will take it to Perseus on his next voyage."

A third man grunted his agreement.

The men continued to talk, but their voices grew softer as they moved away.

Rachel smothered a laugh. Now that surely was an interesting bit of information, but not a whit more useful than what she'd heard from the Middlebrook ladies that morning. What cylinder? What ship? And who were Perseus, Odysseus, Hermes and Zeus?

Too weary and disappointed to consider it further, Rachel returned to the upstairs guest room, changed into her night rail, and surrendered to sleep.

In the morning service, the bishop's homily did nothing to encourage Rachel regarding the revolution. He spoke of obedience, affirming that God's will could be found only in submission to His chosen authority, King George. Seated between Papa and Frederick, Rachel resisted the temptation to yawn.

That afternoon, the *Mingo* reached Mayport by dark, where they would spend the night on shipboard and continue by flatboat to the settlement in the morning.

Once again, Rachel had to sit in the cramped cabin while the other ladies hovered around Lady Augusta and chatted about frivolous matters. Rachel had given up trying to be a part of their society, but found solace in the warmth of Mrs. Winthrop's kind glances.

On Monday morning, her group parted company from the

Amelia Island travelers, much to Rachel's relief. The two flatboats moved westward with ease due to the strong ocean tide flowing inland against the outflow of the wide, shallow St. Johns River.

In the early afternoon, everyone except the rowers had fallen into a lazy, heat-induced stupor. Rachel watched the passing scenery through half-closed eyes until she noticed Lady Augusta's arm hanging over the boat's side, her white dress's wide sleeve flapping like the wing of a wounded crane. A second later, movement in the water sent Rachel scrambling to her feet the instant an alligator rose from the river and clamped its massive jaws on the sleeve. The grunting beast twisted its scaly body as it dropped back, dragging Lady Augusta halfway over the side. She screamed and gripped the gunwale with her free hand.

"Help! Help us!" Rachel knelt and slammed her folded parasol on the beast's snout again and again. The wooden handle broke, and she stabbed at its eyes with the sharp splintered end. Numb to everything but the battle, she struck so hard that her broad-brimmed straw hat flew off.

Behind her, she heard scrambling and cries. Someone shoved her out of the way.

"Augusta!" Major Brigham grasped his wife's waist and tried to pull her into the boat.

"Shoot it. Shoot it," one soldier yelled.

A musket fired. The flatboat dipped dangerously.

"Balance the boat," Papa boomed out. "Moberly, over here, or we'll be swamped."

"Yes, sir," Frederick shouted. "Mrs. Winthrop, over here."

Rachel scrambled to join them.

"Shoot. Shoot." Major Brigham set his feet against the boat side, clutching and clawing to keep a grip on his wife's clothes.

The other two soldiers fired their muskets, then reloaded, a maddeningly slow process.

The battle seemed endless, but neither side surrendered. The five-foot alligator rolled again, and the sleeve became more entangled in its teeth and snout. Rachel could not believe the fabric had not torn loose.

At last the sleeve ripped from the dress. Major Brigham and Lady Augusta flew backward, landing in a heap. The soldiers fired again, and the beast disappeared beneath the murky surface. The boat continued to rock, and the rowers used their poles to steady it.

To her credit, Lady Augusta did not become hysterical. But her eyes were wide, and she shook violently as Major Brigham settled back into the seat and grasped her.

"Oh, my dear, my darling." The major seemed unaware of anyone but his wife. "Thank our merciful God that you are safe." He kissed her temple. "Let me see your arm."

Lady Augusta held out the scraped limb and gave him a trembling smile. "Only a little blood. There, I am the one wounded in battle, not you, my prince." Her expression was filled with sweetness such as Rachel had not imagined her capable of, and their endearments almost moved her to tears. Or perhaps it was her own hysteria, for a sob broke from her unbidden.

Frederick folded her in his arms. "Shh. You were quite brave, my love. We can thank the Lord you were alert and watching."

She nestled against him, still shuddering, still watching the woman whose life she had helped to save. All anger, all hurt feelings, all struggles not to mind Lady Augusta's rudeness floated away like Rachel's straw hat. Beneath her aristocratic exterior, she was a woman who loved and was loved by both God and the man He had ordained for her. Just like Rachel.

"Yes, thanks be to the Lord."

"Well done, Rachel." Papa's eyes sparkled.

She drank in his approval like a thirsty plant. She could

almost feel water filling her. Looking down, she saw the river pouring into the boat through a small hole in the side.

"Water!"

Once again shouts filled the air.

"Row to the bank."

"Bail it out."

"Keep the powder dry."

"We're sinking!"

"Where's the other boat?"

Mrs. Winthrop dispensed cups and bowls from the picnic basket, and everyone except the rowers scooped out the water as quickly as they could. Even the Brighams joined the task.

Papa emitted a mild oath. "I never should have slept. Even then, I sensed we were off course."

"What do you mean, sir?" Frederick scanned the horizon.

"This river has many islands and creeks, as well ye know. From this level, they all look the same. It's easy to go down the wrong stream when ye don't set landmarks in yer mind." Papa tapped his forehead as he studied the area around them. "We've got to put in." He pointed toward a jut of land. "Over there. Put in, I say."

The rowers looked at Frederick.

"Do as he says." His tone was terse.

Amidst the disaster, Rachel felt a measure of pride that Papa still proved himself a worthy commander *and* that Frederick was not too proud to listen to him.

The two rowers gripped their poles and shoved the flatboat through the tall marsh grasses, coming at last to a sandy promontory. All the men jumped out and pulled the craft onto the little beach, then assisted Lady Augusta, Mrs. Winthrop and Rachel to dry land.

For several minutes, everyone looked around without speaking. Then Frederick grinned at Rachel. "Well, my dear, it looks as if we'll end the day with a stroll." He broke into laughter, and Rachel did, too.

The Brighams appeared unwilling to join the merriment, but the three soldiers and even the slave rowers guffawed.

Papa's gaze was directed toward the forest some distance away. Hands on hips, he faced the crowd. "We'll not be walking through that salt grass marsh. There'll be quicksand and water moccasins, not to mention more of those hungry alligators."

Major Brigham exchanged a look with Frederick, and they both turned back to Papa.

"What do you suggest, sir?" Major Brigham asked.

"I'd say Mr. Moberly and I should go for help. We'll take this lad along." He clapped one soldier on the back. "I'm fairly certain he's not the one who blasted that hole in the boat." He eyed the other two soldiers, one of whom appeared unwilling to meet his stare. "We can test our steps with one of these poles." He took one in hand. "And we'd best be off soon so the day don't get the better of us. Not all of the Indians in these parts think kindly of us."

Proud of Papa for taking charge, Rachel nonetheless moved closer to Frederick and looped her arm through his. She longed for him not to leave her.

"A good plan, Mr. Folger." Major Brigham shook Papa's hand. "Do you need any provisions?"

"A jug of water and a bit of bread should do it." Papa motioned to Frederick. "Come along, lad."

Frederick placed a quick kiss on Rachel's cheek. "Will you be all right? Silly question. Of course you will, my brave girl."

Despite his praise, it took all Rachel's inner strength not to beg him to stay with her. She noticed that Papa patted Mrs. Winthrop's hand, and the lady gave him an encouraging nod. Rachel decided she must be as brave as the older woman.

Lightly provisioned, the three men struck out on their venture. While the others made camp, Rachel watched the travelers on their zigzag course across the marsh. Several times Frederick turned back to wave, giving her an incentive to keep her vigil.

When at last they were out of sight, she searched for some task that might help the encampment, but all had been accomplished. The rowers had speared some fish and started a fire to cook them. Mrs. Winthrop had cleaned the cups and bowls and would ration the water. The beached flatboat sat drying in the sun. Even Lady Augusta joined the effort by bringing out the mosquito netting. All seemed in order.

After their humble meal, Major Brigham instructed the ladies to sleep within the boat's protection. The men would take turns standing watch.

Yet despite the comforts of a full stomach, the boat cushions, mosquito netting and the fresh cool breeze off the river, Rachel could not sleep. Alligators grunted in the distance. Frogs and crickets played a discordant symphony. Fish—or something else—splashed in the river all too near them. Never mind that one could not hear a snake if it approached. She could hear Major Brigham ordering his men to keep watch for the Chickasaw, whose attacks on the English had led to many deaths in recent years. Rachel shuddered, then shuddered again, thinking of the dangers Frederick and Papa might encounter. She lifted up a prayer for their safety before lying back to wait for whatever the dawn would bring.

## Chapter Twenty-Three

Following behind Mr. Folger, Frederick felt his admiration for the man grow, for he and Private Martin were forced to push themselves to keep up. Rachel once mentioned that her father limped due to an injury sustained on his last whaling voyage. The limp was not as noticeable today. With an optimism Frederick found contagious, the old man gamely led them across the salt grass marsh, both on sandy ground and through stretches of waist-deep water.

Folger had set their heading toward a thin spire of smoke curling into the afternoon sky, no doubt from the Timucuan village on the plantation's southeastern border. If the Indians would help them, they would be able to get back to Rachel and the others before daybreak.

The strenuous journey took its toll on Frederick. And from the haggard looks of the other two men, he could tell they also felt the stress. The sun beat down on them with fury, and their thirst raged. Folger rationed the water. Frederick and Martin bantered that they must match the older man's endurance. More than once, they sidestepped to avoid water moccasins, rattlesnakes, or snapping turtles, even juvenile alligators. Startled cranes and cormorants took flight at their approach.

Heat forced the men to remove their shirts. Then, shortly before sunset, mosquitoes swarmed over them, biting every bare patch of skin. They hastened to don their garments again.

But persistence proved rewarding, for they reached the tree line before twilight descended, albeit with torn, filthy, wet clothes. Summerlin would have a fit over Frederick's ruined boots, which were soaked both inside and out.

With what seemed to Frederick an uncanny sense of direction, Folger continued to wend his way through the palmettos and scrub that grew beneath the palm and cypress trees. At last they found a path to follow.

Ahead, the torch-lit village hummed with late evening activities. The smell of roasted meat met Frederick's senses, and his mouth watered. Beside him, he heard Martin's belly rumble.

Folger stopped and called out a greeting in the Timucuan tongue. The Indians sent the women and children to their palm-thatched huts, then grabbed bows, arrows and clubs. One man carried a musket, and several others brought torches. Most wore little clothing and bore many tattoos.

"Stop." A tall, burly, gray-haired man stepped from the group. "Who comes?"

"Greetings, Saturiwa. 'Tis yer friend Folger." He lifted both hands and spoke in his jolly, booming voice. "And my two friends." He moved forward.

"Folger." The old chief beckoned to Mr. Folger. "Come." He slapped him on the back.

As Frederick and Martin entered the torchlight, some men pointed to the private's red coat and began to murmur. Saturiwa hushed them.

"You come from the river," the chief said.

"Aye. Yes," Folger said. "Our boat got swamped. Can ye help us fetch the rest of our party?"

Not answering, Saturiwa now set his gaze on Frederick.

"Moberly." The resonance in the chief's voice reminded Frederick of his father. When he had met the chief before, Frederick had been on horseback. Now the man's superior height, well over six feet, proved intimidating.

"Good evening, sir." Frederick shook away his edginess. The trip across the swamp had taken more out of him than he realized. "May we rely upon your help? I shall make it worth your while."

Saturiwa grunted. "When other English kill us, you let us stay on our land. That is enough. You will eat. Then we will talk."

Frederick and his companions sighed their relief as if one man. They followed the Indians into the center of the circled huts and sat beside an open fire, where remnants of the evening meal still hung on a spit. Two old women brought them springwater, roasted rabbit, and a tasty cornmeal mush. Soon Frederick felt his strength returning.

Across the campfire, Saturiwa and two other men conversed in their language. They appeared to reach some agreement, for the chief stared at Folger expectantly. Frederick dismissed the urge to speak up. An old man himself, the Indian no doubt respected age and regarded Folger as the group's leader.

Folger set down his wooden bowl and wiped a damp handkerchief across his lips. "Will ye help us fetch our friends, sir?"

Saturiwa nodded his affirmation. "We will *fetch*—" he grinned using Folger's word "—your friends and take you to the plantation. We will go at first light."

Frederick and Folger traded frowns.

"Could ye consider going now?" Folger waved his hand toward the darkened path. "My daughter and the other ladies—"

"Ah." Saturiwa conferred with another man for a moment,

then addressed Folger. "The little daughter of Folger must be safe, but travel in darkness is not wise. We will go before first light."

Frederick and Folger accepted his decision with reluctance. They would sleep beside the campfire and be rested for their journey.

As the Indians prepared for the night, Frederick noticed Martin's frequent glances into one palm-thatched hut. He nudged the soldier.

"That could be considered rude. Don't give them cause for offense."

"Yes, sir." Martin clenched his fists. "Thing is, sir, I see what looks like one of our uniform jackets hangin' in there. Why would these savages…'scuse me, sir, these people have a British soldier's jacket?"

Frederick took a step toward the hut but found his way blocked by two Indians.

"Moberly." Saturiwa called from across the camp. "Come."

Dreading a confrontation, Frederick walked around the fire. He'd noticed the chief's reference to "our land." If the Indians turned on them in reprisal for the suffering inflicted by other Englishmen, they might be slaughtered, as other white men had been during a recent uprising. The situation did not sit well with Frederick, but he must face up to the chief, whatever the outcome. "Why do you have a British soldier's jacket?"

Saturiwa regarded him for several moments, perhaps sizing him up. Frederick didn't lower his gaze, but he also kept his posture and expression neutral.

"A soldier came to us to flee his evil chief. He no longer wanted to soldier but to live among us." Saturiwa lifted his chin and narrowed his eyes. "We do not turn you away. We did not turn him away."

The hair on Frederick's neck prickled against his sweat-soaked collar. "Where is this man?"

"We do not betray those who put their lives in our hands."

"What's the trouble?" Folger approached, hands on hips, and cast a disapproving glare at Frederick.

Frederick bit back a retort. "I think we may have found the man who burned down the inn and almost succeeded in burning your store." He added that last detail for the chief's information.

Folger spat out an oath. "Where is he?"

Frederick turned back to the chief. "If my suspicions are correct, the man you are protecting murdered two innocent people in the great fire last month. He lied to you about fleeing an evil leader, Saturiwa."

"Ah." The chief looked toward the hut. "He has wounds and fights a fever. Come."

Saturiwa grabbed a small torch to light the hut's interior. The smell of infection and human waste assaulted Frederick, and he covered his nose with one hand. On a raised platform some four feet above the ground lay the soldier he had kept from harming Rachel, the one Brigham had identified as the vengeful arsonist. The sleeping man's pale face indicated his fever had broken.

"Buckner." Frederick reached out and shook him. "Get up, man. You're coming with me."

Buckner groaned but did not awaken.

Saturiwa stepped up beside him. "He cannot walk."

"What?" Frederick stared at the chief.

"Wild boar." The chief lifted his torch and pointed to Buckner's left leg, which was wrapped in blood-stained rags.

Frederick grimaced. "Will you keep him until we can send soldiers for him? I will make certain they do not harass you."

Saturiwa shrugged. "He will be here."

The chief's relaxed demeanor invited Frederick's confidence and soothed his earlier anxieties. "Thank you."

Frederick marveled at finding Buckner still on the plantation. He had ordered his people to leave the Timucua in peace, and no one ever came to this remote corner of the property. But by the strangest of circumstances, God had brought him here to find the miscreant, and Frederick would not rest until the man faced justice.

"*Rachel.*" The impatient whisper came through the darkness from the flatboat's other end.

Rachel blinked away sleep and perceived the shadowed speaker's identity. "Yes, Lady Augusta?" Both drowsiness and impatience filled her voice. The first she could not help, but the second she regretted immediately. She sat up and rubbed her eyes. "What news, madam?"

Growing accustomed to the campfire's dim light, she could see Lady Augusta in silhouette and her husband beside her.

"Major Brigham has told me *you* are responsible for my rescue." Her tone resounded with annoyance.

"Augusta." Major Brigham spoke his wife's name so softly that Rachel could barely hear him.

"Oh, very well." Lady Augusta exhaled impatiently. "I thank you, Miss Folger. We shall reward you."

Raging heat rushed to Rachel's face. *Lord, give me patience.* She drew in a deep, cooling breath. "Your well-being is my reward, Lady Augusta. We may praise God for your deliverance."

Frogs croaked in the distance. The men standing guard murmured around the fire. A dove cooed its mournful night song. But no sound came from the boat's other end.

Rachel lay back down.

"Yes. Well. Nevertheless, I thank you."

With no small difficulty, Rachel held back a rush of tears. She would not have thought this woman could hurt her feelings again, but she just had. When Rachel could speak, she whispered "You are welcome."

She turned on her side and covered her head with her shawl to avoid hearing their quiet conversation. Soon they became silent, but Rachel could not return to sleep. Tears slipped across her cheek and ran down into her hair, but she did nothing to stop them.

*Lord, please grant me kindness toward others, no matter what their station in this world, for You have made us all equal in Your sight. Grant me a stout heart and only courtesy toward Lady Augusta.*

How like her arrogant English monarch this woman behaved. In spite of repeated attempts by the colonists to reconcile with King George, he had spurned their pleas for relief from mistreatment. While Lady Augusta held no such authority over Rachel, she certainly acted as if she did. And the woman continued to snub Rachel, even when Rachel had helped to save her life, and had lost her favorite hat while doing so.

A bit of Papa's playfulness entered her thoughts. *Lord, if You can find a reason to send Lady Augusta back home to England, she would be much happier there, don't You think?*

With the hope that her prayer did not sound too impertinent, Rachel sat up to await the soon-coming dawn. When she and Papa arrived in East Florida, the early arrival of daylight had surprised her. Dawn came early. Twilight descended late. Nights were short, especially in the summer.

Now a thin, horizontal glow split the eastern blackness, and with it a thick fog rose from the St. Johns River. Soon the small encampment became shrouded in gray. Rachel heard a haunting moan and saw hazy tongues of fire floating above the mists, as if the river were burning. Gradually, dark, blurred forms appeared and moved ever closer to the shore.

Major Brigham awoke and grabbed his musket. The two guards rushed to the flatboat and aimed their weapons toward the apparitions.

"Who goes there?"

# Chapter Twenty-Four

Rachel gripped the sides of the yellow pine canoe as it flew through the water like an arrow shot from a bow, thanks to the muscular arms of the Indians at the slender vessel's front and back.

Frederick sat behind her, and she turned to see how he fared. Despite his puffy, bloodshot eyes and slumped posture, he gave her a reassuring smile. "Are you well, my love?" His voice croaked with weariness.

"Very well, thank you, now that the sun is up." She would not mention her lost hat or the heat scorching the back of her neck. This ordeal would soon be over.

What a fright he and Papa had given her, arriving through the heavy fog with a dozen or more torch-bearing Timucuans. Only by God's mercy did they not find themselves shot by the nervous soldiers guarding the encampment. Unlike the men, both white and Indian, who dismissed the incident once identities were established, the ladies had come near to fainting over what might have happened. Rachel hoped never to spend another night in this wilderness.

When the party arrived at the plantation in the late morning, Frederick ordered a carriage to take her home. As a servant drove them toward town, she and Papa had little energy to talk, but she did find comfort in learning that Frederick had apprehended the man who started the fire.

Once home, they placed themselves in the capable hands of Mr. Patch and Inez. Rachel fell into bed and blissful rest.

She awakened to find the sun still up, only to realize by its morning position that Wednesday had arrived. She'd slept more than sixteen hours. Quickly washed and dressed, she hastened downstairs to the store. There Papa waited on customers as if he had never been away.

"There ye are at last." His light tone bespoke good humor. "Run along to the kitchen house, girl. I know ye're hungry."

"Have you eaten, Papa?"

"Enough for a horse, girl." His booming voice filled the store, to the amusement of the tanner's wife and another woman examining bolts of dress fabric. "Now, get ye along."

As she hurried to obey, Rachel shook her head, enjoying Papa's high spirits. Perhaps he and Mrs. Winthrop had come to an agreement and would soon announce their betrothal, too.

Crossing the backyard, she inhaled the aroma of cooking chicken, and her empty stomach cried out for satisfaction. Surprised to find the kitchen house door closed in such hot weather, she opened it cautiously in case Inez was bathing Sadie. Inside she found her servant at work and a young man seated beside Sadie on her bed. Dressed in rough brown breeches and a well-worn calico shirt, he had not shaved in some time, and his auburn hair needed to be combed.

Fear shot through Rachel. "Who are you?"

He jumped up, terror streaking across his face. With a quick glance about the room, he started toward the window.

"Rob, no," cried Sadie. "Don't leave us." She swung her legs to the floor and struggled to stand but fell back, wincing and crying out in pain.

"Sadie girl." The man hurried back to pull her into his

arms. "Don't harm yourself, love." He stared at Rachel, fear widening his eyes. "I'm Sadie's husband, come to care for her."

Hoping to set Rob at ease, Rachel lifted little Robby. The child put his tiny arms around her neck and giggled as she kissed his forehead and nuzzled into his neck.

"You have nothing to fear. I'm merely surprised to find you here." She eyed the pot bubbling over the hearth fire, and her mouth watered at the aroma of the savory chicken. "Inez, I'm famished." Releasing the child to his play, she sat at the table. Although this could not be considered proper manners, she must eat something soon or risk becoming faint.

"*Sí*, señorita." Inez produced a crockery bowl and served meat, rice and bread.

"Does Mr. Folger know you are here, Rob?" Rachel spooned in a mouthful, endeavoring to appear detached. If he did know, surely he would have told her before she came out.

Rob and Sadie exchanged a look.

"No, ma'am," Sadie answered for her husband.

"Hmm." Rachel ate slowly. When Robby leaned against her, she fed him a bite of bread.

"Here, boy, don't annoy the lady." Rob pulled his son away.

"He is no annoyance." Rachel noticed that the others continued to watch her. "Have you eaten?"

"*Sí*, señorita, I feed them." Inez poured coffee for Rachel. "I know you are generous and would not mind."

"Very good." Rachel sent up a prayer for wisdom. Clearly Rob had deserted his soldiering duties, which would make him a criminal to some people. But unlike the horrid soldier who had set the fire, this one deserted for an honorable purpose—to care for his family.

After several minutes, Sadie and Rob seemed to relax. They whispered endearments to one another and talked about what they had done while separated. Rachel tried not to listen, but the room was too small to keep their conversation private.

"The boy's strong." Rob eyed his son with pride. "You've done a good job, love."

Sadie leaned against him. "He needs his pa, he does." Tears covered her cheeks. "Ya did good to come."

Rob kissed her forehead, but his eyes held concern, while Sadie's eyes radiated her love.

Their mutual tenderness moved Rachel. This was the depth of love she felt for Frederick. What would she do if they were forced apart? How could she bear it?

For Sadie's and Robby's sakes, Rachel must hide Rob, must help him avoid detection by the British soldiers who patrolled the settlement randomly day and night.

She finished her meal and stood. "Thank you, Inez."

"*De nada,* señorita." Inez came to clear the table, while Rachel walked toward the door.

"Beggin' your pardon, miss." Rob approached her. "Could you find it in your heart not to report that I've come here?"

Her heart welled up with sympathy. "Of course I'll not report you. But you cannot hide here for long. Do you have a plan?"

Rob glanced back at Sadie, and she nodded.

"We're going to Cuba."

Rachel stared at him. "Cuba? But why? And with Sadie's injuries, how will you travel?"

"Travel where?" Frederick appeared in the open doorway, his eyebrows arched with curiosity. He looked at Rob, then Rachel, then Sadie, and back to Rachel. "My dear, your father told me you were here. Who is this?" He stared at Rob, and his tone, while not forceful, rang with authority. His magistrate voice.

Dizzy with shock and a remnant of exhaustion, Rachel swayed, almost losing her balance. "Frederick."

Rob's face grew pale around the edges of his sunburn, and he began to tremble.

Rachel felt herself blanching, too. How tempting to lie about this situation, especially since she had promised not to betray Rob. But conviction blocked that wicked thought.

"This is Sadie's husband."

Frederick straightened and frowned. He stared hard at Rob. "Are you not in His Majesty's service?"

Rob gulped. "Yes, sir. That is, I was."

Sadie began to sob, and Rob hurried to her side. "It's all right, Sadie girl. I knew what I would face. But I had to come. I had to know about you and the boy."

A painful knot filled her chest, and Rachel could not contain her own tears. "Frederick, please, can we not let them go?" She grasped his arm and gazed up at him. "Please. Give this to me as a wedding gift, and I shall never ask anything else of you."

"Do you know what you're saying?" Frederick shook his head. "It would be treason."

She wiped a sleeve across her damp face. "Treason against whom? An unjust king who cares nothing for the suffering of common people?" If he did not help them, she wondered whether she would be able to forgive him. She stared into his eyes, wishing, praying for him to relent. "They will hang him," she whispered, "merely for loving his wife and child."

He looked across the room again, his struggle evident in his grinding jaw and deep frown. Anger stormed across his eyes. He stared at the floor, and his lips formed a thin line. At last, he slapped his hat back on and pointed at Rob. "Do not be here when I come back." Then he strode out the door, slamming it on his way.

Gulping back tears, Rachel refused to think of all this meant for their future. "You must have help. I'll go to my father." She opened the door.

"Oh, miss, what if he won't help?" Sadie began to sob again.

Rachel shook her head. "I don't know." *Lord, have mercy. Please soften Papa's heart and make him help us.*

She ran to the store and remained behind the burlap curtain until Papa's customer left. Driven by urgency, she rushed into the room and locked the door.

Papa stared at her with a bewildered expression. "What're ye doing, girl? 'Tis not yet closing time."

"Sadie's husband deserted and came here to see her. He's out in the kitchen house right now. Please, Papa, no matter how you feel about it, I beg you to help them get away from here. They want to go to Cuba and—"

"Hold on a minute." Papa held up his hands. "I'm getting yer meaning clear." He scratched his chin. "Go fetch Mr. Patch. He should be at the livery stable. I'll see what I can do."

Rachel reached up to kiss his stubbly face. "Thank you, Papa. I knew you would help."

He grunted. "Go on, girl. Don't waste time."

All the way to the stable, Rachel forced herself to walk instead of run, for she must not draw attention to herself. Now *this* was an adventure. This was something grand to do for someone else. Something so right that she risked displeasing Frederick, perhaps even losing him.

*Dear Lord, please make him understand.*

If he did not, she had no idea what she would do.

Frederick dug his heels into Essex's sides and bent forward in the saddle. The stallion leapt into a gallop and thundered along the road to the plantation. A good, hard ride would clear Frederick's mind and give the horse some much needed exercise.

He had come into town to make certain Rachel and Mr.

Folger had recovered from their ordeal. He also wanted to deliver the news that Buckner had been brought to the fort and would face the ultimate punishment for his crimes, which included not only arson and murder but desertion. And now Rachel wanted him to help another man desert His Majesty's service.

How could she have put him in this position? From her disparaging remark about His Majesty, she appeared not to have changed her mind about becoming a loyal British subject. He had been foolish to think she would alter her allegiance merely because they were in love.

*Love.*

The word struck into his soul, and he reined Essex to a walk that he might have more time to ponder its meaning.

Indeed, he did love her, and all the more for her courageous generosity in helping the poor, unfortunate little family at the expense of her own happiness. Frederick had no doubt she would carry that same courage into their marriage and into their lives in this wilderness. Was this not the reason he had fallen in love with her in the first place?

An ironic chuckle broke through the knot in his chest, and some of his tension dissolved. His little darling would ask nothing but the soldier's freedom. Frederick recalled Mother asking something similar of Father, risking his wrath to acquire freedom for a mistreated slave. Mother and his beloved were much alike, a similarity that pleased him exceedingly.

He should have stayed to help her. Perhaps he should go back now. But this morning Oliver had requested an audience, and Frederick's every instinct required him to tend to that matter first.

He would return tomorrow morning, and they would talk about the disagreements that threatened their happiness, not the least of which was their conflicting loyalties. He must help her to understand that their lives would not be in danger here in East Florida, for the rebellion would not reach these shores. As for her other concern, he would convince her that the plantation slaves would always be treated with fairness. She herself could see to it.

Kicking Essex into a gallop again, Frederick whispered a prayer into the wind. "Lord, You know how much I love her. Please help us to work out our differences."

## Chapter Twenty-Five

Frederick crumpled the letter and flung it toward the hearth. How tired he was of receiving nothing but condemnation from Father. The earl barely mentioned last spring's abundant shipment of indigo and rice. Instead, he harped on the expense of reinforcing the slave quarters and providing occasional meat for the plantation workers. Frederick wondered if it would be worth the effort to tell Father how well the quarters had withstood the recent storm or how the slaves worked harder in appreciation for his generous provision. No doubt the old man would still find some reason to call it wastefulness.

Leaning back in his chair, Frederick put his feet on the desk and toyed with the marble horse figurine Mother had given him before he left home. If not for her, he would have little trouble asking Father to replace him as the plantation manager.

No, that was foolishness. The people here thought well of him as magistrate, and in that position he had to answer to His Majesty, not Father. Furthermore, he would soon have a wife to care for, a fact that precluded any impulsive decisions such as leaving the plantation.

He sat up and retrieved the letter. It had been written over six weeks ago, before Templeton had a chance to reach London. Perhaps now Father's opinion of Frederick had been improved by that worthy captain's recommendations. But what bitter medicine to swallow that the earl would listen to anyone but his own son.

The sound of labored breathing outside the library window interrupted his thoughts.

"No, sir, I won't do it."

Frederick recognized the voice of Betty, the housemaid. She sounded as if she had been running.

"I saved your life, you stupid little wench."

Oliver! What was the man up to now?

"Ow," Betty whined. "Twist me arm all you like, I'll not steal the—" Her words were cut off with a gasping cry.

Rage burned through Frederick's chest, but he managed to move quietly to the hearth and remove the crossed rapiers from their brackets.

"Shall I feed you to those alligators?" Oliver's voice held cruel amusement. "Ow. You little—" Had she stuck him? Bit him?

The unmistakable sound of a slap. A girlish whimper.

Frederick dashed from the library, down the hall, and then out the back door. There on the back lawn Betty knelt weeping with her hands to her face. Several slaves watched wide-eyed from the corner of the house. Oliver stood over Betty and drew back his foot.

"Kick her, and you are a dead man." Frederick raised one rapier and pointed it at Oliver.

The face his former friend turned to him resembled nothing Frederick could recognize—a dark, wild-eyed frown, an ugly grimace, cheeks contorted with hatred. He hurled out a blasphemous curse, words Frederick never permitted at the plantation.

"So you're home after all." Oliver's expression eased into a scornful scowl. "And playing with swords. My, my, Freddy, aren't we brave."

Frederick swallowed his fury and tossed the second weapon toward Oliver. It landed at his feet.

"Pick it up." *Lord, help me.* Perhaps this was not the best way to handle the situation.

Without removing his angry stare from Frederick, Oliver reached down to retrieve the foil. "You know, of course, that I am your better." He emitted an odd snicker. "At fencing, I mean." He bowed the blade slightly and swished it through the air.

Frederick looked beyond Oliver to see little Caddy helping the frightened housemaid to her feet. "What did he want you to do, Betty?"

"Keep your mouth shut, girl." Oliver kept his gaze on Frederick.

"For me to steal the keys from Mrs. Winthrop is what he wanted." Tears streaked her face. "But I wouldn't do it, no sir, not for him nor nobody."

"Good girl." Frederick felt a presence behind him and glanced back to see Summerlin, Cousin Lydie, Dr. Wellsey and several grooms. Old Ben held a pitchfork, and determination filled his black eyes as he glared at Oliver.

"Ah, me." Gratitude filled Frederick, followed by a twinge of disappointment. He truly longed to take Oliver on and prove him wrong about his swordsmanship. "Too much help for a fair fight. Shall we call it a draw?"

"Coward." Oliver flung down the sword and strode toward the stable.

Frederick stopped Oliver with the side of his blade. "We will talk in the library now."

Oliver jerked away and moved toward the house.

"Oh, dear, Frederick." Cousin Lydie touched his arm. "What if he—"

"It will be all right, dear." Frederick patted her hand. "You see to Betty." He motioned to Summerlin and Wellsey.

Inside, Dr. Wellsey closed the library door, and Summerlin leaned out the window and shooed away curious servants. Seated behind his desk, Frederick watched Oliver crumple into a chair and stare at the floor.

"Well, Oliver, out with it." Frederick had difficulty keeping a stern tone, for he would prefer to entreat his lifelong friend to explain his behavior. "Why did you need the keys?"

"Now, really, Freddy, if you had not taken my set of keys, none of this would have happened." Oliver rolled his eyes and shook his head. "I did not plan to take all of your money. Just enough for passage to Brazil. Oh, and a little food along the way." He brushed a bit of dirt from his shirtsleeve. "My needs are modest."

Frederick felt his jaw go slack. "Why did you not simply ask me?"

"I should not have to ask for what I have earned." His hands clenched, Oliver fidgeted, as if ready to take flight. "Simply put, I am leaving. I have depended upon *your* father's generosity for too long. It is time to make my own way in the world."

Frederick caught Oliver's emphasis on *your*. "What happened to prompt this decision?"

Oliver's face pinched into a grimace. "Your man Summerlin here has been with your family since he was fourteen." He glanced over his shoulder. "An excellent fellow, the epitome of uprightness. He, eh, informed me of certain happenings in the year before my birth that precluded some, uh, suspicions I have carried since boyhood."

Wellsey grunted, but Summerlin's neutral expression did not change.

"Ah." Both dismay and relief flooded Frederick. "Whatever the issue may be, I pray you will find peace in its regard."

"Peace? Ha." Oliver leaned back in his chair and stretched out his legs. "Lord Bennington has always treated me as a…treated me kindly and praised my business acumen. I thought to manage this plantation in your stead. But I could do that only if you failed." His eyes narrowed. "What do you think of that?"

At the affirmation of his worst suspicions, Frederick could hardly speak past the lump in his throat. "Did you plan that before we came here? No, I know you didn't. On our voyage over, we were friends as we always have been." He exhaled a labored sigh that hurt clear down to his belly.

Oliver snickered. "I really should consider an occupation in the theater." He rose and walked to the bookcase, where he pulled out the incriminating pamphlet Frederick had hidden in the pages of *Paradise Lost*. "I see your Miss Folger has left something for you to read. Perhaps Lord Bennington would be interested in it, as well."

Frederick felt the blood drain from his face. Rachel had never tried to conceal from him her sympathies for the insurrection. Was she the one who left the pamphlet the night of his dinner party in hopes of swaying his opinions? He glanced at Wellsey, who eyed the paper with curiosity. Summerlin maintained his disinterest.

"We have had numerous guests here, Oliver. Any one of them could have left it." He swallowed hard. "It's nothing but seditious nonsense."

Oliver's face took on a serpent-like slyness. "And yet here it remains, untorn, unburned."

"One does not burn evidence."

"Hmm." Oliver held the paper up as if reading it. "And yet you do not seek to find the guilty party?"

Anger flashed through Frederick—anger at himself, at Oliver and at Rachel. He crossed his arms. "You don't need to do this. You may go wherever you wish without trying to blackmail me." Boyhood memories of better times with this friend filled Frederick's mind. "In fact, you may have your mare, your clothes and thirty pounds to start your new life."

"What?" Oliver stared at him, clearly stunned. "After all I've done and said?"

Frederick walked around the desk and put his hands on Oliver's shoulders, forcing his adversary to look deep into his eyes. "Whatever you felt for me, I have always cared for you like a brother. In fact, closer than my true brothers."

Oliver's face grew pale, and his glance darted between Wellsey and Summerlin. "But—"

Soft rapping on the library door cut into his answer.

"Come," Frederick called.

The door cracked open, and the butler stuck in his be-wigged head. "Sir, Major Brigham's in the drawin' room. May I say you'll see him?"

"Yes. Tell him I shall be there straightaway." Frederick eyed Oliver, but spoke to the other men. "Doctor, see Mr. Corwin out to the stable. Tell Ben to saddle the mare for him. Summerlin, pack his belongings and some food. He is not to set foot in this house again." A quick glance told him they would follow his orders forthwith.

"Oliver, I shall get the money for you shortly. I advise you to take the King's Highway to St. Augustine. 'Tis a three-day ride, and there you will have your choice of ships."

"I—"

"Stubble it." Frederick left the room, swallowing the ache in his throat. He doubted he would ever know whether or not the pain in Oliver's eyes was genuine.

"A moment, sir." Summerlin stopped Frederick and fussed with his clothing and hair. "Now, sir, go meet the major."

Again Frederick tamped down his emotions. Summerlin's faithfulness stood in stark contrast to Oliver's betrayal.

At the drawing room door, he extended his hand toward

his guest. "Major Brigham, I hope you and Lady Augusta have recovered from our excursion."

"Amazingly so." Brigham shook his hand. "In fact, I think she will take great delight in regaling her friends in London with her tale of being rescued from the jaws of a dragon." His eyes glinted with uncharacteristic cheerfulness.

"Very good, sir. Will you sit?" Frederick waved his hand toward an upholstered chair. "I'll send for lemonade." He made motions to the butler by the door.

"I will stay only a moment. I must return to the garrison and supervise the packing."

"Packing?" Frederick digested the thought for a moment. "Aha. Your transfer came through."

Brigham whisked a hand across his red jacket sleeve. "Yes. At last I'll have a purpose for wearing this uniform."

Frederick found his high humor a welcome relief. "Very good, sir. I'm pleased on your behalf. Did you come to take your leave, then?"

"Yes. I will leave in four days and wanted you to know of my good fortune."

"What of Lady Augusta?" Frederick asked. "Will she be regaling those friends in London sooner rather than later?"

A shadow passed over Brigham's brow. "I'd intended to send her home after the incident with the alligator, but the brave girl will have none of it. And there are other officers' wives in Boston. It shouldn't be a problem, as we will hold the city against the rebels. We have several thousand more troops arriving soon."

The butler carried in a refreshment tray and poured lemonade from a cut-glass pitcher into matching goblets. Both men partook.

"Well, then." Frederick eyed Brigham expectantly. "What other news?"

"Ah, yes." He drew out a sealed document from his jacket

and handed it to Frederick. "From Governor Tonyn. He requires your presence back in the capital without delay. I've ordered a flatboat to take you to the coast this afternoon before the tides turn."

Frederick's heart sank. This would delay his getting back to Rachel to assure her he was not angry about the soldier and for them to have their long-overdue discussion about their differences. Yet he had no choice but to obey Governor Tonyn's orders, no matter what the personal cost to him or Rachel.

"The pony cart is almost packed." Rachel sat beside Sadie in the kitchen house while Papa and Mr. Patch helped Rob prepare for their departure.

"Thank you, miss." Sadie reclined on her cot beside her napping son. "With your help and Mr. Moberly buyin' the livestock, we'll be able to make it to Cuba."

Rachel ignored the disquieting emotion stirred by the mention of Frederick's name. Instead, she studied Sadie's expression. "You seem worried."

"Yes, miss. I ain't never known any Indians, and all I've heard is they like to kill us English for sport." She caressed her son's unruly hair.

"Do not be afraid. Papa has made friends with the Timucua people. They respect him, and for his sake, they will take good care of you until you are able to travel."

"I do hope so."

"And Inez will be there to take care of you, as well."

Sadie grasped Rachel's hands. "Oh, miss, will you ever forgive me? I never meant to take your servant. I never thought to *have* a servant, bein' one myself."

Rachel tried to smile, but her lower lip quivered. "But you can see God's goodness in this, can you not? Inez has been separated from her sons for twelve years, since England took possession of East Florida. Now she can go to Cuba with you and find them."

"You're good to look at it that way, miss." Sadie dried her face on her sleeve.

Soon Papa, Mr. Patch and Rob came to collect the other travelers. With last goodbyes said, Rachel watched the little band walk up the road toward the wilderness path.

How she wished she could go to the plantation. But seeking Frederick out, even though they were engaged, would be improper and might offend dear Mrs. Winthrop. He had said he would return, and while she awaited his visit with a measure of trepidation, she anticipated their long-overdue conversation about the revolution. For somehow she must persuade him to the patriot cause.

## Chapter Twenty-Six

Frederick did not come to see her. Even Papa did not return from the Timucua village. At dusk, Rachel bolted the front door, secured the kitchen house and back door, and then carried her dinner upstairs. By candlelight, she managed to force down some stew, although her appetite had long ago been chased away by anxious thoughts.

The evening breeze blew in through the tall windows, carrying a refreshing pine scent and cooling the apartment. Raucous laughter and fiddle music came from the town's remaining tavern a half mile away. The haunting yelp of a dog wafted in from the salt grass marshes, and Rachel shuddered. No doubt some poor pup had fallen prey to an alligator.

She loaded one of Papa's muskets and laid it on the dining table. Other than the man who attempted to burn the store, no one had tried to harm them. But she would not be caught unprepared. New people came to the settlement every week, some like Papa fleeing the war up north, others perhaps to find wealth in the wilderness. But some might wish to cause trouble.

A slender crescent moon rose outside her window. Papa still did not return. Rachel retired, but sleep would not come.

She prayed for Papa's safety, then reassured herself that he no doubt decided to stay the night in the village. He had proved his wilderness mettle, and her worries served no purpose.

She prayed for Frederick, but could find no such reassurance. The Lord remained silent. After a restless night, she rose to open her Bible at dawn. Her ribbon bookmark lay beside Psalm 51, where one verse seemed prominent. *Behold, Thou desirest truth in the inward parts: and in the hidden part Thou shalt make me to know wisdom.*

Certain she had been truthful with both the Lord and Frederick, she wondered why the verse lingered in her mind as she ate the remaining stew and went downstairs to open the store. Customers came and went. Clouds kept the sun's usual heat at bay.

Midmorning, Mr. Patch burst through the front door. "Miss Rachel, come quick." His terror-filled eyes sent fear coursing through her. She hurried outside after him.

"What—" At the front porch, she grasped the railing as light-headedness struck.

Papa straddled his mule and lay against its neck not moving, perhaps not breathing.

"Papa!" Rachel thrust away her weakness and rushed to him. "What happened?"

Small but sturdy Mr. Patch grasped Papa's waist and struggled to pull him down. "Snakebite. Rattler," Mr. Patch managed through clenched teeth.

"Is he alive?" Rachel choked out the question as she tried to help, to no avail. Papa weighed too much for the two of them and might be further injured if he fell to the ground.

"Aye, Miss Rachel, and flaming with fever. It happened early this morning as we made our way home." Mr. Patch blinked away tears. "After he was bit, he climbed up on old Kip here and passed out. I brought him as quick as I could without him falling off."

"You did well, Mr. Patch." Forcing aside the fear that paralyzed her, Rachel looked around for help. Several soldiers on their rounds appeared down the street, and she screamed out to them. Led by her acquaintance, Bertie Martin, the men hastened to pull Papa gently from the mule and carry him upstairs to his bed.

"I thank you all." Rachel wiped away her tears and stared at Papa's swollen calf and torn stockings. "Does anyone know what to do for a snakebite?"

"He'd do best to have a doctor, Miss Rachel." Private Martin's anxious expression spoke of his concern for Papa.

"Is it within your duties to fetch Dr. Wellsey from Bennington Plantation?" And Frederick. Surely he would come, even if he were still angry with her.

"Yes, miss. We can do that." Private Martin tilted his head toward the door, and the other soldiers followed him out.

"Mr. Patch, get fresh springwater and towels from the kitchen house." Rachel pulled off Papa's shoes.

"Aye, miss." Mr. Patch dashed out.

Her hands trembled as she removed Papa's knife from its sheath and cut away the stocking on his wounded leg. Two punctures scarred the outside of his calf, and the skin stretched tight over the red, swollen limb. Rachel examined the wounds, wishing she could squeeze out the poison that even now caused his labored breathing. Perhaps Dr. Wellsey would bring leeches.

"Lord, have mercy on Papa. Please do not let him die without knowing You." Rachel bit back a sob. Papa would be all right. He was strong. He would fight off the poison.

Mr. Patch brought the water, and Rachel washed Papa's face and the wound. They replaced his shirt with a nightgown, and Rachel stepped into the hallway while Mr. Patch removed Papa's breeches. Mr. Patch paced the room and wrung his hands, stopping every few minutes to stare at him, as if willing him to be well. His nervousness made Rachel's struggle to stay calm all the harder.

"Mr. Patch, please go downstairs and manage the store."

Mr. Patch's face crinkled with worry. "Aye, miss." He cast a last glance at Papa before leaving.

Rachel paced for a few minutes herself, but then fetched her Bible and sat beside Papa's bed. She read aloud the third chapter of John's gospel, emphasizing verse sixteen, especially the last part, "whosoever believeth in Him should not perish but have everlasting life," willing Papa to hear and believe. Then she read Mother's most beloved verses, followed by her own favorites. Her voice grew weary from reading and praying.

If Papa heard any of her words, he didn't indicate it but continued his occasional groans and convulsions and his constantly labored breathing.

In the late afternoon, Dr. Wellsey marched into the room carrying a leather bag. "Good day, Miss Folger." He focused immediately on Papa, first checking the wound and then touching Papa's neck and lifting his eyelids.

"Rachel." Mrs. Winthrop entered behind the doctor. "I am grieved for your father."

"Oh, Mrs. Winthrop." Rachel hurried to the older woman's open arms and released her pent-up tears.

"There, my dear." Mrs. Winthrop patted Rachel's back. "We will do all we can." Her voice wavered with emotion.

Rachel lifted her head and peered around Mrs. Winthrop. "Frederick?"

She shook her head. "He could not come, my dear."

Could not or would not? Rachel had thought she could not endure any more heartache, but this cut even deeper.

While Dr. Wellsey studied Papa's wound, Mrs. Winthrop moved to the bed and leaned close, concern deepening the wrinkles around her eyes. "Mr. Folger." She reached a gloved hand toward his cheek, but drew back and seemed to swallow a sob. With a little sniff, she tore off her gloves and reached for the cloth and bowl of water on the bedside table, wiping sweat from his face with a tenderness that caused Rachel more tears.

Dr. Wellsey applied a green poultice to the snakebite. It smelled of bear grease and some sort of weed. Rachel almost gagged, and Mrs. Winthrop coughed discreetly.

All this time, a question nagged Rachel. Now it burned too much to keep it to herself.

"Mrs. Winthrop," she whispered, "you said Mr. Moberly could not come." She hoped her tone didn't convey an accusation of neglect. "Did plantation business keep him?"

Mrs. Winthrop arched her eyebrows. "Why, no, my dear. He is fond of your father and certainly would have come if he were home. But he was summoned back to St. Augustine."

"St. Augustine?" Hope lifted Rachel's heart. He had not disregarded Papa's life-and-death struggle, after all.

Mrs. Winthrop glanced at Papa. "Your father is in Dr. Wellsey's capable hands. Let us go to the drawing room." She led Rachel to a chair by the hearth and sat opposite her. "After our party left the city, Governor Tonyn received further information about the fighting up north. This is no longer a minor civil war easily dispensed with. The rebels are growing stronger. In May, they overran Fort Ticonderoga in New York colony and stole British cannons and ammunition to use against our own soldiers. In June, Boston suffered a siege, and many of our soldiers were killed or wounded."

Rachel's heart made several leaps. Praise God the patriots had conquered a British fort and secured weapons. And no doubt the siege of Boston included the Breed's Hill event Mrs. Middlebrook had whispered about in those early morning hours in St. Augustine.

"But why did that news require Frederick to go back to the capital?" A nauseating premonition swept through Rachel.

"According to the letter from the governor, more loyalists are coming to East Florida to escape the insurrection. Hidden among them are spies for the rebels. The governor has evidence that some are already here. Can you believe it? Spies, right here in our peaceful colony." She exhaled a weary sigh. "Why do people do such things?"

"But…Frederick?"

"Why, my dear, as His Majesty's representative in this area, he must learn all he can so as to apprehend those spies." Her tired eyes shone with pride. "When Mr. Moberly read the governor's letter to me, you could see his outrage. You can be certain no rebel sympathizer will go undetected. No spy will escape."

"He was angry?" Rachel's voice was thick.

Mrs. Winthrop nodded soberly. "You know our dear Mr. Moberly is a moderate, even-tempered young man, but he stormed about the house, slamming doors and muttering under his breath. Were he not such a gentleman and a Christian, I fear he might have, well, uttered an oath. He was quite upset."

Rachel swallowed hard, and the ache in her chest restricted her breathing. Frederick knew where her sentiments lay, and all this time he had hinted he had no quarrel with the patriot cause. What a fool she'd been. Now her morning verse made sense. God desired that truth should dwell in His children, and she had endeavored to be truthful. But Frederick had done nothing short of lying to her. He would never support the revolution, would do all he could to stop it. If she learned anything helpful and tried to relay it to her fellow patriots, Frederick would be required to have her arrested.

Sick with dismay, she forced her thoughts back to Papa, whose danger was more imminent than her own. "We must see how Papa is faring."

"Yes, of course, my dear." Mrs. Winthrop rose. "And let

your heart be encouraged. Dr. Wellsey has used that snake-bite ointment on several slaves to good effect. He learned of it from the Indians."

When they returned to Papa's bedchamber, Dr. Wellsey was checking the poultice.

"It would have been more effective if I had applied this right after the bite." He seemed to speak to himself. "Nevertheless, we hope it will draw out the poison." He looked at Rachel. "I will be happy to stay with you until his crisis passes. Mrs. Winthrop insisted on accompanying me for propriety's sake."

"I'm grateful to both of you." Rachel's head and heart had been buffeted from all sides, but she must see to her duties. "I'll order food from the tavern."

Throughout the rest of the day and into the night, Papa rolled about, sweating and vomiting. From time to time, violent seizures struck, and Mr. Patch came to help the doctor hold him to the bed. Everyone took a turn at sleeping and eating to maintain their strength. They also knelt in turn to pray for Papa's life and health.

After midnight, Rachel sat in the darkness of the drawing room, too weary to decipher all that Frederick's dishonesty meant to their future. Of course she could no longer think of marrying him. But how could she face him to break off their engagement?

The swish of Mrs. Winthrop's skirts interrupted her thoughts.

"Your father is not quite so restive now." She sat beside Rachel on the settee. "I thought I should come and give you another bit of news." The warmth in her tone generated Rachel's curiosity.

"Yes, ma'am?"

Mrs. Winthrop leaned toward her. "Major Brigham has been reassigned to Boston. He and Lady Augusta will be sailing there this Friday."

An unexpected giggle bubbled up in Rachel's throat, and she found it difficult to subdue it. The Lord had answered her selfish prayer for her adversary to leave.

But a sobering thought cut short her mirth. Now she had a new adversary, and he was none other than the man she loved with all her heart.

In the dim light of a whale oil lamp aboard the *Mingo*, Frederick studied the pamphlet, and his heart grew heavier with each reading, even as his mind became enlightened. Too long he had shrugged off the seriousness of the strife in the thirteen rebelling colonies. He should have comprehended what was to come when he learned the colonists had organized their auspicious-sounding "continental congress" in Philadelphia last September. That a large group of educated, landed gentry would gather to write such an articulate and well-reasoned appeal to His Majesty could not be dismissed out of hand. Especially when the war might now extend to East Florida, including his own settlement. Including his own upcoming marriage.

He could no longer lightly regard Rachel's passion for the colonists' cause, though he had dismissed his earlier concern that she might already be spying for the enemy. Her sentiments, whether serious or sanguine, always radiated from her dark brown eyes, a quality he valued, and she would have given herself away long ago.

The ship rose and fell in the undulating surf. The lamp swayed, casting grotesque shadows about the small cabin. The fetid odors of waste and dead fish reached his nostrils, and he longed to ascend to the deck so the fresh sea air might cleanse him inside and out. Simply reading this pamphlet befouled his soul and made him feel like a traitor.

Yet he could not argue with the colonists' claims to the historic rights of all Englishmen, rights he himself took for granted. Should not the present generation of English descendants on American soil have those same rights? It all made sense to him and was, in fact, the way he dispensed his own authority.

As manager of his father's plantation, he held a king-like power and endeavored to wield a temperate scepter over the servants and slaves. They responded by working harder, thus producing more and finer crops than they had under Father's imprudent former agent or would have under Oliver's iron hand. Why could His Majesty not treat his colonies in like manner? Did not the Scriptures teach that a laborer was worthy of his hire? Moreover, a king should serve his people rather than bleed them dry through taxation. He should permit them to gather lawfully in order to deliberate on how to present "their dutiful, humble, loyal, and reasonable petitions to the crown for redress." The men who wrote this document were articulate, God-fearing gentlemen.

Exhaling a weary sigh, Frederick folded the pamphlet, tucked it in his coat, and then retrieved the governor's letter. This missive convinced him that, instead of a civil conflict propagated by a few unruly dissidents, a full-blown war raged between his homeland and thirteen of her American colonies. The rebels' successful raid on Fort Ticonderoga and the many British losses at Breed's Hill demonstrated that the colonists were endeavoring to sever their ties with England. The news that they might bring their rebellion to East Florida portended many unpleasant days ahead. Before he could decide what part to play in this tragedy, Frederick had much to consider and much to pray about, not the least of which was how it affected his marriage to Rachel.

## Chapter Twenty-Seven

"Perseus."

Rachel jolted awake in her chair beside Papa's bed and rushed to his side. Darkness shrouded the room, but she could make out his form.

"What is it, Papa?" She caressed his brow, grateful his fever had broken earlier.

Mumbling unintelligible words, he tried to roll toward the side of his injured leg, but returned to his back with a deep groan.

"Shh. It's all right, Papa."

Unshaven but wearing a clean nightgown, he smelled of lye soap from the bath Dr. Wellsey and Mr. Patch had given him.

"Take it to Perseus."

There. He said it again. She hadn't dreamed it. Her scalp tingled, and a shiver ran down her neck.

"Who is Perseus, Papa?"

"Uh?" He rose slightly. "Water."

She struggled to lift him while raising a glass to his lips. He drank greedily, then fell back on the pillow and began to snore. His noisy but even breathing mitigated her disappointment that he hadn't answered her question. The crisis had passed, as Dr. Wellsey informed her before he and Mrs. Winthrop returned home.

Once Papa awoke, however, she would hound him until he confessed. She had not the slightest doubt he was the third man she heard talking in the night in St. Augustine. In spite of her constant grief over Frederick, this truth about Papa tickled her insides. To think, Papa was a patriot. Why, that must mean Cousin Jamie was, too. Though exhausted, she remained by Papa's bed, shaking her head over the absurdity. All this time she had never suspected either of them.

Then another thought took hold. Why had he never told her? Why had he not let her stay in Boston to spy on General Gage? He and Jamie had shut her out, calling their secret discussions "men's business." Pain ripped through her, rivaling her agony over Frederick's lies. She didn't have to ask Papa why. Their exclusion of her in their plans said it all. They did not trust her.

Tears scalded her cheeks, and her body ached. Minding Dr. Wellsey's instructions to get her own rest, she lit a candle and examined Papa's color. As best she could see, it appeared normal. Now she could safely leave him and go to bed.

Once there, she still could not surrender to sleep for the turmoil in her mind. She had heard at least three men in St. Augustine, but one only grunted rather than speak. *Zeus.* Why, that was the ruling god of Greek mythology. If Papa had chosen that name for himself, he must be the leader. And that meant he had the cylinder. He was to deliver it to...*Hermes.* Hermes, the messenger god. That must be Jamie! Who would take it by ship to...*Perseus.* But who was Perseus? And why had they chosen these names from Greek mythology? Could it be to show that some Greeks in East Florida supported the revolution? That must be the reason Papa had spoken with the Greek prisoner. She wondered what he had told the guards to gain such a privilege.

With Papa likely to be sick for some time, with Jamie in England for who knew how long, someone needed to deliver the cylinder to Perseus. If only she knew where it was and where to take it, she could prove herself worthy of helping the revolution.

She would search Papa's belongings at first light. As a child, she'd discovered a false bottom in his sea trunk. She also knew of a hollow chamber beneath the finial on one of his bedposts. A brick on the hearthside had been loosened and might hide a cavity. She had no doubt Papa would keep something that valuable close by. She would find it somehow.

*Lord, please show me where it is. Please reveal to me who Perseus is and how I can find him. And help me to forgive Papa and Jamie for treating me like an inconsequential child.*

A map. Of course. Rachel marveled at the clever ploy. The topography of northern East Florida drawn on doeskin as thin and pliable as a lady's gloves, then rolled tightly into a brass cylinder resembling a sea captain's collapsible telescope, lay in the top drawer of Papa's chest. If Rachel had not grown frustrated in her search and retrieved the supposed telescope to stare out the window for amusement, she never would have found the map.

What amazed her even more was the discovery of a fake red beard and a heavily lined coat under the false bottom in Papa's trunk. But Papa could not be the patriot who had tried to stir up the settlement, for he could never hide his limp. And dear Mr. Patch was far too short.

But now she must discover the identity and location of Perseus. If Jamie was to take the map to the man on his next voyage, the place could be anywhere, but most likely in the colonies. Most likely Boston. But Rachel could not be certain.

Still, the idea of Boston grew with such strength that she began to think it was God's leading. She must find a way to get there, even if forced to humble herself and ask to travel with Lady Augusta. Providing, of course, Papa felt well enough by Friday for her to leave him in Mr. Patch's care. If Frederick would stay away until then, she would not have to face him to break their engagement. By implying he supported her belief in the revolution when he actually stood against it, he had hurt her too much to deserve an explanation. Indeed, how could she explain to him that, now and forever, they were enemies?

In the afternoon, Rachel read to Papa, interspersing prayers with Bible verses. His even breathing encouraged her regarding his health, but his lack of faith still concerned her. She had just begun a passage in James, when he mumbled, coughed and opened his eyes.

"Rachel." His gravelly voice sounded like music to her.

"Papa." She set aside her reading and kissed his unshaven cheek. "Dear Papa." She laid her head on his chest and wept.

For once, he didn't dismiss her display of emotion, but patted her hair and coughed. "There now, daughter. All's well 'cept for my voracious thirst."

She dried her tears and poured water, which he managed to drink by himself.

"Are you hungry?" Rachel straightened his sheets, trying to anticipate what he might need.

"No." His reddened eyes turned toward his chest of drawers, and a worried frown crossed his brow. "Doubtless I will be soon." He grimaced. "'Tis a frightful thing, a snake-bite. Never have I felt such pain."

"Not even when you broke your leg?"

"My what?" His eyes widened briefly. "Ah, yes. Even more painful than the broken leg."

"Oh, dear Papa, I'm so sorry." Rachel glanced toward his once sturdy limbs. "My heart grieves for your suffering, but we may thank God for your life."

She braced herself for his usual dismissal of her faith, but he merely grunted, even gave her a little smile. "Well, I suppose this'll go down in the family lore about yer old father. Do be sure to write yer sister all the details." Now his eyes lit with a bit of their old sparkle, though dark shadows hung beneath them.

Rachel's mind turned. This could be the answer to everything. "Papa, what would you think if I went to Boston and told her myself?"

"What?" He tried to sit up, but fell back against the pillow. "Hmm. Aye, aye. East Florida's turned out to be a dangerous place. Not that Boston's any safer these days." He closed his eyes for a moment, then stared at her with tender concern. "But what of Mr. Moberly?"

She looked away, forbidding herself to cry. "Haven't I been foolish, Papa? You saw it, I am certain. That is why you were reluctant to approve our engagement. Mr. Moberly is a Tory, a loyalist. We would not make a good match." Another thought intruded. "Nor will you and Mrs. Winthrop."

"Me and Mrs. Winthrop?"

"Of course. I know you are fond of her, but you must not deceive her about who you really are." Rachel fussed with his sheet corner. "You see, Papa, I know you are a patriot...Zeus."

Papa inhaled sharply. "Did I speak that name in a delirium?"

She patted his shoulder. "Don't worry. You and I were alone when you mentioned Perseus." Briefly, she told him all that had transpired during their trip to St. Augustine, including when she had overheard him with his cronies. "If you had spoken that night, I would have recognized your voice right away. But I did not realize until you said 'Perseus' in your sleep that you were the third man."

With each incident, his eyes widened and his mouth hung open. "Rachel, my girl, I'd have never thought..." Perspiration beaded on his forehead, and his face grew pale.

"Please rest now, Papa. We can talk more later."

He rolled his head from side to side on the pillow. "No. This must be decided." His gaze became steady, even harsh. "Ye must go to Boston to deliver a gift to Charles, but ye must tell no one of it. Keep it deep in yer travel bag, and never let it out of yer sight. Can ye do this, girl?"

"Yes, of course." Excitement spun through her like a storm. Now he would trust her. Now she had a chance to prove herself. "May I assume Charles is Perseus?" She never dreamed her sister's mild-mannered husband possessed such courage.

Papa's eyes narrowed into a wily expression. "I know not what ye mean, girl. Have ye been reading Greek myths again?"

At last, she permitted herself to laugh. "No, sir." But she must make one more attempt to win his soul. "These past few days, I have found great comfort in the Scriptures."

"Ah, that answers it." He scratched his scruffy chin. "Many a dream I had these nights of yer mother reading those same Scriptures to me. But ye left out my favorite passage, John 6:68–69. In my travels to many ports of this world, 'twas the one that kept me from the seductive spells of strange religions."

Her pulse racing, Rachel snatched up her Bible and quickly found the passage. "'Then Simon Peter answered him, Lord, to whom shall we go? Thou hast the words of eternal life. And we believe and are sure that thou art that Christ, the Son of the living God.'" She could barely finish for weeping. "Oh, Papa, you believe. Why have you never told me?"

Weariness seemed to overtake him, for he closed his eyes and sunk deeper into the pillow. "Not every man wears his opinions…or his faith on his face. Sometimes 'tis better not to bare yer soul."

As she considered his words, she longed to discuss them further. But he had drifted back to sleep, and she would not disturb him. Nor would she urge him to reveal the identity of the other local patriot.

How often he had chided her for her emotional displays, which she rarely tried to contain. Could such a person be trusted to spy or even keep a secret? Not likely. Even falling in love with Frederick had been fraught with too much emotion and too little temperance. Had she been wise, she would have required a definitive answer regarding his sentiments on the revolution. But she had disregarded the proverb to keep her heart with all diligence and blinded herself to the truth, seeing only what she wished to see.

Now she had the opportunity to do something truly important for the cause she held dear, but only if she could hide her deepest feelings. That might not be possible if Frederick returned from St. Augustine before she left.

"You have made a wise decision, Rachel." Lady Augusta fanned herself as they sat in the cabin of the British frigate three days later. "Marital happiness cannot last when the wife's rank is inferior to her husband's."

Bracing herself against the woman's hurtful remark, Rachel ran a finger over the ornately carved arm of her mahogany chair beside the captain's desk. "But isn't Major Brigham the son of a baronet, while you are the daughter of an earl? I do not pretend to understand much about English rankings, but doesn't that mean you married beneath your station?" She smiled sweetly and blinked several times.

Lady Augusta's eyebrows lowered, and her pretty mouth twisted into a snarl. "My connections have made it possible for my husband to advance in His Majesty's service, whereas an inferior wife will always be a detriment to her husband's aspirations."

Rachel stared down and bit her lower lip to keep from responding. She was no match for this woman's cruel tongue.

Further, any discussion of her former engagement to Frederick would be pointless. She inhaled deeply to soothe her ravaged emotions, drawing in the mouth-watering aroma of beef stew. They would soon be dining with the captain here in his quarters, and Rachel consoled herself that during the meal she might gather some helpful information to pass on to Charles. Posing as a loyalist rankled, but it also gave her a heady sense of dangerous excitement.

Her emotions now under control, she again looked at Lady Augusta. "I hope you will find Boston more pleasant than St. Johns Settlement."

Lady Augusta sniffed. "At the very least, the society will be an improvement."

At a knock on the cabin door, Lady Augusta said "You may enter."

The captain's uniformed steward stepped in and bowed. "Ladies, if you will excuse us, we must prepare the cabin for supper." He turned to Rachel. "Will you be joining us, miss?"

"Don't be ridiculous." Lady Augusta marched toward the door, her wide panniers brushing against the desk and almost knocking over the chairs. "She will eat with the servants."

Trailing after Lady Augusta as she left the cabin, the scent of orange blossoms struck a double blow to Rachel's already aching heart. The sweet, delicate fragrance would always remind her of this unfeeling woman, but worse, of pleasant walks with Frederick in his orange grove. Papa had promised that the pain would lessen one day, but Rachel doubted she would ever stop hurting.

"To Boston?" Frederick stared at Mr. Folger, not believing his words. "Sir, why would you send her back there when the city is under siege?"

Mr. Folger sat propped against his pillows, pale and sweating. But he had assured Frederick he was on the mend.

"Would she be any safer in this wilderness?" Mr. Folger pointed to his leg. "Snakes, alligators, mosquito hordes...I was wrong to bring her here."

Frederick paced the wooden floor, trying to make sense of all that had happened while he was away. Mrs. Winthrop had related the horrifying news of Mr. Folger's snakebite, but she made no mention of Rachel's leaving. This news would break his cousin's gentle heart.

He stopped beside the bed, his mind torn between wanting to shake more information from Mr. Folger and sending for Dr. Wellsey to be certain the old man was indeed improving.

Feeling as if someone had sliced open his chest and ripped out his heart, Frederick dropped into a bedside chair and lifted his hands in supplication. "Sir, I implore you to tell me the reason she left. Did she fear I would not forgive her for harboring the deserter?" He stood and paced, then reclaimed the chair. "We agreed we must talk about our differences regarding the revolution. Why would she leave before we could do that?"

Mr. Folger shrugged. "Ye knew of her devotion to that cause. Did ye think she would lightly abandon it?"

Frederick ran a hand through his hair, loosening several strands from the queue. "I know you have no interest in the conflict, sir, but I do. Rachel's passion for it has forced me to examine the issues more deeply." He paused, wondering how much to trust Mr. Folger. "This second trip to St. Augustine was...enlightening."

Mr. Folger's eyes flickered. He yawned and stretched. "Yer pardon. These past few days, I'm not myself."

Shame filled Frederick. "Forgive me. I will take my leave and let you rest." He stood and walked toward the door.

"Sit down, boy." Mr. Folger's hoarse tone resounded with authority.

Frederick did as he ordered. "Yes, sir."

"As ye said, Rachel's passion for the revolution makes a

man think, that and my comin' near to death's door. Mayhap I've been a coward not to choose sides. What think ye?"

Frederick stared into the old whaler's dark brown eyes, searching for some indication of his opinion. Now who was the coward? Perhaps the time had come for him to state his own opinion regardless of what others thought, regardless of the outcome.

"My visit with Governor Tonyn was informative, but not the way he intended. All of England's colonies in this hemisphere are feeling the same pressures, may I say, *injustices* from the Crown. Only thirteen of them are willing to do something about it. It takes courage to break off from one's parent, especially when that unjust parent tries to control his child by any possible means." As he said the words, Frederick's heart swelled with affirmation. His course of action had not yet become clear, but he knew where he would stand.

Mr. Folger grunted. "Speak ye of the colonies or yer own father?" A grin lifted one corner of his lips.

Frederick returned a rueful grimace. "I should go to her."

Mr. Folger's gaze grew intense. "Aye. Ye could do that…if ye've no doubt about yer sentiments bein' equal."

The sly old fox. He had said nothing to incriminate himself, yet everything to bestow his blessing on Frederick.

Yes, he *would* go. For he could not think of staying in this wilderness without Rachel by his side.

# Chapter Twenty-Eight

"Mind your stitches." Susanna studied eight-year-old Eliza's handiwork. "Loose stitches lose his britches."

Rachel and the four other ladies in the sewing circle hummed their agreement to the instructive rhyme and continued with their harmless gossip.

Susanna mentioned a stray sow in someone's garden and warned everyone to keep their gates closed. Mrs. Arthur told of her concern for a peacock whose hen had vanished. Mrs. Brown expressed the wish that someone would shoot a mad dog causing distress in the city. With the British controlling Boston, those who favored the revolution needed to avoid drawing attention to themselves. Thus, gossip about minor things became the only fodder for wagging tongues, other than an occasional outburst by a passionate patriot.

With the map safely in Charles's hands, Rachel felt adrift, no longer important to the cause. Her brother-in-law had forced a promise from her not to attempt anything on her own.

"But I might be able to gain a position in General Gage's house," she said. "Mrs. Gage hired me before. Think of what I could learn as her servant."

"All of the necessary people are in place," Charles said.

"We're relaying information to General Washington daily. You've done your part. In due time when we've built our strength, we'll pass this map to the patriots in Georgia and South Carolina. Taking the revolution to East Florida will be their responsibility." He patted her shoulder. "I am proud of you, sister. You have done well."

After that, no one in the family mentioned the war, and the red-coated soldiers who patrolled the city received their every courtesy.

Rachel sometimes saw Major Brigham at a distance but avoided him. He had been kind to her in East Florida and on the voyage to Boston, but now he was the enemy, just like Frederick. At least the officer had never deceived her, but Frederick's lies still pained her. Many nights she fell asleep with tears drenching her pillow.

With October approaching, Rachel consoled herself by sewing winter clothes for her nieces and nephew and helping to harvest her sister's kitchen garden. As a supposed Tory, Charles did not suffer as many others in the city. The family sat in church side by side with known loyalists. Unlike years past, no soldiers quartered in their home, and a rare shipment of goods reached Charles despite privateers lurking at the mouth of Boston Harbor.

The leaves turned bright red and orange, then faded to brown and fell to the ground. November arrived, and hearth fires were lit, filling the air with the smell of burning wood. One afternoon, Rachel donned the long woolen shawl she had left behind when she and Papa sailed to East Florida.

"I'm going to Granny Jones's house with her dinner." Rachel lifted the covered basket, enjoying the aroma of chicken, spiced apples and pumpkin pie. "She'll want me to eat with her."

"Come home before dark." Susanna frowned. "The soldiers…"

"Yes, I know." Rachel shuddered. Once darkness struck, not all British soldiers behaved as gentlemen toward the ladies of Boston.

She hurried through the narrow cobblestone streets toward a poorer section of town. Granny Jones lived alone and always enjoyed company. Rachel could not be certain, but she guessed that the widow's sons had joined the Continental Army encamped around the city. If they invaded, Rachel wondered who would keep the feeble woman safe.

They sat at a rough-hewn old table, and Mrs. Jones devoured her meal while Rachel munched some chicken.

"Shall we have pie?" Rachel lifted the pie tin from the basket.

"No, dear. I'll save it for later." Mrs. Jones blinked behind her spectacles, her eyes not focusing.

"Since I must go before dark, I'll eat some now." Rachel plunged a knife into the creamy orange pumpkin.

"Don't—"

"What on earth?" Rachel pulled a small square of oilcloth from beneath the piecrust. Wrapped inside was a piece of parchment containing dates and names of familiar places. "Why, Mrs. Jones, what is this?"

The widow's eyes focused sharply on Rachel. "Tell Charles it'll be delivered."

Rachel stared at her for a moment, her heart racing. That rascal. He *was* using her for the cause. How many other messages had she unwittingly delivered to this *bright* old woman?

"Now get on home."

Rachel wrapped a blanket around the woman's feet. "Yes, ma'am." She took her basket and hastened from the cottage, shoving away the hurt feelings that tried to take hold. With every person under suspicion by the British, Charles was wise to keep secrets from her.

Two blocks from home, she cut through an alley to save time, almost bumping into Mrs. Arthur from the sewing circle.

"Oh, good evening, Mrs.—"

The words froze in her throat as Major Brigham stepped from the shadows. "Good evening, Miss Folger. What a surprise to see you out so late."

"Oh. Yes. It is." Rachel stared at Mrs. Arthur, the plump, pretty wife of a church deacon. Had she interrupted an assignation?

The woman's eyes narrowed. "Miss Folger, you should be at home at this hour." Her lips formed a thin line, and she stared up at the officer. "Major Brigham, perhaps you should escort this young woman to Charles Weldon's house. He is her sister's husband."

The sly look of understanding that passed between them could not be regarded as lovers' gazes. No, this woman, who just yesterday had sat in Susanna's house and whispered with passion about the revolution, was conspiring with the enemy. Why, she had been baiting Susanna.

"Tell me, Miss Folger, why do you look so alarmed?" Major Brigham cocked one eyebrow and gave her a smile that sent a shiver of fear down her spine. "And where have you been just now?" He took her basket and lifted the embroidered linen napkin. "Empty." He glanced at Mrs. Arthur.

"I, uhm, that is, I took supper to an old widow." Rachel forced a smile but could feel her lips trembling.

"Ah, yes. Granny Jones." Mrs. Arthur snickered.

"Yes. Poor dear." Rachel swallowed. "Well, if you will excuse me—" She turned to go.

Major Brigham caught her arm. "I think you should come with me."

"Ouch." Rachel leaned away from him, longing to run. But he would easily catch her.

"Come along, my dear." From his tone, he might be asking

her to tea. He handed the basket to Mrs. Arthur. "Take this to Weldon and tell him you found it on the street."

"Poor Susanna." Mrs. Arthur muffled her laughter with her hand. "She will be in such despair over her sister's disappearance."

"But why—?" Rachel's eyes stung, and she struggled not to give way to tears.

"Really, Miss Folger, do not be tedious. We're merely going to visit General Gage." Major Brigham gently shoved her along the street, glancing back at Mrs. Arthur. "I'll see that someone calls on Granny Jones."

"Thank you for bringing these letters, Captain Templeton." Frederick held a stack of correspondence from his family. "I trust Mr. Folger has apprised you of the situation here." He moved closer to the fire blazing in his drawing room hearth, thankful for the warmth this chilly November morning. After three years, he preferred East Florida's warmer days.

"I surmise you're referring to Rachel removing to Boston." Templeton lounged in a wingback chair, a frown of concern darkening his eyes. "You have my sympathy, sir."

Frederick took a seat opposite his guest. "Thank you. I trust you found my family well."

"I did. You come from hospitable people. They were eager to hear of your endeavors." Templeton puckered his lips as if smothering a smile, and his eyes now radiated high spirits. "Your sister sends a particular greeting."

"Marianne." Frederick glanced at her unopened letter, eager to read what the little darling had written. She'd been almost seventeen when he left home and would soon turn twenty. "Did she say something that is not in her letter?"

Templeton shifted in his chair. "It would be better if you read the letter first, but may I say that I found...that is, she is, I, uhm—"

Comprehension filled Frederick, and he burst out laughing. "Good show, Templeton. You know a true gem when you see one."

Templeton's eyebrows rose. "That sounds very much like approval."

Frederick shrugged. "My approval is not required." Yet this man could become a closer brother to him than the three with whom he shared Lord Bennington's blood. "But I will gladly grant it if you like."

Templeton's high humor returned. "That's all we need. God willing, we'll find our way to happiness."

"You understand my father will never approve."

Templeton flung out his hands, palms up, and shrugged. "Nor will he approve your marriage to Rachel."

Frederick noticed the calluses on Templeton's broad, work-roughened hands, unlike those of the dandies who graced London's balls, but much like Frederick's own since he had been in East Florida. "I suppose Mr. Folger told you she broke our engagement. I hope to change her mind."

"Yes, he told me." A sympathetic frown furrowed Templeton's brow. "He also said you hadn't yet found a ship willing to brave the privateers outside Boston Harbor."

"No." The old wound broke open, flooding Frederick with pain. "Furthermore, I could not in good conscience leave the plantation before the last harvest. Then a fever struck the settlement, requiring me to stay. But now, if winter were not upon us, especially in the north, I would ride the length of the continent to pursue her."

Templeton stood and strode to his side, thumping him hard on the shoulder. "What's the matter with you, man? Settle your affairs here, and we'll sail for Boston."

Objections flew through Frederick's mind, but hope quickly dismissed them and lifted him from his chair. "If you're willing to run the gauntlet, so am I."

"Ha. That's the spirit." Templeton clapped him on the same shoulder, almost knocking him over. "That's the man who's worthy of my cousin Rachel."

Recovering from the friendly battering, Frederick felt less eager to read his parents' letters. Had Templeton persuaded Father that Frederick was no failure? Had Mother been aware of the romance blooming in her own drawing room? Of only one thing was he certain: Marianne's words would feed his soul in unexpected ways.

Not until Templeton left did Frederick realize he had no idea where the man stood regarding the revolution.

## Chapter Twenty-Nine

Standing tiptoe on a crate, Rachel peeked out the small round window at the gray sky. If she were a little taller, she could see down to the street or perhaps as far as the harbor. As it was, she saw only an occasional airborne seagull or wren. She heard only horses' hooves clopping past General Gage's house and the muffled voices from the rooms below. Try though she might with an ear to the floor, she could not distinguish one word from another.

Since her imprisonment almost a month before, Rachel had dredged up memories of sewing circle conversations and prayed none of the other ladies had revealed important information to the traitor. Only one clue surfaced. The peacock had lost his hen, and Major Brigham's dreadful wife had sailed home to England. Perhaps the stray sow in the garden referred to none other than Mrs. Arthur. Had Susanna suspected her?

To furnish Rachel's tiny attic prison, Mrs. Gage had provided a narrow cot with a feather mattress and two blankets. Three times a day, either a British lieutenant or Major Brigham himself brought her meals and hot water, no doubt to keep her from talking to servants or kind Mrs. Gage to beg that a message be sent to Susanna. Rachel's poor sister must be worried sick. Charles might make a few inquiries about her, but his position must not be compromised.

With only a borrowed Bible for comfort, she spent her days and weeks reading and praying for a way to escape. Once she had tried stacking the crate on a trunk to reach the window and climb out. But the scraping sound had alerted the soldiers, and they took away the trunk. After many tears and prayers, Rachel decided her post in the revolution was to be a prisoner. By delivering the map to Charles, she had done all that she was supposed to do. One thing was certain: her face would always betray her heart, as proven by her confrontation with Major Brigham.

Snow brushed over the round window, dimming the attic. Huddled against the chimney's warm bricks, Rachel pulled her woolen shawl closer. Soon winter would arrive in full force. Never had she expected to miss the heat of East Florida, but oh how she would welcome it now.

The key turned, the door opened, and Major Brigham stepped into the attic. "Miss Folger, gather your things." His placid expression gave her no indication of whether or not she was in imminent danger.

She glanced about the attic. "I have nothing to gather." Hugging her shawl, she toddled across the room on legs aching from want of exercise and stopped in front of her captor. "Am I to be p-punished?" Would they hang a woman? "If so, would you please explain why?"

Amusement rippled across his aristocratic face. "No, my dear, you will not be punished. You have been our guest these weeks past to prevent your divulging, ah, how shall I say it? A certain friendship of mine. Now you will be delivered into the hands of a loyalist sea captain who in turn will deliver you back to your father, from whom I never should have separated you."

"Sea captain?" Irrational hope sprung up within her.

"Yes," Major Brigham drawled. "I believe you know the chap. This way, Miss Folger."

Her legs shook as she descended two flights of stairs to the drawing room. Near the door stood Frederick, and he took a step in her direction.

"Rachel!"

Her heart seemed to rip in two. She pushed past him and flung herself into Jamie's arms.

"Oh, Jamie, take me home."

To her shock, Jamie gripped her upper arms and stared sternly into her eyes. "Cousin, do you not wish to greet your betrothed?"

The imperative message in his gaze penetrated her cloudy mind.

"Oh." She turned around. "Frederick. Darling." Surely no one would be fooled by her cold tone. She walked across the room on wooden legs, seeing beyond him that Major Brigham stared at her through narrowed eyes.

Frederick pulled her into his arms and kissed her forehead. "Dearest," he whispered, "trust us."

She nodded her assent, but only because Jamie had come, too.

"Enough." Major Brigham moved closer. "Our bargain is that you will return her to East Florida forthwith and keep her out of trouble once she's there." He leaned so near that Rachel could smell cherry tobacco on his uniform. "Understand, Miss Folger, I am releasing you only because—" Abruptly, he stepped back. "Really, I am not a brute. But we are at war, and—" He exhaled impatiently. "I owe you much for saving Lady Augusta from the alligator. This should balance our accounts."

Rachel's knees buckled, but Frederick held her fast. She tried to form a response.

"Furthermore," Major Brigham continued, "your courage

during the fire impressed me. Take that boldness back to the wilderness and raise loyal British subjects—"

"Enough!" Rachel straightened and stepped out of Frederick's embrace. "You have prattled on far too long." She glanced at Jamie. "Shall we go?" Forcing strength into her legs, she strode toward the hallway door.

"Sir, forgive her." Jamie's voice reached her. "Naturally, she's a little overwrought."

"Naturally." Sarcasm laced Brigham's tone. "As I told you, you will have an armed guard until your ship sails, in case she tries to—"

"She will behave, Major Brigham." Frederick's voice sounded like music to her traitorous heart.

No, she would not behave. Not if she could help it.

"Please believe me, Rachel." Frederick stood beside Jamie, blocking the door of the ship's cabin. "Your sister and her family are in no danger."

Rachel looked at Jamie, wondering what safe response she could give. Anything she said to Frederick might cast suspicion on her cousin. Like Papa, Jamie had never claimed to be a patriot, thus keeping their revolutionary activities secret. But Jamie's brotherly smile gave her no indication of what she should say.

"It's true, Rachel." Jamie nodded. "We visited with Charles. He said to tell you the stray sow in the garden has been put back in her pen."

Cautious relief crept into her. "That is good news. Do you know what happened to...to a certain old woman?" Rachel could not bear to think of Granny Jones being imprisoned, too.

Jamie put a warning finger to his lips. "When we're out to sea, I'll tell you everything. For now, will you please stay here and not try to jump ship?" His face creased into a pleading expression.

Rachel pursed her lips at his humorous remark. "I won't jump ship." But only because she could not swim.

The two men traded a look of relief.

"I'm going on deck," Jamie said to Frederick. "We'll want to sail beyond the harbor before sunset."

Once he left, Frederick sat behind the oak desk and toyed with a long, slender package.

Rachel fussed with her shawl. "This is against all propriety."

He glanced up. "What is?"

"Our being alone. Is there no other woman on board?"

Frederick set aside the package. "Tsk. An oversight. How shall we amend that?"

Despite the cold, heat filled Rachel's cheeks. "*You* could jump ship."

Merriment lit his face. "Ah, but I promised your esteemed father that I would deliver you safely home."

"Nonsense. Jamie can do that." She could not comprehend why Jamie seemed all too willing to leave her alone with Frederick.

"Or we could secure the services of a vicar, who could marry us before we are out to sea. Then you would be safe in my care."

"What?" Rachel crossed her arms and glared at him. "Oh, forgive me. I forgot to tell you. I have released you from our engagement."

Hurt clouded his gaze, but his smile remained. "Rachel, I know of no other way to tell you this. I have come to believe the revolution is the only right and righteous course for England's American colonies—all of them." Fervor burned in his eyes, and he came around the desk to kneel in front of her. "Believe me, my darling. You and your father have convinced me."

Shivers swept down Rachel's back, and she drew her shawl

tighter around her. "You expect me to believe you? You implied all this before, yet it was a lie."

Frederick moved to the chair beside her and grasped her hand. "I did not intend to lie, but I know I misled you. By doing so, I failed to respect your opinions, your most cherished beliefs. But your father and I have had many talks these past months. We are convinced that the revolution will come to East Florida after all. Every man will have to decide where he will stand. I have made my decision."

Tears coursed down Rachel's cheeks. "You have?" Hope burst through her grief like sunlight through the falling snow, but caution gripped her once more. "How will I know you're telling the truth this time?"

Frederick stared at the floor for several moments, then rose and left the cabin. Within minutes, he returned with Jamie.

"Captain Templeton, we have often skirted this discussion, but the time has come for me to tell you that I support the patriots and their revolution. If you do not, then kindly permit Rachel and me to leave this ship...or return us to Major Brigham."

Rachel gasped. "No, Jamie. He does not mean it."

"Shh." Frederick grasped her hand once more. "I do mean it. Captain, what say you?"

Jamie chuckled. "I wondered how long it would take for you to tell me."

Frederick chortled, obviously not surprised by his response.

"You have known?" Rachel thought she might like to smack her cousin.

Jamie crossed his arms and leaned against the door. "Yes, since returning from England."

"All this time." Frederick scratched his head. "You see, my dear, everyone except you has been reticent to expound on their opinions. You have more courage than all of us." He glanced at Jamie. "Or perhaps just more than I."

Her face flamed again, this time with pleasure at his praise. "Oh, Frederick, I have missed you so much."

He brushed a hand across her cheek. "Will you make me the happiest of men and become my wife?"

Sniffing back her tears, Rachel whispered, "Yes."

"Ahem." Jamie shuffled his feet. "May I take my leave now?"

Rachel shook her head. "We cannot sail until Frederick and I are married. We must go ashore and find a minister."

"Hmm." Jamie scratched his chin. "I think I might have a stray parson somewhere on board." He hastened from the cabin.

"What?" Rachel started to follow him.

"Wait." Frederick gripped her hand and gently tugged her back into her chair. "You see? We came prepared."

She huffed out a bit of artificial indignation. "You are very sure of yourself, are you not?"

His rueful wince contradicted her. "Not when it comes to you." He leaned his forehead against hers. "Beloved, the coming days will not be easy."

"But God will be with us and guide us."

"Yes. And I believe He will bring about a new day for all of the colonies."

Rachel searched his eyes. "Do you think the people of East Florida will join the revolution?"

He shook his head. "There's no way to know right now. We only know that each of us must do his part."

Jamie returned with his first mate and Rachel's former minister.

Rachel jumped to her feet. "Reverend Wentworth, how kind of you to come."

The elderly vicar gave her a gentle smile. "My dear, it

gives me great joy to unite you and this young man in marriage."

He opened his well-worn prayer book. "Dearly beloved, we are gathered together here in the sight of God, and in the face of this congregation." He glanced around the small cabin and chuckled. "Wherever two or three are gathered in His name." He continued with the rites and led Rachel and Frederick through their marriage vows, then invited them to sign his Bible, gave them a blessing and thereafter took his leave.

Jamie embraced Rachel and shook Frederick's hand. "God bless you both." He hustled the first mate from the cabin. "See you in the morning."

Her face burning, Rachel could not look at her new husband until he cleared his throat.

"My dear, I have a wedding gift for you." He retrieved the package from the desk.

"Oh, my." She took it in hand and tore off the paper, revealing a white lace parasol. "Why, it's beautiful." Her heart pounded as she began to push it open.

"Ah, ah." Frederick stayed her hands. "Tomorrow is soon enough."

She started to reach up and kiss him. But the memory of their first such encounter held her back. "You may kiss your bride, Mr. Moberly."

The love shining from his eyes swept away the last of her doubts. "Why, Mrs. Moberly, I think I might just do that."

# Chapter Thirty

*July 1776*
*Bennington Plantation*

"Papa, I am exceedingly displeased with you." Rachel spoke in soft tones and kept an eye on the drawing room doorway, lest a servant should happen by. With one hand on her well-rounded belly, she shifted in discomfort on the red brocade settee. "How can you marry Cousin Lydie without telling her of your nighttime activities on behalf of the revolution?"

Seated in the adjacent wingback chair, Papa leaned toward Rachel with a glower. "What makes ye think I haven't told her? Do ye think I lack the integrity to be honest with yer future stepmother?"

"But she has never mentioned—ah!" Rachel gasped as the new life within her made his presence known with a pointed kick to her rib cage.

Papa's glower turned to a playful smirk, the only indication that he noticed her plight. "O'course she hasn't mentioned it nor even given anybody a hint. As I've told ye before, not everybody wears their feelings on their faces."

Rachel did not acknowledge Papa's comment, for Frederick often told her how much he loved her openness. Not a helpful trait if one wished to be a spy, but then God had made clear His will for her in that regard.

To think that dear Cousin Lydie did not oppose the revolution. In the eight months of living here at the plantation, Rachel never would have guessed the old dear's views had changed. Indeed, it was a topic Rachel and Frederick discussed only in whispers, only to each other. If the war came to East Florida, many families might find their loyalties divided.

"Where is my bride?" Frederick's voice echoed down the front staircase, and soon he strode into the drawing room. "Ah, there you are, my darling." He bent over the back of the settee and kissed her cheek. "Mr. Folger, welcome." He extended a hand to Papa, who shook it with his customary enthusiasm. "Cousin Lydie will be down in a moment." He sat beside Rachel and flung an arm behind her across the back of the settee. "Darling, are you certain it is wise for you to take a turn around the grounds?" He glanced at her belly, then at Papa and his ears reddened. "I mean—"

"Oh, yes." Ignoring his chagrin, Rachel drew in a quiet breath so he would not see her discomfort. "Walking is the very best thing for me these days."

"And for me, as well." Papa patted his left knee. "Disuse makes a body unusable."

Rachel puckered away a giggle. "Just make certain you do not forget to limp." She still had difficulty comprehending that Papa's claim to have broken his leg while whaling had been a ruse so that he could walk naturally in his patriot disguise. And now that his snake-bitten limb had healed, he could walk without difficulty.

"Indeed." Papa clicked his tongue. "Do keep reminding me, daughter. I fear these days my mind's on other things."

One of those *other things* walked into the room, her lightly wrinkled face smoothed by a radiant glow. "Good morning, Lamech."

Papa stood and hurried to her—without a limp—and kissed both of her hands. "My dear Lydia, how beautiful you are this fine day."

Rachel traded a look with Frederick. They had discussed how Papa's speech improved in Cousin Lydie's presence, as did his manners, and his changes amused them both.

"Shall we go?" Cousin Lydie grasped Papa's hand and led him from the room.

Frederick helped Rachel rise from the settee. She placed a hand on her aching lower back and was grateful for the loving sympathy emanating from her husband's eyes.

Little Caddy opened the front door for the party, and Frederick rewarded her with a confection. Rachel touched the child's shoulder as she passed by.

As she descended the front steps, with Frederick's hand cupped under her elbow, she surveyed the distant indigo fields where most of the plantation's two hundred slaves bent over the tender green plants. Rachel prayed that when the British were driven from these shores, freedom would come for these slaves as well as for the white colonists.

"You are frowning, my love." Frederick kept a supporting hand under her arm. "Are you in pain?"

She gave him a little smile. "No more than usual."

"But you are not happy, are you?" He bent and kissed her forehead.

Rachel leaned against him. "I am happy with you, my darling. But—" She looked toward the fields again. "If East Florida joins the other colonies in their fight to dissolve its ties with England, what will become of these people when the revolution succeeds?"

* * *

When Frederick gazed down into his beloved's dark brown eyes, the love that welled up in his heart felt almost painful. How he longed to grant her every wish, even going so far as to free the slaves. Yet until Father responded to Frederick's news, it would be madness to make such a drastic move as to set the slaves free.

"Perhaps we will have our answer when Jamie returns from London." Frederick expected it to take a long time to straighten out the lies Oliver had told Father. If Father would listen to reason about that tangled matter, perhaps he would look favorably on other matters.

Frederick had spent much time on his knees imploring the Almighty that his marriage to Rachel might find favor in Father's eyes. Whether or not the earl forgave him for following his heart, Frederick would never regret doing so. Further, he had proven to himself that he could work with his hands, that he could manage money without wasting it, and that he could be a loving husband. If Father banished him from the plantation, Frederick and Rachel would be able to face whatever challenges life might bring them. What more should a parent ask of his child than that he might be self-determined and capable? Much like the colonies who strove for freedom from their mother country, England.

Frederick had written all his thoughts in a diary to keep until the day when his son—or daughter—found someone to love. Simply reading his own words on the page deepened his convictions.

"Would it not be wonderful if Jamie brought Lady Marianne back with him?" Rachel gave him a playful grin. "Married to her, of course."

"Of course." Frederick tweaked her pretty little nose. "But have you no mercy? My father may be a tyrant, but Mother should not be bereft of both of her children." He would await their child's birth before telling her of his letter to Marianne. He wrote that his sister must accept with grace Captain Templeton's decision to break with her. One day, both she and Rachel would understand.

"Jamie deserves to marry the woman he loves." Rachel's eyes twinkled. "As you did."

Frederick observed that Mr. Folger, whom he had not found courage to call Father, had found a wrought-iron bench under a spreading oak tree. There he sat with dear Cousin Lydie, both of them clearly besotted with love, if one could judge by the tender expressions passing between them. Frederick leaned down and placed a gentle kiss on Rachel's lips.

"Will you always have the last word, my little rebel?"

"Why, Mr. Moberly, I certainly do hope so."

And Frederick found that admission not at all discouraging.

\* \* \* \* \*

Dear Reader,

As strange as it may seem, I never expected to write about Florida, even though it has been my home state these past thirty years. But when my fellow author Kristy Dykes (1951–2008) suggested that I write a historical novel about Florida, the setting just seemed right. Digging into my state's history has been a great joy for me.

One thing I never knew before was that England owned *more* than thirteen colonies in the part of North America that became the United States of America. What fun to discover that while the patriots in those thirteen colonies were struggling to form an independent nation, two other English colonies called East Florida and West Florida had the potential of becoming the fourteenth and fifteenth states. Such was not to be, however. Instead, loyalists fled to East Florida to escape the American Revolution and held the line against patriots who tried to breach their defenses.

Another interesting fact has to do with my fictional setting of St. Johns Settlement. I chose the site because it was near an old French fort on the St. Johns River. Imagine my surprise when I interviewed Fort Caroline Park guide Bill Johnson and he informed me that there actually had been a burgeoning English village named St. Johns Towne on the very spot I had chosen. What fun to have the fictional meet up with reality!

That you for choosing *Love Thine Enemy*, the first book in my Florida series. If you enjoyed Rachel and Frederick's love story, look for the romance of Rachel's cousin, Captain Jamie Templeton, and Frederick's sister, Lady Marianne Moberly, coming soon from Love Inspired Historical. In both stories, I hope to inspire my readers to always seek God's guidance, especially when making the decision of whom they will marry.

I love to hear from readers, so if you have a comment about *Love Thine Enemy*, please contact me through my Web site, www.Louisemgouge.com.
Blessings,
Louise M. Gouge

## QUESTIONS FOR DISCUSSION

1. As the story begins, Rachel is angry because her father has brought her to Florida when she would rather be back home in Boston helping to fight the revolution. How does that affect her thinking and her manners toward the young Englishmen? As a Christian, is she justified in her thoughts and behavior?

2. Frederick is a trusting person until he is betrayed by his boyhood friend. What caused Corwin to "bite the hand that feeds him"? What effect does this have on Frederick, and how does it help him finally stand up to Corwin? How does this help him decide to stand up to his father regarding his love for Rachel?

3. According to the customs of the day, it was shocking and inappropriate for a man to kiss a young lady before their engagement. Considering their respective levels of society, why does this denote particular disrespect on Frederick's part toward Rachel? How might their relationship have progressed differently if Rachel had welcomed the kiss?

4. Frederick's mother has had a stronger influence on his opinions and actions than his father. Why is he still seeking his father's approval? Are there people in your life whose approval you are seeking? Why or why not? What is the solution?

5. Why don't Mr. Folger or Jamie Templeton trust Rachel with their true sentiments about the revolution? Are their motivations justified? How?

6. Mr. Folger is adept at keeping secrets, not only about his spying but about his faith. While it is obviously necessary to keep his spying a secret, why might he be remiss in hiding his spiritual beliefs from Rachel? How might it have affected their relationship if he had told her of his faith in Jesus Christ? Are you able to discuss spiritual matters with your family and close friends? Why or why not?

7. Rachel tries hard not to be affected by Lady Augusta's arrogance, but the woman still manages to hurt her feelings. How would you feel in similar circumstances? How does the noblewoman's behavior mirror King George's treatment of the colonists?

8. Frederick seemed to take his English loyalties for granted. What influences cause him to change his opinion about the Americans' "Glorious Cause"?

9. Sometimes sincere Christians can find themselves on opposing sides of an issue. Rachel and Frederick fall in love before they reach an agreement about several important matters. On some points, they are willing to compromise, and on others they postpone a much-needed discussion. How might this story have turned out differently if Frederick had remained a loyalist?

10. Rachel keeps trying to find the unknown patriot or at least some bit of information to help the revolution. What does this reveal about her character? Why is she unsuccessful at spying?

11. At the end of the story, Frederick has no trouble letting Rachel have the last word. Does this in any way diminish his leadership in his family? Or does this show his determination not to be as dictatorial as his father?

12. Which character changes the most in the story? Rachel? Frederick? In what ways does each one mature and become stronger?

Dumped via certified letter days before her wedding, Haley Scott sees her dreams of happily ever after crushed. But could it turn out to be the best thing that's ever happened to her?

*Turn the page for a sneak preview of*
*AN UNEXPECTED MATCH*
*by Dana Corbit,*
*book 1 in the new* WEDDING BELLS BLESSINGS
*trilogy,*
*available beginning August 2009 from Love Inspired®.*

"**I**s there a Haley Scott here?"

Haley glanced through the storm door at the package carrier before opening the latch and letting in some of the frigid March wind.

"That's me, but not for long."

The blank stare the man gave her as he stood on the porch of her mother's new house only made Haley smile. In fifty-one hours and twenty-nine minutes, her name would be changing. Her life as well, but she couldn't allow herself to think about that now.

She wouldn't attribute her sudden shiver to anything but the cold, either. Not with a bridal fitting to endure, embossed napkins to pick up and a caterer to call. Too many details, too little time and certainly no time for her to entertain her silly cold feet.

"Then this is for you."

Practiced at this procedure after two days back in her Markston, Indiana, hometown, Haley reached out both arms to accept a bridal gift, but the carrier turned and deposited an overnight letter package in just one of her hands. Haley stared down at the Michigan return address of her fiancé, Tom Jeffries.

"Strange way to send a wedding present," she murmured.

The man grunted and shoved an electronic signature device at her, waiting until she scrawled her name.

As soon as she closed the door, Haley returned to the living room and yanked the tab on the paperboard. From it, she withdrew a single sheet of folded notebook paper.

Something inside her suggested that she should sit down to read it, so she lowered herself into a floral side chair. Hesitating, she glanced at the far wall where wedding gifts in pastel-colored paper were stacked, then she unfolded the note. Her stomach tightened as she read each handwritten word.

*"Best?* He signed it *best?"* Her voice cracked as the paper fluttered to the floor. She was sure she should be sobbing or collapsing in a heap, but she felt only numb as she stared down at the offending piece of paper.

The letter that had changed everything.

"Best what?" Trina Scott asked as she padded into the room with fuzzy striped socks on her feet. "Sweetie?"

Haley lifted her gaze to meet her mother's and could see concern etched between her carefully tweezed brows.

"What's the matter?" Trina shot a glance toward the foyer, her chin-length brown hair swinging past her ear as she did it. "Did I just hear someone at the door?"

Haley tilted her head to indicate the sheet of paper on the floor. "It's from Tom. He called off the wedding."

"What? Why?" Trina began, but then brushed her hand through the air twice as if to erase the question. "That's not the most important thing right now, is it?"

Haley stared at her mother. A little pity wouldn't have been out of place here. Instead of offering any, Trina snapped up the letter and began to read. When she finished, she sat on the cream-colored sofa opposite Haley's chair.

"I don't approve of his methods." She shook the letter to emphasize her point. "And I always thought the boy didn't have enough good sense to come out of the rain, but I have to agree with him on this one. You two aren't right for each other."

Haley couldn't believe her ears. Okay, Tom wouldn't have

been the partner Trina Scott would have chosen for her youngest daughter if Trina's grand matchmaking scheme hadn't gone belly-up. Still, Haley hadn't realized how strongly her mother disapproved of her choice.

"No sense being upset about my opinion now," Trina told her. "I kept praying that you'd make the right decision, but I guess Tom made it for you. Now we have to get busy. There are a lot of calls to make. I'll call Amy." Trina dug the cell phone from her purse and hit one of the speed dial numbers.

Haley winced. In any situation, it shouldn't have surprised her that her mother's first reaction was to phone her best friend, but Trina had more than knee-jerk reasons to make this call. Not only had Amy Warren been asked to join them downtown this afternoon for Haley's final bridal fitting, but she also was scheduled to make the wedding cake at her bakery, Amy's Elite Treats.

Haley asked herself again why she'd agreed to plan the wedding in her hometown. Now her humiliation would double as she shared it with family friends. One in particular.

"May I speak to Amy?" Trina began as someone answered the line. "Oh, Matthew, is that you?"

*That's the one.* Haley squeezed her eyes shut.

\* \* \* \* \*

*Will her former crush be the one
to mend Haley's broken heart?
Find out in AN UNEXPECTED MATCH,
available in August 2009
only from Love Inspired®.*

# Love Inspired.
# H I S T O R I C A L
## INSPIRATIONAL HISTORICAL ROMANCE

Mary Randolph is determined to help the orphans of St. Louis, even if that means battling with by-the-book police captain Samuel Benton. Sam had a rough childhood, but Mary's feistiness is reigniting his faith—and showing him how true love can fulfill dreams.

**Look for**

*The Law and Miss Mary*

**by**

# DOROTHY CLARK

*Available in August
wherever books are sold.*

**www.SteepleHill.com**

Steeple
Hill®

LIH82817

# REQUEST YOUR FREE BOOKS!

## 2 FREE INSPIRATIONAL NOVELS
## PLUS 2
## FREE
## MYSTERY GIFTS

*Love Inspired*
### HISTORICAL
#### INSPIRATIONAL HISTORICAL ROMANCE

**YES!** Please send me 2 FREE Love Inspired® Historical novels and my 2 FREE mystery gifts (gifts are worth about $10). After receiving them, if I don't wish to receive any more books, I can return the shipping statement marked "cancel". If I don't cancel, I will receive 4 brand-new novels every other month and be billed just $4.24 per book in the U.S. or $4.74 per book in Canada. That's a savings of over 20% off the cover price. It's quite a bargain! Shipping and handling is just 50¢ per book.* I understand that accepting the 2 free books and gifts places me under no obligation to buy anything. I can always return a shipment and cancel at any time. Even if I never buy another book, the two free books and gifts are mine to keep forever. 102 IDN EYPS   302 IDN EYP4

| | |
|---|---|
| Name | (PLEASE PRINT) |

| | | |
|---|---|---|
| Address | | Apt. # |

| | | |
|---|---|---|
| City | State/Prov. | Zip/Postal Code |

Signature (if under 18, a parent or guardian must sign)

### Mail to Steeple Hill Reader Service:
**IN U.S.A.:** P.O. Box 1867, Buffalo, NY 14240-1867
**IN CANADA:** P.O. Box 609, Fort Erie, Ontario L2A 5X3

Not valid to current subscribers of Love Inspired Historical books.

**Want to try two free books from another series?**
**Call 1-800-873-8635 or visit www.morefreebooks.com**

\* Terms and prices subject to change without notice. Prices do not include applicable taxes. Sales tax applicable in N.Y. Canadian residents will be charged applicable provincial taxes and GST. Offer not valid in Quebec. This offer is limited to one order per household. All orders subject to approval. Credit or debit balances in a customer's account(s) may be offset by any other outstanding balance owed by or to the customer. Please allow 4 to 6 weeks for delivery. Offer available while quantities last.

**Your Privacy:** Steeple Hill Books is committed to protecting your privacy. Our Privacy Policy is available online at www.SteepleHill.com or upon request from the Reader Service. From time to time we make our lists of customers available to reputable third parties who may have a product or service of interest to you. If you would prefer we not share your name and address, please check here. ☐

LIH09

**HISTORICAL**

# TITLES AVAILABLE NEXT MONTH

## Available August 11, 2009

**THE LAW AND MISS MARY by Dorothy Clark**
It's disgraceful how St. Louis's orphans are treated.
Mary Randolph is determined to help them, even if she has
to battle by-the-book police captain Samuel Benton every
step of the way. A poverty-stricken childhood left Sam
hungry for the social acceptance now within his reach. Then
Miss Randolph's feisty perseverance begins to give him
second thoughts, reigniting his faith—and showing him how
true love can fulfill all their dreams....

**THE OUTLAW'S LADY by Laurie Kingery**
Rebellious rancher's daughter Tess Hennessy seeks
adventure—and finds herself abducted by the Delgado gang!
Gang member Sandoval Parrish captured her as a means to
an end, seeking retribution for the sister Delgado ruined. Yet
when his plan puts Tess in danger, Sandoval must choose
between the drive for revenge and a newfound love.